I0817865

WARRIORS OF WRATH

BOOK TWO

AE WINSTEAD

This is a work of fiction. Names, characters, places, and incidents either are the product of the author's imagination or are used fictitiously. Any resemblance to actual persons, living or dead, events, or locales is entirely coincidental.

First paperback edition March 2022

Cover design by MiblArt

ISBN 978-1-7352-709-5-1 (hardback)
ISBN 978-1-7352-709-4-4 (paperback)
ISBN 978-1-7352-709-3-7 (ebook)

www.aewinstead.com

TO MY READERS, *you are the real ones—*

the ones who kept me from giving up.

I have commanded those I prepared for battle; I have summoned my warriors to carry out my wrath…

Isaiah 13:3 NIV

DAY ONE

ONE

Church of the Holy Sepulcher
Jerusalem, Israel

Armageddon.
Apocalypse.
The end of the world.

Such words had been tossed around all of Lindsay Martin's forty-eight years, mostly in reference to some new book or blockbuster movie, not real-life events.

And even though her husband, James, had harbored an almost unhealthy obsession with the idea of "being prepared for anything" since the birth of their daughter almost eighteen years ago, Lindsay had never dreamed that the terror and destruction depicted in those stories could ever befall the world, let alone that her daughter would be embroiled in the midst of it.

The gray gloom of the Israeli afternoon leached its way into the basement room that had been Lindsay's prison for the past three days. Clouds cast long shadows through the high, stained-glass windows that lined the tops of the stone walls.

The first two days in this dank and dusty space had been hell, spent daydreaming of nothing but escape. But the past twenty-four hours had spawned a shift in perspective. She'd stay here forever, she decided, if it meant her family could be safe from the extermination happening outside these walls.

Outside, thunder rumbled and rain pattered against the building. It seemed the dismal weather of their small Kentucky town had followed them halfway around the world.

Lindsay closed her eyes, trying to imagine herself back on her farm, curled on her sofa, a cup of coffee in hand, listening to the soothing rain outside her living room window.

She opened her eyes to take in the room around her, a stark reminder that those days were long over.

How could I have missed so much?

News of hurricanes, earthquakes, floods, and volcanoes had buzzed through their home for years. Perhaps overcompensating for her daughter's intense fears, Lindsay had played it down. *"It's just the natural cycles of weather—nothing to worry about."*

Lindsay, like most everyone else, hadn't thought much of the bizarre weather…until it had almost killed her.

Two of the men—or angels, rather—who stood guard around their underground sanctum had brought her and James to this church after they'd all but died in the flood that'd destroyed their hometown back in Kentucky.

Lindsay couldn't say she'd believed in angels before, but there was no denying; she and James *had* almost drowned on one continent and woken on another. So, Lindsay was inclined to believe.

To her dismay, James had been oddly compliant with the angels and their strange orders. And even though she relished the fact that she wasn't responsible for nixing an attack on a group of Archangels, she'd been nothing short of surprised at James's nonchalant attitude to the situation.

"Let's just see what they have to say," he'd said when they'd woken in the presence of these imposing strangers.

James had never been a *lets-see-what-they-have-to-say* kind of guy. He was more of the *shoot-first-ask-questions-later* type.

Lindsay would have expected James to scoff at the probability of angels and demons, Heaven and Hell, but she guessed the saying was true: Seeing *was* believing.

Even so, James surely would have coordinated their escape by now if not for the sudden appearance of their only child yesterday in the company of a shaggy-haired boy named Ethan and a handful of other angels.

Sitting on her cot now, Lindsay couldn't take her eyes off her daughter, wanting to soak in every ounce of her. Two days ago, Lindsay had been certain she'd never see Camryn again. Yet here she was, completely unharmed, because apparently, she and Ethan were angels, too. Or had been in a past life. *Whatever the hell that means.*

Lindsay massaged her temples as a waif of a woman sat next to her.

"Want a pretzel?" Elizabeth Reyes asked, holding an open bag out to her.

Lindsay shook her head and moved over, making room for Ethan's mother on her cot. Lindsay had tried to calculate the probability of all five of them—James, Elizabeth, Camryn, Ethan, and herself—ending up in *Jerusalem* after an earthquake in *Kentucky*, but it just made her head hurt.

She tried not to think about the absurdity of it all. She would've been happy to have her daughter delivered to her by aliens if that had been her only option.

Lindsay watched as Camryn stood alone next to a stack of crumbling cardboard boxes, her honey-blonde hair pulled into a knot on top of her head, arms outstretched, palms down and straining as if trying to summon a snake from the floor. She wore a ridiculously small, lilac t-shirt that Lindsay *knew* Camryn would never have chosen for herself—she preferred clothing that hid her curves—but in their situation, clothing options were limited. Lindsay looked down at her own mud-stained jeans and sighed.

"What's up with the hair?" Elizabeth cast a pointed glance toward Michael, whose silver locks would have made any human look nothing short of elderly.

"Right?" Lindsay agreed, taking a pretzel from the bag. "I can't stop looking at that one," she gestured with a nod toward Raphael, the one who had delivered the three adults halfway across the world to be reunited with their children. "I've only seen that shade of red once before on a teenager at the mall downtown. And then there are those two," Lindsay said, pointing to the other two Archangels in the room—Samael and Japhael. "Brown and blond. How unfortunate for them." She chuckled.

"It's strange." Elizabeth squinted at the unnatural hue of Michael's hair. "It doesn't even make him look old. More like..." Elizabeth faltered, searching for the right word.

"Eternal," Lindsay finished for her. The word had been on the end of her tongue since she'd first laid eyes on him.

"Eternal..." Elizabeth repeated softly. "That's exactly it."

Michael, the presumed leader of the angel group, flitted back and forth between the two kids like a mother hen, attempting to help Camryn and Ethan harness their powers while they waited for instructions from—

While they waited for instructions from the one they all referred to as Elohim.

The Creator, Michael had explained, had sent Camryn and Ethan here on some grand mission at the end of their previous life. The problem: neither of them remembered a lick of it.

So, while the two kids waited for some divine inspiration, they were stuck in the musty basement of this church practicing skills they'd spent their whole lives trying to suppress.

"She's supposed to make a windstorm in this stuffy basement?" Lindsay scoffed, shaking her head. Michael may as well have told her to make it rain in here with no clouds to draw moisture from.

Lindsay's frown deepened at Camryn's fruitless struggle, knowing her efforts would garner no results. Lindsay had once watched Camryn completely shut down: no eating, no sleeping. She'd even stopped talking for two whole days because of a science project that wasn't going the way she'd planned. Lindsay had seen it too many times. Camryn's worry that her creation would grow out of her control would make it impossible for her to even start.

Being her mother, of course Lindsay wanted to help, but she knew that under the circumstances, Camryn needed to figure this out on her own. Besides, what wisdom could she, a mere human, offer her celestial daughter?

Lindsay glanced back to the corner of the room where Japhael, the blond angel Camryn referred to as Jay, stood beside her husband. Much like the other Archangels, he was clad in military fatigues, his shoulders broad and his stature muscled.

Taking them all in, Lindsay understood why they chose human soldiers as their disguise. It was likely a choice between that or professional wrestlers.

Dwarfed in Jay's shadow, her naturally intimidating husband now reminded Lindsay of a child wielding a giant sword, his face lit with awe. The sword looked as if it should be too heavy for even a brawny man like James to handle, but he swung it from side to side as if it were no more than a plastic toy. Jay stood, hands on hips, gazing down like a proud father.

All men are the same. Lindsay smiled. *No matter the species.*

Lindsay's eyes shifted forward just in time to see flames shoot from Ethan's outstretched hands. The blaze reached higher and higher into the air, illuminating the large underground room before flickering and vanishing without a trace.

Two younger-looking angels sat on another cot nearby. Akira cheered, and Ronan whooped his approval. Lindsay's eyes lingered on the two a moment longer than necessary.

They were just so peculiar.

Akira, who seemed more like a snarky teenager than an ethereal being of higher intelligence, had a petite frame, wild red hair, and pale white skin standing stark against her all-black wardrobe; while Ronan, with his tight black curls, dark brown complexion, and kind, encouraging expression had his crisp polo tucked into pressed khakis.

Lindsay wondered how two celestial creatures could have such contrasting images but then considered the human race and all the intricate differences between them and wondered if perhaps the same were true for the angels.

Lindsay sighed as Camryn huffed and turned away from Ethan's fire, still concentrating on her gust of wind.

"Good. Now try projecting," Michael instructed Ethan. "A little farther this time. Try to reach that painting in the corner."

"That looks important," Ethan replied. "What if it's some priceless artifact or something?"

Michael almost rolled his eyes. "It's worthless, I assure you. But you're trying not to leave a trace. If you do it correctly, the painting won't be harmed."

"If you say so." Ethan shrugged before whipping his hand in a circle, appearing to draw fire from the air and side-arming a ball of flame smoothly across the room.

"Blow it up!" Ronan shouted from the sidelines, eliciting a swift elbow to the ribs from Akira.

"Pull it back. Pull it back!" Michael yelled, but the painting had already burst into flames. Ethan grimaced as Michael slapped out the blaze.

"Hell yeah!" Ronan laughed while Michael glared at him.

"Sorry," Ethan called, waving smoke from the air.

Michael looked as if he might blow his own flames out of his ears at any moment. "Are you two sure you don't have any other powers? This is all we have to work with?"

"Does crippling anxiety and untreatable anger issues count?" Camryn called from the corner. "If so, then definitely yes."

Michael cursed and turned his attention back to the smoldering canvas.

Lindsay watched Ethan jog over to her daughter and put a hand on her back. Lindsay couldn't hear the words Ethan spoke to Camryn, but the girl visibly relaxed. All of a sudden, Lindsay didn't feel so bad about not being able to help her daughter. Camryn had others to help her now. Others with the same burden to bear.

"I never thought I'd see him like that with anyone," Elizabeth said.

Lindsay put a hand on the woman's knee. The two women had spent the morning watching their children try to conquer their long-suppressed powers. All in an effort to ready themselves to take on the Fallen angel responsible for the mess this planet had dissolved into.

While Lindsay tried to wrap her mind around it all, she glanced at the fragile-looking woman.

"You know," Lindsay said softly, trying not to disturb the practice, "when I first made the connection between our town's strange weather and Camryn's toddler moods, I thought I was crazy." She paused, remembering the sleepless nights.

"I'd lay awake at night, wondering if I'd eventually have to send my daughter off to wizarding school or if she'd be collected by some government agency when she turned eighteen."

Lindsay ran through it all in her head, remembering the crazed frenzy of those first few years, trying to figure out what the hell was wrong with her baby.

"I studied my ancestry, asked my husband some very strange questions. But this..." She gestured at the group of angels in the room. "This never crossed my mind."

Elizabeth picked at her cuticles, her chin trembling as she whispered, "At least you didn't abandon her."

Lindsay glanced at the woman. In the past twenty-four hours, she'd learned of Elizabeth's drug addiction and her time in jail—the jail that Raphael had rescued her from after the earthquake had destroyed the building.

Lindsay knew Ethan had been placed in foster care with their neighbors, Dale and Grace Morgan. That's how he and Camryn had come to meet. And if Camryn had Ethan to share her very unique experience with, Lindsay had Elizabeth. But even though she shared such a special bond with this woman, Lindsay realized how little she actually knew about her.

"Looking at him now," Elizabeth continued, "I see the sweet boy who tried to take care of me all those years. But back then..."

She struggled to get the words out. "I'm ashamed to say...I was terrified of him."

Lindsay recognized the shame in Elizabeth's eyes—the same shame she'd seen in the mirror so many times.

"I can't blame any of it on him," Elizabeth went on. "I had my own stuff going on, but I justified it, you know? There were legends around the reservation where I grew up, legends of dark and evil spirits who could walk the earth like you and me."

She stared down at her fingers in her lap. "And that's what I saw when I looked at him sometimes. Just darkness and—"

The last words caught in her throat. She buried her face in her hands, her shoulders racked with silent sobs.

"Oh, honey." Lindsay put her arm around the woman's thin shoulders. "You think you're the only one who's ever been afraid of your child?" she asked with an incredulous look. "Try staring into the face of your screaming toddler when lightning strikes next to you out of a completely blue sky."

Elizabeth wiped her hands down her face and sniffed.

"She was three." Lindsay shrugged. "We were at the park, and I told her it was time to go. You can imagine how that went." She chuckled at the memory. "Talk about terrified. I almost got in my car and left her right there on the merry-go-round."

Elizabeth hiccupped a laugh and wiped a tear from her cheek.

"I mean, who wants to get in the car with *that*, right?"

"I guess." Elizabeth gazed at Ethan, a sad smile haunting her lips.

"Kids are resilient," Lindsay said. "Look at him. He couldn't be happier to have you here with him now."

"Kids..." Elizabeth muttered. "They *are* still our kids, aren't they?" she asked as Ethan playfully tugged on a loose strand of Camryn's hair and laughed at Michael trying to clean up his mess.

"They are," Lindsay confirmed. Even if it wasn't entirely true, she couldn't think of her daughter any other way. She just couldn't connect her anxious, antisocial child with a wise, eternal being. Camryn was still the same little girl who would pour an entire bottle of shampoo into her bathwater to make "the most epic mountain of bubbles." And who would sneak downstairs at night to eat a gallon of ice cream straight from the carton.

In the corner now, even with Ethan's help, Camryn still struggled to make use of her powers. Lindsay rubbed her hands together, itching to rush over to her.

"She needs to be outside for that to work," Akira called from her spot beside them.

Michael scowled in her direction. "It's too dangerous."

"Well, we can't stay here forever." Akira said what everyone seemed to be thinking. "Whatever their mission is, it isn't inside this basement."

Michael shot her a hard expression that Lindsay thought he wore more often than not. Of all the Archangels, Michael was the only one who bore a perpetual scowl—but not one meant to strike fear. As a parent, Lindsay recognized the expression—not one of malice or derision. It was the look of someone whose shoulders bore too much responsibility.

"Can you believe this?" Lindsay asked Elizabeth. "What kind of nightmare are we living right now that our children are honing their powers while waiting for the literal devil to come after them?"

Elizabeth's tears were gone now, her gaze intent on her son. "That darkness that I used to be so afraid of." She raised her chin the tiniest degree. "It will serve him well when that day comes."

Lindsay's eyes traveled back to her daughter's face. Did Camryn have this darkness inside her as well? If you asked

Camryn, she would probably say yes. But Lindsay had to disagree. To her, Camryn was the embodiment of light. Brilliant. Luminous. The long-awaited sun in the eventide of Lindsay's life.

No. Camryn didn't have darkness inside her. But she did have...something. Something just as dangerous. Behind those round, amber eyes and button nose lurked an earnest determination that remained unrivaled to anything Lindsay had ever seen. Camryn just had to figure out how to use it.

And quickly.

Her very life—and the world—might depend on it.

TWO

Shaking the fatigue from her hands, Camryn threw back her head and groaned. She'd been working for hours to conjure the stupid wind storm Michael had tasked her with, but nothing had worked. All morning she'd tested herself, trying to rouse her power, but for all her efforts, she'd only managed to turn a few glasses of water to ice.

"I'm never going to figure this out," Camryn said as Ethan propped himself against the wall beside her, twisting his plastic good luck charm between his fingers.

The sharp angles of his face were made less severe in the dim light of the darkened alcove, his russet skin appearing even darker, and the silver ring of metal in his lip all but disappearing in the shadows.

He stared at the ivory-colored piece of plastic for only a moment before flicking his gray eyes in Camryn's direction. When their eyes met, a familiar heat flushed her cheeks, and she glanced away, pressing her lips together.

Despite her frustration, Camryn's stomach flipped. For a moment, she wasn't a human-born angel training to take on the Fallen leader of the underworld. She was just a teenage girl staring into a pair of dazzling eyes and wondering what twist of fate would ever allow such a beautiful boy to look at her the way Ethan was looking at her now.

"Come on," he said. "That's not the Camryn I know."

"Oh really?" Camryn replied, as if she weren't bothered in the least. "Then you clearly don't know me very well."

Ethan smiled as he unhitched himself from the wall. "Akira's right, you know? We have to get out of here."

Camryn watched him drop the token into his pocket, remembering the story he'd told her on the Navy ship—the same ship where they'd received their angelic memories before traveling with Michael and the others here to Jerusalem.

She'd lain in the medical bay and listened to Ethan explain how his mother had given him the Lakota token and what it told him about his family. They'd not had a chance to talk about it, but Camryn imagined it was important to him for more reasons than one. The ivory-colored medallion displayed two arrows surrounded by a thin circle and bore the weight of all the stories his grandmother had ever told him about her tribe—the only information he really knew about his family.

Camryn blinked, tearing her eyes away from Ethan to glance around at the Archangels guarding each exit. "I don't know how we're going to get by those guys, but if you think we have a shot, I'm right behind you."

"We can hear you," Samael called from across the room.

"Stop eavesdropping," Ethan grumbled, turning his back to the room and addressing Camryn with a whisper. "I can't stay in this room one more day." His eyes shouted his desperation. "We have to figure something out."

Camryn massaged her palms. "I feel you. I really do, but…what are we going to do out there? I mean, you can at least start a fire. Unless someone needs some ice chips, I'm useless."

"You need to stop saying stuff like that. I'd trust you with my life over anyone else in this room. Including the ones with wings."

Camryn couldn't help the grin that snuck onto her face. "I just wish I had one memory—just one—of some kind of victory. Some kind of success. Because all I remember about our life before is failure after failure, and that isn't really great for the confidence, you know?"

Ethan came to stand in front of Camryn, placing one hand on each of her shoulders. "Listen to me, okay? You can do this. You just have to have faith. You'll figure this out. I know you will."

Camryn blinked twice. "Are you kidding me with that?" She tried to suppress the smile twitching at her lips. "That was the worst pep talk I've ever heard."

Ethan drew his arms protectively around his middle as she poked him in the stomach. "Okay," he laughed. "That *was* pretty lame."

"That's one word for it." Camryn turned away before Ethan could witness the smile fall from her face. She knew Ethan believed his own words, even if he wasn't the best at delivering them. She felt his confidence in every glance, every brief touch of his hand. She just couldn't find that same assurance within herself.

Once upon a time, she had. She'd been a fearless warrior who'd led armies into battle. She'd looked Lucifer in the eye without blinking. She'd fought against the most powerful Archangel in Heaven and actually thought she could win.

Yeah, because I was stupid.

Stupid or not, Camryn wanted nothing more than to feel that powerful again.

Apollyon had to be stopped. And soon.

"I just don't understand. Why does it have to be us? Look at these guys." Camryn gestured around at the four imposing warrior angels in their midst. "If they couldn't stop him, why do we think we can?"

Ethan opened his mouth to answer, but no words made their way out. His explanation turned to a shrug as Raphael called to them from the front of the room.

"Come look at this," Raphael beckoned as he placed his small, black tablet on the table in front of him—the same type of device that Jay had used back in Kentucky when they'd only known him as the nice medic trying to help Camryn find her parents.

She had thought it an odd device at the time but now recognized it as celestial technology that the angels jokingly referred to as a Halo.

"I know you've only seen these used for communication or tracking," Raphael said to Camryn, "but we've discovered a few more uses for them with the advancement of human technology."

A light shot into the air, and Camryn found herself watching an actual news broadcast, the Halo picking up a satellite signal intended for local television stations and projecting it into the air above the device.

The signal picked up just as a middle-aged, raven-haired woman with sharp eyes and even sharper cheekbones strode into view. She wore a black pantsuit and a stern gaze, the picture of power and authority.

"That's the president of Turkey," Ronan said.

Ethan looked confused. "I thought she was that SEF lady."

"She is," Akira answered without taking her eyes off the projection.

"Huh?"

"Same person," Camryn whispered under her breath. The woman on the screen was Harriet Kaya. The same woman who'd appeared on the news almost every night for the past few years, warning the world about the dangers of carbon emissions and overpopulation. Her Save the Environment Foundation had gained a lot of attention in the past year as her warnings about global warming had begun to come to fruition.

When the string of hurricanes, wildfires, and droughts began to spread over the globe, she'd amassed quite a following. And she did all this humanitarian work while being the leader of a thriving country.

Camryn had always wavered between a sense of awe for the lady and thinking her a sensationalist. Her father opted for the latter.

"This lady is a loon," her father said, as if on cue.

Camryn grinned in appreciation. *God, I love that man.*

"Good morning, ladies and gentlemen," Harriet Kaya began from behind the podium on the front lawn of the Turkish Capital Building.

"I want to thank you all for coming to this press conference on such short notice. I called you here today, as I have become aware of a grave threat to our region."

Her deep brown eyes stared straight into the camera, not even acknowledging the press who had gathered on the lawn.

"I will give you what information I can and address the hostiles directly, but for security purposes, I will not be taking questions at this time." An audible groan swept through the crowd.

"At five pm last night, I became aware of two hostile agents taking refuge in Jerusalem, and reliable intel suggests them to be a direct threat."

"What is—" Camryn started, but the words froze in her throat like the fragile ice she'd managed to create. Two pictures had popped up on the screen. One, of a girl in a lilac t-shirt, hair pulled into a loose ponytail, the other of a black-haired boy with a lip ring.

"Holy shit..."

"As your president, it is my duty not only to protect you from such threats but to do everything in my power to stop the threat from becoming more perilous. With that being said, I want to speak to the hostile cell in Jerusalem." She paused, tightening her grip on the podium.

"To the two American terrorists: we know where you are. Your location is under close surveillance, and we are working closely with Prime Minister Gaba of Israel to extract you at the earliest opportunity. He has agreed to lend as many forces as it takes to get you into our custody and out of his country." She took a deliberate pause that Camryn assumed was meant specifically for her.

"We don't want anyone else to be hurt, so I'm asking you now to turn yourselves in. I will be at the Turkish embassy in Tel Aviv in a few hours and will remain there until noon tomorrow. If you surrender peacefully, you will not be harmed.

If we have to take you by force, there is no way to guarantee your safety or the safety of those with you. You have until daybreak. After that, we will be forced to take other actions. Please do the right thing. Don't let anyone else die because of you."

With that, she turned and walked off the stage. The swarm of reporters erupted into a barrage of questions, all of which went unanswered.

A festering fire traveled over Camryn's body, burning away her flesh until she had none. Her skin disintegrated, her bones vanished, and she floated outside herself, viewing the scene from above as a numb, impartial spectator. She watched as the body she'd once inhabited gripped Ethan's arm to keep from falling to the floor.

Ethan…

She watched him grab her, cradle her head to his chest. She watched her parents rush over to her.

Mom…

Dad…

Her mother took her arm, trying to lead Camryn to her cot, handling her in that maternal way she had.

But even from above, something tugged at Camryn's gut, a string of fierce protectiveness that pulled her back toward her body. Her family was in danger, and she would be even more useless to them if she were unconscious.

It wasn't even a decision. She pulled herself along that invisible string, struggling as if swimming against a strong current, until finally…finally, she saw the world through her own eyes again.

Camryn pulled back from her mother's grip on her arm, and Lindsay paused, blinking.

"I'm…okay," she said, her gaze traveling over the room from Akira, who stood with arms crossed and brows furrowed, straight to Ethan, whose entire body appeared rigid with concern.

Camryn closed her eyes, trying to orient herself. She smiled despite the fog that overtook her brain like the aftereffects of a bad migraine. She'd done it. She'd fought against the current that had tried to take her under, and she'd won.

It wasn't a huge victory, but it was something.

THREE

Ethan recognized the glazed look that flashed in Camryn's eyes. He'd first seen it after they'd met Jay back in Kentucky—after she'd almost drowned and then found out her parents were most likely dead. That look hadn't faded until hours later, when they were safe on the Navy ship, in the medical bay, after he'd told her the story of the good luck charm in his pocket.

No. That wasn't the first time.

He'd seen the same haunted expression on his mother's face when he, at eight years old, had dialed 911 after finding her passed out on the kitchen floor. And again, those same blank eyes had stared straight through him from the bathroom floor of the bar downtown. And from the alley behind the River View Motel.

Ethan walked over to stand beside his mother, who sat rocking on her cot, staring at the floor, evidently rattled by Camryn's episode.

Ethan couldn't say he wasn't rattled as well. Seeing Camryn like that—even for a moment—so detached and unresponsive, left him with a familiar hollowness in his gut. Ethan focused on the feeling, tried to give it a name.

It was hopeless.

Helpless.

It was *weakness*.

Ethan watched as Lindsay whispered to Camryn and rubbed a reassuring hand over her daughter's back. Camryn sniffed and nodded but seemed oblivious to her mother's words. She'd fixed Ethan with a pleading stare, overwhelming him with the urge to knock Lindsay out of the way to get to her.

I should be the one helping her.

But who was he kidding? He'd never been able to help his mother. Why should he think Camryn would be any different?

Ethan lowered himself down beside his mother and wrapped an arm around her shoulder to stop her rocking.

I can't protect her here. I can't protect either of them.

"I'm really okay," Camryn said, pulling away from her mother, looking sheepish. "We need to focus on who that woman is… Who she *really* is. And how she knows who we are."

"She has to be working for Apollyon," Ethan offered. "It's the only explanation."

Michael seemed to concur. With the crisis with Camryn averted, he now glowered at Akira with silent rage blazing behind his eyes. "If that's true, why is this the first I'm hearing of her?"

Akira recoiled. "How was I supposed to know about this?"

"It's your job to know these things," Michael said through his teeth. "*How* does she know our location?"

"You know what, Michael? You can kiss my ass." Akira whirled away from him but seemed to think better of it as she turned back to face him, her face red with anger.

"I don't know how something like *this* slipped past me," she said, gesturing toward the Halo. "But you know as well as I do that I've had us covered since we got here. There's no way she knows where we are. She has to be bluffing."

"Hold up," James interrupted. "Covered? What does that mean?"

"Akira is a Tracker," Samael replied.

"That means she's very good at finding people," Jay added.

"It also means she's good at keeping people from finding her," Raphael finished, "or the people she's with. That's why it's been so important to have her join us on this mission."

James looked as if he were puzzling over an impossible riddle. "The church isn't protection enough? Camryn said the…demons," he hesitated on the word, "can't come in here. They're forbidden, right?"

Akira's eyes widened as she gestured to herself. "Hello. Fallen angel here."

James looked to Jay, still not understanding. "But…"

"We're not technically in the church," Samael, the quietest and least intimidating of the Archangels explained. "We're under it and far enough removed from any holy ground that Akira or any others of her kind could tolerate any discomfort this glorified storage closet might impart."

"Why aren't we in the church then?" James's face reddened.

"Because even though they couldn't get into the church," Michael chimed in, "they could still detect our presence without Akira's shield. And since Akira can't enter the church…" He trailed off as if the effort to grant any further explanation had become too burdensome.

"So, this power you have?" James challenged. "You're sure about it? I mean, it sounds like this Harriet lady is important, and *that* got by you. Any chance that something else might have slipped, too?"

Akira's eyes hardened. "You know, I'm going to give you a pass because you don't know me, but—"

"Okay, hear me out," Ronan cut in. "What if—" he glanced around the room with a mischievous glint in his eye, "—we wait till everyone is boarded on the plane, then we blow it up. *Blam*! Problem solved."

"Enough!" Michael shouted. "These are innocent human lives we're talking about. There will be no blowing anyone up just yet. We don't even know who this woman is." He turned to Raphael. "Get over there. See what you can find out. I want to know everything we can about her before we start talking about killing her."

"On it." Raphael looked to Jay and Sam. "You two are coming with me."

"Why do I have to go?" Jay asked. "Two can stay here, and two can go."

Samael checked his weapons to find not even a stitch out of place. "You heard Akira. There's no way Harriet Kaya knows where we are," he said. "They are perfectly safe here."

James scoffed, eliciting a look of disdain from Akira.

As the angels prepared to leave, Ethan caught Akira's eye, holding his breath while holding her gaze. He'd seen that look before, her expression pleading, and it left an unpleasant burn in his throat. She couldn't give two shits about what anyone else thought of her, including Michael, but she *needed* Ethan to believe her.

He gave her the slightest nod, enough to appease her before turning away. He couldn't have Akira doing something stupid just because she'd gotten her feelings hurt. Keeping Camryn and his mother safe remained his only concern, and if he had to lie in order to do that, then so be it.

But it wasn't a lie. Not really. He did trust Akira—she'd never done anything to warrant anything less—but if Camryn had taught him anything, he needed to be prepared for anything.

Just in case.

FOUR

Ethan's black hair fell into downcast eyes, and he didn't bother pushing it away.

With the dusty ground under him and the stone wall at his back, a foreboding chill leached through his clothes, cooling his skin, seeping into his bones. But the iciness did little to douse the flickering embers inside him.

Ethan stretched his neck, his back aching from immobility, but he couldn't make himself move. Camryn lay beside him on her cot, her blank eyes staring at the ceiling.

He strained to keep his hands in his lap. Not because he didn't want to touch her but because he so desperately did. He wanted to lay his hand on hers, wanted to prove to her that as long as he was around, no harm would come to her. But he was afraid—partly because her father hadn't stopped glaring at him since their arrival. But mostly because he knew it wouldn't be enough.

The primal magnetism that had held him in Camryn's orbit even when he'd tried so desperately to leave seemed to be growing stronger. He could barely touch her now without feeling her essence ripple through him, touching every part of him, inside and out. And feeling that bond, that connection that had been lost so long ago...he never wanted to lose it again.

"It's been an hour," Ethan said. "Shouldn't they be back by now?"

Michael's eyes shrank into slits. "Sometimes these things take time."

Camryn didn't acknowledge the exchange, barely blinking as the hands resting on her stomach moved up and down with her even breathing.

Ethan felt the restless energy seeping off of her even though she insisted she was okay. But her parents sat quietly nearby and didn't seem concerned, so maybe he shouldn't be either. They knew her best.

Didn't they?

Looking at Camryn's parents now, Ethan realized they were not at all what he'd been expecting. Walking into the basement room the day before, Ethan had been too distracted by his own mother to notice, but now he studied them with tepid curiousity.

When Camryn had talked about her parents before, he'd pictured them more like Dale and Grace, his foster parents back in the sleepy farm town of Kentucky Bend. But the pair across from him now more resembled a hippie and a lumberjack than two rural Kentucky farmers.

Lindsay's long, light brown hair fell over each of her shoulders, and she wore a patterned blouse with loose-fitting jeans. Beside her, James rubbed his rugged beard and adjusted the flannel button-up that stretched over his wide shoulders.

Noting James's dark eyes and hair, Ethan couldn't help thinking that Camryn clearly got her looks from her mother.

"But he hasn't even contacted you?" Ronan asked.

Michael paused a beat before shaking his head.

Ethan groaned. The Archangels had had plenty of time to get to Turkey and have *something* to report by now.

Michael stood by the door like a statue. His stony face gave nothing away, but as Ethan turned, he caught a glimpse of a warm yellow mist rolling off the Archangel like fog. Ethan jerked his head back, but the haze had vanished.

He's nervous.

Ethan could tell. He shouldn't be able to...but he could.

Camryn didn't so much as blink as Ethan stood and stretched his back.

"Where are you going?" Michael snapped.

"I've gotta take a piss. Is that okay with you?"

Michael seemed to actually contemplate the question before nodding toward the bathroom.

As Ethan washed his hands in the dingy sink a few minutes later, he ran over their situation again in his head. *Harriet Kaya is working with Apollyon. We don't know how, but she is. She's given us till dawn to turn ourselves in, but Michael is unwilling to even entertain the idea*.

Could they do it without him? *Probably not.*

The probability of talking Akira and Ronan into transporting them remained low, and sneaking away from three angels undetected would be impossible.

Ethan heaved a heavy sigh. Time seemed to be running out for all of them, and Elohim had yet to reveal any divine mission.

Why is he making us wait while people continue to die?

Why seemed to be the question of the week.

Why?

Why any of this?

When Ethan finally looked into the square piece of plastic hanging above the sink with a reflective coating to serve as a mirror, his image returned to him wavy and distorted. Exactly how he felt—like a warped version of himself. As much as he wanted to project their situation into something completely normal, he understood Camryn's struggle with relating to the angel she used to be.

The angel of his past had been submissive, a follower. Uriah protected Arael, but he seldom made decisions based on anything else. He just did as he was told. Surely more would be expected of him now. Or maybe…

Maybe protecting Camryn was his only job. His only purpose. Ethan took a moment to wonder—would that be enough. "Yes," he answered aloud. Did he want to watch the life leach out of Apollyon's eyes at his own hands? Also, yes. But if protecting Camryn was the most he could contribute, he would execute that task with elite precision.

Stepping back into the dark corridor a few moments later, Ethan wasn't surprised to see Akira leaning against the wall, arms crossed, waiting for him. Ethan averted his eyes from the pale white skin of her stomach that stared at him from under the hem of her tiny crop-top.

"What do you want?" Ethan whispered.

Akira's eyebrows pinched together. "God, when did you become such an asshole? I'm just trying to talk to you. You've been doing an impressive job of ignoring me since I got here."

Ethan turned back toward the others. "I can't do this with you right now," he said, raking the hair out of his eyes.

Akira stopped him with one small but firm hand on his arm. "I'm not trying to *do* anything." She spun him back toward her. "What's wrong with you?"

Ethan tried to pull away from her. "Nothing. Nothing's wrong."

"Are you mad at me about something?"

Ethan took a breath. The hurt in Akira's eyes betrayed her flippant attitude. He didn't want to hurt her. He just—

"I'm not mad. I just know how easily things could get complicated." Ethan looked back down the corridor toward the room where Camryn lay on her cot. "You two already aren't on good terms. I don't want things to get worse."

Akira raised a thin eyebrow. "Let's see. The earth is imploding. We're stuck in this basement being hunted by the ruler of the underworld, and the only hope we have of getting out lies with two human kids who can't figure out how to use their powers. What could possibly make the situation any worse?"

"Akira, I swear to God. If you say anything to her—"

Akira rolled her eyes. "Don't worry. I'm not going to tell her. Believe it or not, I *am* here to help you."

Ethan felt the tension drain from his body. "Good. Glad we can agree."

Akira raised her shoulders and wrinkled her nose. "On the other hand…"

"No," Ethan said. "There is no other hand."

"Do you think it's a good idea to keep secrets from her?"

Ethan grabbed Akira by the arms and pressed her into the wall at her back.

"So much aggression," Akira said, her red lips turning up into a smirk. "I like it."

"Stop that," Ethan said, releasing her. "That's not funny."

Akira made a show of straightening her shirt. "Sure it is. You just never had much of a sense of humor."

"Just trust me about this, okay? She doesn't need to know about anything that happened between us."

Akira shrugged. "Whatever you say."

Ethan took a few uneasy breaths before speaking. "I'm sorry…" He paused. "…for pushing you."

"Don't worry about it. I'm an angel. You can't hurt me, remember?"

FIVE

Arael stood panting on a jutting mass of rock that protruded from the tunnel from which she'd just emerged. Footsteps pounded and shouts echoed from the chamber.

Someone was chasing her.

A lake of boiling lava rolled and hissed below her, lighting the cavern with an orange glow. She turned to see Akira on an adjacent cliff, her auburn hair matted with sweat and blood and a barely conscious Uriah on her shoulder.

His misery evidenced by his pained expression and tense posture, Areal could imagine the agony that must be rippling through him, taking all the pain and suffering of this place as his own.

Uriah's eyes widened when he caught sight of Arael. He tried raising his head, but it swiftly lolled back onto Akira's shoulder.

Akira nodded to Arael in what looked to be some kind of salute—the first time she ever remembered Akira looking at her with anything less than contempt.

Arael glanced around, just then realizing where they were—the perimeter of the Void. Unlike the inner sanctum, Akira could transport from there.

"Go! Get him out of here!" Arael shouted as voices grew closer from the tunnel behind her.

Akira gave Arael one last apologetic look before she and Uriah disappeared.

Camryn bolted upright on her cot. Fragmented memories expunged themselves like this sometimes, like shards of shrapnel extracted from her mind.

Most of the time, they were just flashes—moments frozen in time—nothing useful, but they pulled Camryn's heart to a screeching halt every time.

This memory left her feeling sick. He'd looked so bad. Her eyes searched the room for Ethan to reassure herself that he'd actually made it out, but he was nowhere in sight. Neither was Akira.

Camryn planted her black and white converse on the floor, preparing to push herself to her feet, but her mother suddenly appeared in front of her, a worried expression on her face.

"He's fine," her mother said, lowering herself down beside her daughter. "He's in the bathroom."

Camryn breathed out a laugh and relaxed back against the wall, leaning her head into Lindsay's shoulder. Camryn had spent so much of the past week thinking her mother dead that every moment spent with her now was like waking from a bad dream.

"So that was pretty cool what you did earlier, huh?"

Camryn shrugged. "I guess..."

Her mother pursed her lips as if looking for the right words. "Remember last week when I called you from Franklin after that first earthquake?"

"Um…" Camryn did remember. "Yeah."

"I was so mad at myself for leaving you alone. I just knew that you needed me, and I wasn't there. I was packing a bag as I dialed your number."

Camryn remembered the frantic phone call, her mother's bewildered voice on the other end of the line when Camryn had answered with relative calm.

"And then I talked to you, and you were fine." Lindsay shrugged. "Rational even."

Camryn smiled against her mom's shoulder.

"It was because of him, wasn't it?"

Camryn swallowed hard, her smile quickly fading. There was only one *him* her mother could be referring to. "He was with me, yes."

Lindsay nodded. "That's what I thought."

They were silent for a moment longer before her mother straightened. "I'm glad he's here then," she said. "Even if it's just to help you see how incredibly strong you really are."

Camryn stared after her mother as Lindsay stood and strode back over to join James on the other side of the room.

"Where have you two been?" Michael snapped as Ethan and Akira emerged a moment later from the darkened corridor.

"Nowhere," Akira said.

"Nothing," Ethan said at the same time.

Michael frowned.

Camryn cocked her head at them.

"Smooth," Akira whispered before sauntering back to her cot.

Heat flushed through Camryn's body at the sight of them, her mother's words squashed in one enlightening moment. Watching the two of them emerge from the darkness, Camryn realized she'd never seen them—just the two of them—together like that. She hated that it bothered her. Being the jealous girlfriend was the last thing Camryn wanted. But what troubled her more than her own insecurity was how perfect they looked together.

With Ethan and his ragged appearance and Akira in full goth attire, they just *fit*. A startling realization.

Camryn wanted to speak up, to ask what they'd been doing down a dark hallway together, but one look into Ethan's stormy eyes reminded her of the terrible vision that had so terrified her just moments before.

"That was nothing." Ethan gestured toward Akira, apparently alarmed by Camryn's expression.

Camryn twisted her hands in front of her. "Yeah." She waved him off. "I know."

Ethan's face relaxed, but he seemed to waver. "Well, what's wrong then?"

How to answer that? She didn't have anything new to share. Not even a real memory. Only a picture of him, clinging to life in the Void.

"Maybe we should do what this Harriet lady says," Camryn said, first to Ethan, then turning to Michael. "Maybe we could just go talk to her and—"

"Camryn," Michael said with forced patience, "you aren't going to go to the embassy and just sit down and have a conversation with this woman. *If* we go—and that's a big *if*—it will be to dispose of the threat. Not to completely and irrevocably destroy this mission."

"Dispose of the threat? Do you even hear yourself right now? We're not assassins, Michael."

Michael turned away from her. "It doesn't matter anyway. What you're suggesting is exactly what Raphael and the others are doing. We just have to be patient."

"Well, what's taking him so long?" Camryn shouted.

"I don't know!" Michael shouted back. "I've been trying to contact him, but—"

Michael froze, a petrified look crossing his face. He shuddered as if he'd been shot with a thousand-volt current of electricity.

"What's wrong with him?" Elizabeth's mousy voice squeaked from her spot on the floor.

"What?" Ronan stood. "What is it?"

"It's Raphael," Michael managed to say.

Everyone straightened, passing questioning glances around the room.

"I–I don't know what's happened." Michael stammered. "He's gone. I've lost my connection to him."

"I thought you said he hasn't contacted you," Ronan said.

Michael looked at Ronan, dazed, before shaking the uncertainty from his head. "Th–the *qanima* bond is a very tangible thing. I can always feel him on the other end. But now…" Michael looked up, desperation etched in every crevice of his face. "Nothing."

Camryn and Ethan exchanged a look. They both knew the excruciating loss associated with having one's *qanima* bond severed like an injured limb.

"He's just gone?" Akira asked.

Michael's look of utter devastation answered for him.

"Is he hurt? Did they capture him?" Ronan asked.

"I don't know!" Michael shouted, more out of pain than anger this time.

A few silent moments passed before Ronan spoke again. "What are we going to do?"

"I–I don't know." The look on Michael's face took Camryn back to the valley of the Alborz, a bloody and weak Michael standing before her as Dagon and his demons dragged him through the portal. The hopelessness on his face the moment he realized her betrayal matched his grim expression now.

Ethan marched over and put a hand on Michael's shoulder. "You have to find him."

"No." Camryn insisted. "He can't leave us here."

Ethan's eyes found hers. "Akira and Ronan are still here. We're not alone."

"But—"

"Camryn, listen. I remember waking up after that first battle and finding you gone. There was no force in the universe that could have stopped me from tracking you down." He offered Michael a sympathetic look.

"He doesn't want to leave us. And he would try to ignore the pull for as long as he could, but eventually…he'd have to go."

"I can't," Michael whispered. He looked as torn as the bond that had just been ripped from him. Then, as horror crossed his face, he almost fell into the chair next to him.

"Does this mean…"

Camryn understood his hesitation to finish the thought: *"Does this mean he's been exiled?"* The idea brought bile into her throat.

No way," Ethan said. "That could only happen by the weapon of another Righteous angel. That's not possible, is it?" Ethan glanced between Ronan and Akira.

Michael stood abruptly, his senses apparently returning to him. "Ethan's right. I have to go." He pulled his Halo from his breast pocket and tossed it to Akira. "You're in charge until I get back."

Camryn huffed out a breath and looked away. Michael was abandoning them *and* leaving Apollyon's messenger in charge. *Great.*

"I will be back," Michael said to the group. "Until then, for the love of the Creator, listen to your parents. And you all," he said directly to the three adults. "Don't let them leave this room."

Lindsay nodded. James puffed his chest as if he'd just received his first secret agent mission, and Elizabeth looked as if she'd burst into tears if anyone so much as looked at her.

To Michael's credit, he did hesitate a moment more before vanishing from the room.

"Okay," Camryn said as soon as Michael had gone, "we can't really just stay here indefinitely, can we? That can't be what Elohim wants."

Ronan pulled a dagger from the air and inspected it in the beam of light shining in through the window. "I agree. It seems we're just wasting time here."

"I don't know," Lindsay looked uncertain. "Michael did say—"

"Yes," Akira said. "Michael said we stay put. That's what we're doing."

"Let's talk about this for a minute," Ethan said. "I think Camryn is right."

"Of course you do," Akira mumbled.

"You said so yourself, Akira. Whatever our mission is, it isn't inside this church." Ethan's gray eyes found Camryn's. "She's only given us until dawn. If they aren't back before then, we make a new plan."

DAY TWO

SIX

Minutes ticked by like agonizing hours as Camryn lay staring at the small window atop the basement wall, waiting for the first sign of morning to shine through. As soon as the blackness lifted to a dark gray, she swung her feet from her cot and marched over to where Ronan stood guard against one of the four exit doors.

"They're not back."

Ronan pressed his lips together and nodded. "I see that."

"Okay, so…" Camryn slapped her thighs. "It's almost dawn. What are we going to do?"

"What? You mean you don't have a plan?" Ronan raised an eyebrow.

Camryn chewed her bottom lip and folded her arms over her chest. "My plans don't usually pan out the way I want them to."

"Well, that's never stopped you from making them." He smiled.

Camryn almost smiled back. "Ronan, come on. This is serious. If we're going to the embassy, we have to do it now."

"That's the one thing we definitely aren't doing." Ronan looked as if the idea pained him. "You heard Michael. And besides, I'm positive that Akira's cover is solid."

Camryn bit her lip to keep from screaming.

Akira dislodged herself from her post and sauntered over to where Camryn and Ronan stood. "Don't pretend your little brain hasn't been whirring away all night, coming up with some spectacular way to get us all killed," she said. "Let's hear it. What's your terrible idea?"

"Well," Camryn began timidly, "I may have thought of something." She hesitated. "But even I don't like it."

Akira closed her eyes and waved her fingers in a "give it to me," gesture.

Camryn tucked her chin and breathed out the words before she could think better of it. "If I remember correctly, there are safe rooms under the church. Bomb shelters, right?"

Akira and Ronan exchanged a questioning glance.

"If it's just the two of us," Camryn said, gesturing to herself and Ethan, "then the two of you could transport us to the embassy. We can still make it there in plenty of time."

"You mean to take your parents to one of these shelters and just leave them there?" Ronan looked horrified at the idea.

Camryn squeezed her eyes shut. "I agree, it isn't optimal, but what choice do we have? Maybe this is what we're meant to do." She glanced at the faces staring back at her.

"Like in chess… Sometimes, in order to take the queen, you have to sacrifice a few pawns. Maybe we're the pawns, and once she's distracted with us, you two can take care of her, and our families can go back to whatever's left of our homes. This will all be over, and the world will be safe."

"Oh. My. God." Akira rocked back on her heels. "Life really is all sunshine and rainbows in your head, isn't it?"

Camryn glared at her. "It's actually hell in here, if you really want to know, but you don't, so why don't you go fu—"

"Ladies," Ronan stepped in. "Let's focus, please."

"Okay." Camryn waved an arm at Akira. "Let's hear your genius idea then, since you seem to know everything."

"I never said I know everything, but I do know that Harriet Kaya doesn't give a rat's ass about you two. It's Apollyon who's put out the hit, and since I have spent more time with him than any of you, I can assure you, turning yourselves in would stop nothing. Things have progressed too far, and capturing the two of you is only a small part of his plan. Why do you think he's set this random woman on your trail instead of coming after you himself?"

Camryn's jaw tightened. That possibility had never crossed her mind. "But she said—" Camryn slammed her mouth shut before making herself look even more foolish. Promises meant nothing to people who aligned themselves with Apollyon.

Akira rolled her eyes. "It isn't just you he wants. Apollyon has been trying to destroy this earth since its creation. This is just his latest and possibly most successful attempt. There is only one way to stop any of this."

"So...what are you saying?" Camryn thought she knew the answer but hoped she was wrong.

"We have to kill him. It's the only way."

Ethan picked that moment to unfold his long frame from his cot and join them. "Sounds awesome. But how the hell are we gonna do that?"

Akira and Ronan stared at each other as if they'd asked themselves that exact question more than once.

"Could we find others to help us?" Ethan yawned. "I've been thinking about our life before, and we never did anything alone. We always had an army behind us." He gestured to Camryn.

"She had soldiers loyal to her for centuries. Maybe we could use them now."

"She had soldiers loyal to Apollyon. Not her. And definitely not this version of her," Akira said, wrinkling her nose as if catching wind of something foul. "You aren't going to find enough Fallen or Nephilim willing to betray Apollyon like that, even if they wanted to."

"What about Michael's army, then?" Camryn interjected.

"You can't command a spiritual army from the physical realm. Besides, Michael's army only takes orders from Michael. They'd laugh in our faces if we tried to pull them into something like this."

"Well, what if they don't know the orders are coming from us?" Camryn looked pointedly at Michael's Halo sticking out of Akira's back pocket.

"Oh, no." Akira waved her arms in the air. "No way. No one knows that I'm working with Michael except you guys. They'll never believe he just gave this to me. If they find out I have it, I'm dead."

"It couldn't hurt to try," Ronan said.

Akira backed away from them. "It couldn't hurt to *try*? We're not talking about baking an apple pie here, guys. This isn't something we just *try* and hope for the best."

"Excuse me," James interjected, woken by their not-so-quiet conversation. "Didn't Michael leave us in charge? Do we not get a say in what happens with our own daughter?"

"No, actually," Akira said. "He left me in charge. Sorry." Though she didn't look sorry in the least.

Lindsay and Elizabeth sat up, blinking at the commotion.

Akira threw her arms in the air. "Oh good, the gang's all awake. I'm sure they'll have ideas, too. Let's waste a ton more time arguing about pointless endeavors."

"If you don't want to do it, hand it over," Ronan extended his hand for the Halo. "They'll believe me."

A tense moment passed before Akira clenched her jaw and jabbed the device toward him. "*Bloody hell,*" she murmured under her breath. Ronan took it and tapped out a brief message, then tucked the device away in the pocket of his still-pressed khakis.

Camryn finally released the breath she'd been holding. "Now what?"

"Well," Akira said, looking uncomfortable. "I have to admit...your plan wasn't complete trash."

"I'm sorry, what?"

"Yeah," Akira's gaze shifted to the hovering adults. "No matter what our next move is, we can't have them slowing us down. We probably should move them to a safer place."

James shot forward. "Absolutely not. I am not leaving my daughter here waiting for God-knows-what to happen."

"And what are you going to do to protect her, James?" Akira demanded. "You have no weapons, no superhuman powers. We are fighting a spiritual war here. Even your daughter is more useful than you."

James's eyebrows knit together, and he raised his finger as if he were about to give Akira the sternest talking-to she'd ever received until Lindsay put a hand on his arm.

"Honey," Lindsay spoke to her husband but met Camryn's eyes as she said, "I think Akira's right."

James looked at his wife as if she'd grown another head. "Right about what? Leaving our daughter here alone?"

"She isn't alone, and she isn't unprotected. If you believe everything we've been told, and I think we kind of have to, Camryn has a protection over her greater than any human parent can provide. And she's here for a reason. I think we have to trust that...and trust her."

Camryn swallowed the lump in her throat as she walked over and threw her arms around her mother. She closed her eyes and breathed in Lindsay's honeyed scent, desperately trying to commit to memory the feel of her mother's arms around her. *This could be the last time I see her.*

When she finally forced herself to pull away, Camryn turned to Akira. "Thank you," she said to the fiery-haired angel who stood staring down the hall into the darkness, her foot tapping the floor in an unsteady rhythm.

Akira shrugged. "Their incessant prattling is getting on my nerves anyway."

After a few more moments of discussion, it was decided that Ronan would be the one to take the adults to the bunker while Akira and her shield would stay behind with Camryn and Ethan.

"I'll be back in twenty minutes," Ronan said.

Camryn turned to her parents, fighting back tears. She wanted to say so much but didn't even know where to start.

"I know, honey." Lindsay pinned Camryn with steadfast eyes. "I know this is what we have to do. I knew when you walked through that door two days ago that I wouldn't have much time with you."

James came and wrapped both women in his thick, strong arms. He kissed Camryn on top of the head before grasping her by the shoulders. "I would never have wished something like this for you," he said, his voice strained. "But if I've done my job correctly, you'll be ready for whatever comes."

Camryn managed to roll her eyes as she swiped at her tears. "Ready for *this*?" she gestured around the room at the mishmash group of angels.

"I mean it." He lowered his eyes to hers. "We've been preparing your whole life for this. You know how to handle yourself. Now it's time to rock and roll."

Camryn tried to smile. Her dad had been ready to "rock and roll" his whole life. Well, for as long as she could remember, at least. The expression was his motto—what he lived by. Camryn's interpretation: Be prepared for anything at all times.

"Time to rock and roll," she repeated, rolling her eyes again, grateful for something as simple as a corny catch-phrase to cling to in that moment. Camryn leaned forward to hug him again even though he was wrong about one thing.

"But I don't have any weapons, Dad. And even if I did, I don't think they would help me here."

"That doesn't matter." The intensity in his dark eyes rooted Camryn to her spot. "You've got this." He tapped her forehead. "And this is all the weapon you need."

Lindsay hugged her daughter again. "Your dad's right," she said. "You've fought these demons every day. Even if you couldn't see them, they were there…in your fear. But you fought them, and you won." Lindsay's voice came out strained as if she were holding back tears. "You won every time before, and you'll win again."

Camryn had never heard her mother talk this way. So much conviction filled Lindsay's voice that Camryn almost believed her.

She flicked her gaze toward Ethan, saying his own awkward goodbyes with his mother. Elizabeth Reyes clung to her son as her body shook with tears. Ethan shot Camryn a tortured glance, and her heart ached for him—for both of them.

Camryn didn't think they'd spent much time together that didn't include arguing or fighting or screaming at each other. Neither of them seemed to know quite how to handle the love between them.

The adults slowly detached themselves from their children and made their way toward the darkened doorway at the end of a short corridor where Ronan stood waiting.

James turned around, looking as if he'd changed his mind entirely, but Lindsay grabbed his arm. The regret in his eyes almost took Camryn's breath, but she nodded for him to go.

"It's okay, Dad. I'll be okay."

Only with another tug from Lindsay did he turn back to the door and follow the others through.

Camryn wanted so badly to reach for Ethan's hand, but Akira's warning still haunted her. "You're not this weak," Akira had said on their trip to Jerusalem, the words attaching themselves to one of Camryn's deepest fears.

Screw that.

Camryn reached for Ethan's hand, not caring how it made her look, and was surprised to find his fingers reaching for hers in the shadows. His sharp intake of breath when their hands met told her all she needed to know, and suddenly, Akira's warning seemed ludicrous. Needing physical contact didn't make her weak. It made her *human*. With that realization came another, perhaps more important, nugget of truth.

Camryn had been fighting so hard against her humanity, trying to be the angel from her memories, wondering why Elohim would have so inhibited them with these human limitations. But so much about humanity remained a mystery to the angels.

Maybe this mission couldn't be accomplished by celestial understanding.

Maybe her humanity was just what she needed.

SEVEN

Watching his mother disappear through the doorway with Ronan, the fragile sense of security Ethan had warily allowed to take shape in his mind shattered into a thousand jagged shards, piercing him from the inside out.

They'd had so little time together.

At least you got to see her again, the more sensible side of him tried to reason.

But the mental drawer in which his anger had been laid to rest had already burst open, loosing the monster within. Ethan was almost relieved.

His chest tightened. His muscles tensed.

It wasn't enough.

Ethan reached for Camryn's hand, and she leaned into him, collapsing in his arms as if she could no longer keep herself upright.

Seconds ago, he'd wanted to punch something. He'd wanted to burn this whole place to the ground. But Camryn's breath, her touch, her scent became the antidote to the poison dripping through his veins.

His pulse slowed. His body relaxed the tiniest degree.

"They're going to be fine," he said, his fingers weaving into her hair. "Ronan will make sure they're safe." He spoke the words more for Camryn's benefit, but he had to make himself believe them as well.

"They'll be fine," Camryn repeated, almost to herself. The hard set of her jaw sent Ethan's escaping anger back into its resting place, slamming the drawer tight. Ethan suddenly wished Akira had left them alone after all.

He rubbed his thumb over the impossible softness of Camryn's cheek. How could something so small be so incredibly strong?

Ethan parted his lips to speak. If he'd learned anything from his stolen time with his mother, it was to never leave anything unsaid. If you wanted to say something to someone, just say it. Shout it. Scream it through the streets if you had to.

But this was different. *She* was different. The words he wanted to say to her were nothing any seventeen-year-old would ever expect to say to another person. Besides, Akira's guaranteed gagging would ruin the moment.

Camryn's eyes glistened, Ethan's unspoken words dancing in the air between them. But before she could catch them, a soft thud rumbled in the distance. Ethan might have mistaken it for thunder if not for the sprinkling of dust and mortar that showered down on them from the ceiling above.

Akira rushed to the door leading to the outside world and disappeared up the aged, stone stairs.

This wasn't what Ethan had in mind when he'd wished for a few moments alone with Camryn. They could do nothing but stare at each other before another rumble shook the building, closer this time.

Ethan's heart hammered, and his mind clicked into overdrive, quickly slashing "stay in the basement" off their list of possible options and calculating which mode of escape held their best chance at survival.

Akira popped her head back through the doorway and beckoned to them. "Bombs." One word to set them into motion. They rushed toward Akira and up the stairs toward the outside world.

Taking the steps two by two, they stopped short when another earth-shattering explosion sent a huge chunk of stone splintering from the wall and landing on the stairs in front of them.

"Other way!" Camryn turned and shouted.

They all turned and ran back down the steps, through the door, and across the floor toward the exit on the other side of the room. Hitting the bottom of the stairs and sprinting across the vast stone floor, another deafening explosion sent Ethan's instincts into overdrive. He dropped and covered his head just as everything went dark around him.

EIGHT

Metal.
Sulfur.
Blood.

The smell of the bombs still lingered in the air, finding Camryn's nostrils even before she became aware of the crushing weight on top of her.

"Camryn!" a voice called. "Camryn, can you hear me?"

Camryn tried to respond, but couldn't inhale the air needed to push out the words.

Her heart rate accelerated, using her oxygen faster, and stars formed behind her eyes.

Calm down or you're going to die, she tried to reason with herself, but she already knew...death would find her either way.

She tried moving her arms, but found herself completely immobilized by the chunks of debris on top of her. Squeezing her eyes shut, a pleading prayer formed in her mind.

Is this Hell?

It had to be. She couldn't move. Couldn't breathe. Couldn't see a thing—all of her worst nightmares rolled into one.

Akira's growl of effort reached Camryn just as a rush of air entered her lungs and a blast of light blinded her dilated eyes.

"Pull her out!" Akira screamed as she heaved a chunk of stone over her head, and Ronan reached in and extracted Camryn from the rubble.

Camryn's body screamed in pain. She brought both hands up to cradle her throbbing head, the dizziness making her stomach churn.

Blood ran down her dust-covered arm and dripped onto the ground, but as far as she could tell, no bones were broken.

"Are you okay?" Ronan caught her as she stumbled.

"Careful," Akira said, releasing the stone slab and letting it fall back into the pile of debris that had just held Camryn prisoner. "She probably has a concussion."

Breathe, Camryn instructed herself. *Just Breathe.* For several moments, Camryn could think of nothing except getting oxygen into her lungs. Then, as the panic began to subside, she looked up to take in the devastation around her.

Much of the church had been destroyed, the whole area decimated. Small stone columns stood in defiance, the sections of yellowed rock a grim reminder of the precious history that had been lost to the attack.

The impact of the blasts had blown the windows from the walls that dared to remain standing, and glass littered the ground like parade confetti.

From where they stood, she didn't suspect there would be any casualties—not in this nonresidential area, anyway. Nevertheless, the city burned around them.

They stood in some sort of plaza outside what used to be the Church of the Holy Sepulchre. Where shops and other places of worship once stood, piles of smoldering rubble covered the ground.

Camryn turned quickly toward Akira, her questions ready to burst from her lips, but the Tracker anticipated them. "Your parents are fine," she said. "They're safe for now."

Camryn blew out a heavy breath, but the panic refused to release her. "Ethan?" She jerked her head around, looking for him. "Where is he?"

Akira and Ronan exchanged a dismal look. "He's not here," Akira said.

"What do you mean?" Camryn demanded. "Where is he?"

"We don't know. By the time I got back…" Ronan paused. "He was gone."

"No. He has to be here somewhere." Camryn bent over and picked up a stained-glass window that had somehow remained intact. She would move every piece of this church by herself to find him if she had to.

"He's not here," Akira said evenly. "I can tell. The same way I can tell there are no Nephilim in the area anymore either." She glanced at the skyline.

"What–what does that mean?" Camryn followed her eyes, looking at nothing.

"It means they have him." Ronan looked down at his feet. "And they've retreated."

"They *have him*?" Camryn exclaimed. "Well, why the hell are we still standing here?" Camryn stepped down off the pile of rubble and stumbled into Akira.

"Hold up there, Cowgirl." Akira grabbed her arm. "You're staying right here with me. Ronan's going."

"Alone?"

"Well, I certainly can't go with him. I'm supposed to be on their side, remember?"

"I can go," Camryn said. "*I'm* going with him."

Akira rolled her eyes. "No, you're not."

Camryn leaned forward, pointing a finger back at herself. "If Ethan is in danger, there's no way this is happening without me. I can help."

Ronan pulled one shoulder into a shrug and said in a sheepish tone, "I can transport in, grab Ethan and be out in less than a minute."

"You think they won't have barriers up to prevent that? You might be able to get in, but getting out of there won't be easy."

When neither of them immediately argued, she hammered the nail one more time. "You know I'm right," she said, glancing between them.

The corner of Ronan's lip twitched.

"Why are you doing that with your face?"

"Smiling?"

"Yes. Stop it. This is not the time."

"I just find it amusing—this confidence you have when it comes to the people you love."

Camryn's mouth slammed shut. Confidence was not the word she would use to describe her intentions here. She wasn't so sure that she could be helpful to Ronan in this rescue.

But she could be a distraction.

No, not confident. Suicidal, maybe. But not confident.

"You can't go in there alone," she said. "Not after everything that's happened."

Ronan looked to Akira, asking a silent question. She shrugged as if to say, "It's up to you."

"Fine," Ronan said, flicking a glance up to the horizon. "But we have something to deal with first." Akira and Ronan looked up into the distance at something Camryn couldn't yet see.

Camryn's best guess was that Ronan's call had been answered. Michael's army had arrived.

"Let me talk to them," Ronan said, vanishing from Akira's side.

A few minutes later, Ronan returned with four very skeptical-looking angels. The one with black hair and kind eyes, Camryn recognized; the others weren't as familiar.

To Camryn, they all faded into one duplicated mold. Same intense eyes, same set jaw, same fighting stance. They all donned warrior armor, always ready for battle. The looks on their faces made Camryn think they expected one now, and all eyes were trained on her.

Camryn cast a questioning glance at Ronan.

"I told them who you are, but they had to see for themselves."

Camryn shifted her weight. "Well, did you tell them that I'm practically useless? Because it looks like they're ready to battle me right here in the street, and I'm clearly not prepared for that."

Zephaniah, Michael's second in command, let out a raucous laugh. He stepped forward and slapped a hand on Camryn's shoulder. "By God, it really is you."

Camryn chuckled nervously, unsure what to make of his laughter. As the Fallen angel he'd warred against for centuries, should she be treated so...cordially?

"I'd heard you were back, but they didn't say you were a kid." He bent down and stared into her eyes. "And completely human." He put his hands on his knees and leaned in to examine her more closely. "Amazing. Absolutely amazing."

"Well, not completely human." Camryn held up her hands and wriggled her fingers. "I can do some weird stuff with these."

Zephaniah laughed again, straightening to include Ronan in his address. "You all shouldn't be out on the street like this. Apollyon is searching for you." Then his gaze flicked to Akira, standing at a distance with her arms folded over her chest, pretending to look at the sky. "I suppose that's why the Tracker is here, ay?"

"Yeah, something like that," Camryn said. "You won't say anything, will you?"

Zephaniah gave her a knowing look. "Not everyone agrees with me…" He shot a glance over his shoulder at the accompanying men. "But I think what you did was heroic."

"Heroic?" Camryn grimaced. That wasn't a word she would choose to describe anything she'd ever done. In any lifetime.

"There are still a few bits that she doesn't remember," Ronan explained.

"Of course." Zephaniah straightened. "But suffice it to say—" he flicked a glance back to Akira. "—your secret's safe with us."

He rested his hand on his sword and cleared his throat, assuming a more business-like tone. "Ronan says Michael left you last night and hasn't been heard from since?"

"Yes, uh, that's correct." Camryn wished he would have this conversation with literally anyone else. "And we haven't been able to reach Raphael via Halo either."

A look of confusion crossed Zephaniah's face.

His apprehension set Camryn's nerves humming again. "What do you think it means?"

"If none of the Archangels are answering the beacon, they are likely in danger." He turned as if preparing to leave. "We must find them."

“Wait!” Camryn dared to reach out and grab his arm before thinking it through. She straightened, trying to mimic Zephaniah’s authoritative stance. “Please. That’s not the only reason we called you here.” She looked back to Ronan. “If you saw the news last night—”

Zephaniah’s eyes narrowed ever-so-slightly.

“Okay, maybe not. Anyway. Apollyon has an operative in Turkey—”

“Apollyon has operatives everywhere.”

“Yes, but this one is…different. And she’s taken Ethan. My *qanima*. You knew him as Uriah. She has him, and we need your help rescuing him and figuring out who this woman is. Could you spare a few men to help us?”

“Of course, I could. Our numbers are immense.”

Camryn didn’t like the apologetic tone of his voice.

“But I won’t.” Zephaniah eyed Akira again before turning back to Camryn. “You know we can’t interfere unless directly ordered to do so.”

“Michael has risked his life so many times to keep us safe. You don’t think he would order you to help us if he could?”

“He’s kept us out of it so far. I have to assume there’s a reason for that.”

Akira cursed and turned away from them. “I knew this was a waste of time.”

“Zephaniah.” Camryn attempted her most pleading expression. “We can’t do this alone.”

Zephaniah returned her gaze. “Obviously, someone thinks you can.” He looked over the group one last time. “We will locate Michael. That is the best we can offer.”

And with that, the five angels extended their immense wings, lifted off the ground, and shot into the morning sky.

The farther they rose, the heavier the desperation clawed at Camryn's chest, the feeble hope of finding Ethan retreating with every beat of their wings.

"Where do you think they took him?"

Akira exhaled. "He's at the embassy, obviously."

"How is that obvious?" Camryn quipped. "Unless you know something we don't."

"Because this is clearly a trap, dumbass. They're using him to lure you to them. And they already told us where that is."

Camryn glared at Akira through slitted eyes. "Fine," she said. "Let's go."

NINE

The pounding in Ethan's head and the screaming pain gnashing at his back almost drowned out the angry female voice screeching from across the room.

"Where's the girl?" the voice shouted.

With his eyes still closed, Ethan could garner only two bits of information about his situation: One, he'd been burned. Badly. And two, he was tied to some kind of a chair. Not a folding chair, but a cushioned chair with wooden arms.

Assessing all he could about his physical state, he turned his attention to the conversation in the room. "*Where's the girl?*" the woman had asked. She must mean Camryn, right? Ethan monitored his breathing, his heart rate, did his best to appear unconscious, listening.

"The girl couldn't be located, ma'am," a male voice replied.

A surge of hope shot through Ethan's veins. *They don't have her.* But then he remembered how he'd gotten the burns...

"What do you mean? She was there, wasn't she? Why would you leave without her?"

Only then did Ethan realize the voices in the room weren't speaking English.

The words being tossed about the room were...*Turkish?*

"We detected hostile forces approaching." The male voice sounded ashamed. "We had to evacuate quickly."

"We only found this one by chance," another voice added.

"Well, *he* is not the one Apollyon wants," the woman seethed.

Ethan heard clacking footfalls tracing from one side of the room to the other and felt the woman's uncertainty as if it was his own.

"You had better hope—for your sake and mine—that she comes for him. Otherwise, it's the end for all of us."

Ethan groaned internally. If Camryn were still alive—and he couldn't hope for anything less—of course she would come for him. Unless Akira and Ronan could stop her, which he wasn't sure they could.

The footsteps started again and approached, stopping directly in front of him. "You can cut the act, dear. I know you're awake."

Well, damn.

Ethan pried open his eyes against the brightness of the room. He wasn't surprised to find Harriet Kaya—the Turkish president, the leader of the SEF, the woman working for the epitome of evil himself—standing in front of him.

With her hair slightly disheveled, she wore the same pantsuit she'd donned for the press conference the day before. Two men dressed in military fatigues and wielding long rifles stood behind her on either side of the door.

When Ethan's gaze landed on the two guards, he groaned. One was a stranger. But the taller one, Ethan knew intimately well.

"Dameon," Ethan drew out his name. "How the hell did you get assigned a grunt-level job like this one?"

Dameon shot Ethan a venomous glare. "I volunteered."

Ethan licked his lips with a pondering squint but didn't respond, unsure what that meant for him. He and Dameon had history, but did it warrant Dameon taking a demotion just for the opportunity to point a gun at him?

Ethan eyed the scar that ran down the length of Dameon's face and remembered how it had gotten there. The fact that Dameon allowed the scar to remain on his skin like a hardened reminder of their feud told Ethan that the angel might hold a grudge.

Did Harriet Kaya know what these men were? What Apollyon was? Ethan tore his eyes from Dameon's to take in the rest of his surroundings.

They seemed to be in some type of small office, but all the furniture had been pushed to the edges of the room. Ethan sat in the middle of the mess in a plush office chair. Too wide to tip over, he noted.

"Game's over." The woman stood glaring down at him. "We have you. And soon we'll have the girl, too." Harriet Kaya crouched in front of Ethan. She ran her fingers reverently over the dark skin of his forearm.

"You are human." She appeared mesmerized by what she saw. "Not an angel cowering in a human body as before. It's...amazing." Her eyes shot to Ethan's. "How is this possible?"

Ethan would have pulled away from her if his hands hadn't been cuffed to the chair.

"I was born this way, same as everyone else."

Harriet stood, looking down her narrow nose at him. "But you're not like everyone else. Surely you know that."

Ethan did know that. Had known it his entire life. But he didn't know the answer to her question. Everyone wanted to know—Camryn and himself included. But the answer remained buried in their illusive angelic memories.

"What I know, lady," Ethan responded, "is that Apollyon is using you. And when he's done with you, he'll throw you away like the trash that you are."

Harriet drew back her hand and slapped Ethan hard across the face. "You have no idea what you're talking about," she said through her teeth.

Ethan ran his tongue over the ring in his lip, tasting blood. "I'd like to keep that if you don't mind."

Harriet glared at him. "Apollyon and I are a team. We are one." She tugged at her lapels. "Something you know a little about, correct?"

"Apollyon has no *qanima*, and you are no angel, lady. So whatever special bond you *think* you have with him, it's worthless." Ethan knew his words would likely land him in deeper shit than he was already in, but he couldn't help himself.

"Did he tell you he loves you? Is that it? Because he doesn't. He isn't capable of love."

Ethan expected another blow. But this time, Harriet only ran a manicured finger over the top of his hand.

"He's shown me the things you can do."

Ethan reclined his head on the back of the chair and laughed a humorless laugh.

"Yes, he's been watching you." Harriet smirked. "But you knew that, didn't you?"

A cold chill ran over Ethan's body as visions of shadow monsters danced across his memories. "He doesn't know anything about me."

"On the contrary," Harriet replied. "He knows everything about you. Every fight you've started. Every hour you spent in detention. Every fire you've ignited." She leaned down and let her eyes roam over Ethan's face. "Every night you cried yourself to sleep."

Ethan clenched his jaw and jerked against his bindings.

"Your Watchers knew you were special from the day you were born. Your aura was all the evidence they needed." She tilted her head to the side. "An aura you lost in exile, but have now mysteriously regained." She looked at him conspiratorially, as if she'd caught him in the middle of a naughty act.

"We would love to know about that as well." She strode over to the desk and leaned back, crossing her ankles in front of her.

"Your Watchers didn't know exactly what to make of you until you met up with the girl, but we were certain that keeping tabs on you would eventually pay off. And I do believe we were right."

"We?" Ethan scoffed. "You act like you've been around for all this. Who the hell are you?"

Harriet ignored the question. "Any other talents we need to know about before Apollyon's arrival?"

"I thought you knew everything about me."

"You're an Empath. You hold the essence of fire in your palms." Harriet shrugged. "That's what we've seen. But we all know that new powers can emerge, and usually do, in fact. Perhaps there's more you've hidden, even from yourself." Her eyes widened as if she were hungry for more information, like a scientist on the verge of discovering a new species.

Ethan closed his hands into fists. "Untie me and I'll show you exactly what I can do."

"Or we can do it the hard way." Harriet sighed. "All Apollyon needs is a little time, and he'll find out everything anyway. Like where your little friend is, for instance."

Just then, a radio crackled on the shoulder of one of the guards. "We have movement in the back alley," came a voice through the device.

Harriet's face lit with delight. "Speak of the devil."

Ethan rocked the chair back and forth, trying to free himself, knowing it was no use.

Harriet turned and pointed to the shorter guard. "You. Get down there and show our guests in." She muttered to Dameon as she passed, "Find out what we're dealing with here."

Dameon grinned and advanced on Ethan.

"Come on, Dameon," Ethan said in a playful tone. "Can't we work this out?"

But they were long past that.

Well, shit, Ethan groaned. *This is going to hurt.*

TEN

Fifteen minutes earlier, Camryn, Akira, and Ronan had stood outside the remains of the church, taking one last look around at the piles of concrete and glass that had once been a city.

Camryn couldn't help but feel some responsibility for the destruction around her. She knew, deep down, that Akira was right. If they'd gone to the embassy, if they'd met President Kaya's deadline, it wouldn't have changed anything.

This would have happened eventually. Apollyon's hatred of this planet and what it represented flowed much deeper than one irrelevant angel. But Harriet's words still stabbed her in the chest.

"Don't let anyone else die because of you."

Ronan let her soak in her pity for only a moment before he put a hand on her shoulder and found her eyes.

It was time to go.

Akira eyed them with apprehension. "I can hide your aura, but I can't make you invisible. Don't do anything stupid."

Ronan grinned. "I'll leave that up to you."

Akira backed away and Camryn allowed Ronan to scoop her up like a child, one hand under her knees and the other around her back. Camryn shouldn't have been surprised at the firmness of his arms and the ease with which he lifted her. He may have been half the size of the larger-than-life Archangels, but he was still an angel.

"Hang on," Ronan said as two radiant wings appeared in a shimmering flurry from his back. Camryn sucked in a breath. With two majestic beats, she and Ronan were in the air.

Camryn wrapped her arms around Ronan's neck, and as they rose higher, she fought the urge to bury her face in his shoulder.

At first, she concentrated on the span of the massive feathered appendages that had materialized before her eyes. They were blindingly white and shimmered with an iridescent glow. Moving gracefully up and down, Ronan's wings brought an overwhelming ache to Camryn's gut.

She'd had wings once. Wings just as powerful and beautiful as Ronan's.

As Camryn willed her stomach to relax, the nausea disappeared, replaced by giddy excitement. They were in the air above the city and they were flying.

Flying.

Well, flying might not be the right word—more like ascending—but it was thrilling just the same. The fire of her excitement was doused, however, by the carnage flowing like an ocean below her. The city lay in ruins, a smoldering sea of destruction. The Old City of Jerusalem, divided into four neighborhoods, each holding their own rich religious significance, had been lost to the world forever.

The wall around the city had been destroyed, laying in heaps and piles, the round golden dome from the Temple Mount the only recognizable landmark left. The Western Wall, the Via

Dolorosa…all gone. So much history and tradition just decimated, and playing as a soundtrack in the back of her mind—all of Apollyon's ranting about the destruction and chaos he wanted to bring to the world.

He's finally done it.

"Ready?" Ronan asked.

"For what?"

He grinned. "This might be a little unpleasant."

"Wait, wh—"

But before Camryn could protest, they were spinning, spirals of color whipping past her face, distorted and smudged. Her stomach churned like a washing machine spin cycle.

It lasted only a moment, but when the ground materialized under her feet again, she couldn't stop the bile from rising in her throat. She lurched forward, expelling the contents of her stomach.

"Oh, whoa—" Ronan put a hand on her back. "You okay?"

"Yep. Yep." Camryn raised a hand to him. "Just… Just need a second."

The disorientation of the transport on top of the dizzying effects of her concussion, and Camryn didn't know if the spinning would ever stop.

With her hands planted firmly on her knees, urging her stomach to calm, the acrid odor of vomit and old garbage hit her like a wave, making her heave again. Camryn extended a hand to steady herself on the green garbage bin in front of her.

Unsticking her shoes from the goop seeping from under the bin, she followed Ronan to the verge of the alley and leaned out to peer up the street.

"There it is," Ronan said, pointing up the road.

Camryn had expected a more subdued scene; at least some acknowledgement of the disaster that had happened in

Jerusalem just hours away. Instead, she found a busy city street, honking horns, cars speeding past. "Don't they know Jerusalem has just been bombed?"

Ronan peeled his eyes from the embassy to shoot Camryn an uneasy frown. "This traffic is about half what it is on a normal day, but unfortunately, this is a way of life for them. War and death are what they're used to."

Camryn straightened, thinking of her life of relative safety back in Kentucky and the constant fear that had consumed her. She couldn't imagine a world in which the threat of war was a normal part of life.

She tucked that thought into the back of her mind to irrationally obsess about later and switched her focus to the building Ronan seemed to be studying.

The Turkish embassy in Tel Aviv was a pleasant surprise. She'd expected a secluded place set on a green lawn with some kind of security fence around it. Instead, they were staring at an unassuming brick building on a regular city block—four stories tall with large windows facing the street, much like every other office building on the block.

Score one for us, I guess.

"He's on the second floor. Third window from the left," Ronan whispered. "We won't try transporting again so soon." He looked back to her excrement on the pavement behind them. "Not after *that* episode." He turned back to point across the street. "We should probably go up that block and circle around to the back. The stairwell will be easier to access from there."

He looked at Camryn as if he expected her input.

"Um, sure. Sounds great." Camryn waved for Ronan to lead, as she knew nothing about this city or breaking into buildings.

She followed at a trot across the street and around the block. They approached the embassy from the back alley, stopping to assess when they drew closer.

"The building's been cleared out." Ronan's eyes studied the embassy. "It's only the president and two guards."

"Minimizing witnesses," Camryn said.

Ronan nodded. "So, what's the plan?"

"You're asking me?" Camryn hissed. "You're the angel here."

Ronan turned to look at her, his face a flat sea.

"Oh. Right." Camryn kept forgetting—she had been an angel once, too. And she had been the one to lead hundreds of battles against enemy forces. She bit her lip, struggling to think *what would Arael do?*

She shook her head, her face a mixture of humiliation and regret. "I don't—" She could guess at what Ronan expected her to say, but she couldn't risk Ethan's safety on such a game.

Ronan gave her shoulder a reassuring pat. "There's one guard on the ground floor. Looks like he's making a perimeter sweep." His voice came out slow and patient, as if he were teaching a toddler to play a board game. "He's moving," Ronan said. "Let's go."

Camryn followed close behind as Ronan shot down the alley toward the embassy. Nearing the building, they stopped. Ronan listened, and with his signal, they entered through the back door.

They stood for a long moment, listening to the silence expand around them. When they finally moved, Camryn's shoes squeaked against the tile floor causing them both to flinch.

Shadows spread across the floor, and with the sun covered by threatening gray clouds, the row of windows did little to illuminate the space.

Ronan shook his head, indicating that he didn't hear anything.

"That was too easy," Camryn said.

"Yeah." Ronan looked around as if he expected someone to jump out from behind the front desk with a news camera.

Camryn spotted the stairwell by the elevator, her eyes darting, ready for attack. They reached the door and silently eased it open. Once inside, the door clicked shut behind them. Ronan held up a finger.

After a moment, he motioned for them to move, and they began making their way up the stairs.

One stair.

Stop.

Listen.

Another stair.

The silence grew louder by the second as they reached the landing and turned, inching their way up the next flight toward the second-floor, each step sending Camryn's heart galloping faster. They'd almost made it to the top when Ronan put a hand out to stop her.

President Harriet Kaya stepped down onto the landing, a serene smile plastered across her face. "Oh good," she said. "You're here."

Camryn couldn't believe this was the same woman she'd seen on television nearly every night for the past two years. President Kaya wore an expensive tailored suit, her coal-colored hair straggling out of her bun. But somehow she still managed to maintain her picture of professionalism.

Camryn had so many questions for this woman, but none would be answered in this stairwell. Not with Ethan so close.

Ronan's hand tightened on her arm as Harriet Kaya lowered herself onto the step above them. Camryn assumed Ronan was about to pull her behind him when the door they'd just entered through burst open and two guards tumbled through, their guns immediately trained on Camryn and Ronan.

Ronan turned and, with one leap over the railing, sailed down the length of the landing. Feet outstretched in front of him, he met the first guard's chest and knocked both men to the ground.

Harriet Kaya took another step toward Camryn. "There's nowhere to run."

The sound of the scuffle from the bottom of the stairs melded Camryn to her spot. "I'm not running."

Only because there are two guards with guns in the other direction. If she were getting past any of them, it was more likely this middle-aged woman than two armed guards.

Camryn waited for the woman to take another step, then just as she came within arm's reach, Camryn dove for her. She wrapped her arms around President Kaya's waist and tackled her to the ground. Harriet landed with a thud on the stairs, her mouth open in a silent scream.

Camryn recognized that expression. "Ew… Get the air knocked out of you? That sucks."

Taking advantage of the woman's immobility, Camryn scrambled up the remaining steps. As she lunged for the second-floor door, her fingers slid from the handle. A hand had wrapped around her ankle and yanked, bringing Camryn slamming to the floor.

Camryn screamed and kicked with all her strength, but President Kaya's grip remained firm.

Camryn was reaching for the metal railing to pull herself away when the grip of the hand suddenly disappeared from her leg.

Camryn looked back to see Ronan standing over Harriet Kaya with a dagger pinning her arm to the rubber matting of the stairs, a stream of light escaping the wound.

Camryn and Ronan exchanged a bewildered look before they sprang into action again.

Add that to the list of things to talk about later.

Ronan practically shoved Camryn through the door before they heard the president's scream from the stairwell.

"Get them, you idiots!"

But Camryn and Ronan were already gone.

ELEVEN

"Locked. Damn it!" Camryn slammed her shoulder into the door with a growl, but nothing happened. She should have expected that, though. Human shoulder versus metal door. The door was the obvious victor in this fight.

Still, she pulled back to go another round. But just before her shoulder connected with metal again, Ronan stopped her with a bemused smile. He lifted his foot and kicked open the door without so much as scuffing his shoe.

Camryn almost laughed with relief, but all traces of humor died as she beheld the sight before her.

Ethan was struggling with his restraints but looked up in surprise when the door burst open, his left eye swollen and purple and blood covering the front of his shirt.

Camryn rushed to him, taking his face in her hands. "Oh my God."

Ethan grunted a few noises, but his words were garbled over his swollen lips.

"Don't try to talk." She turned to Ronan. "We have to get him out of these," she said, examining the cuffs on Ethan's hands. *Maybe I could freeze them off.* But before Camryn could even fathom how to do that, Ronan wrapped his hand around Ethan's wrists and squeezed. The cuffs snapped like a plastic toy.

God bless celestial strength.

"Can you stand?" Ronan prompted.

Ethan groaned as Camryn lifted his arm over her shoulder.

"He might have some broken ribs," she said.

"He'll be lucky if that's all that's broken."

In the hallway once again, Camryn glanced back toward the stairs. Heavy footsteps fast approached, the guards abandoning the injured president to chase after their escaping prisoners.

"This way." Ronan nodded in the opposite direction. They ran to the end of the hall as fast as Ethan could manage.

"Stop right there!" a voice shouted. The click of the guard's gun echoed behind them.

Camryn froze in her tracks with a frustrated growl. She glanced at Ronan who supported a limp Ethan with one arm and had the other slung across Camryn's chest as if he were a parent who'd just slammed on his brakes.

If only she'd stayed behind like Akira had wanted, maybe Ronan could get Ethan out. Now, instead of one human to take care of, Ronan had two.

Camryn turned to the approaching guards then back to Ronan with panicked eyes. "*What are we going to do?*" She'd never wished for a gun more desperately in her entire life.

Camryn didn't like the look on Ronan's face when he glanced at the window behind them. "We're going to jump."

With one arm already around Ethan, Ronan folded Camryn in his other. Camryn realized what was about to happen at the same instance the guards opened fire. Before she knew it, Ronan had breached the window, bursting into the grim daylight in a shower of glass and bullets.

Camryn squeezed her eyes shut, bracing for the two-story fall. Just as they departed the window, though, Ronan's wings caught the wind, and they floated gracefully to the ground.

Once her feet connected with pavement, Camryn almost vomited again. "I cannot believe you just did that." She gaped at Ronan. "There were at least seven ways that could have ended *very* badly."

Ronan pushed Camryn forward with his free hand. "Well, we're not out of the woods yet." The words were barely out of his mouth before gunshots rang out from the window above.

"I can walk," Ethan managed to say, wriggling out from Ronan's grip. There was no time to argue as they all rushed toward the garbage bin that sat about twenty yards down the narrow alley, the only refuge from the barrage of bullets.

They'd just ducked behind the metal barrier when Camryn heard shouting voices, yelling with the level of abandon reserved only for the young.

She squeezed behind Ronan to peer between the bin and the brick wall. Her mouth fell open at the sight of five teenagers, three of whom had phones pointed at the Turkish soldier hanging out a second story window shooting bullets down the alley.

"I think those boys saw us."

No sooner had the words left her mouth than the guards vanished from the window only to materialize in the alley, their guns now pointed at the group of boys.

Camryn turned to Ronan, expecting the same gallant fighter who'd fought off the two guards in the stairwell—two celestial guards, she now realized. Ronan would know what to do.

"He's shooting at those kids!"

Ronan seemed preoccupied with Ethan's wounds, his hand hovering millimeters above Ethan's skin, roaming over his body like a metal detector. "Camryn, they aren't our problem right now."

His words were an insult flung carelessly at her feet. "What the hell is that supposed to mean?" Camryn stood.

Ethan winced as he reached for her hand, but she pulled away.

"Enough people have died because of me," Camryn said as she stepped out from behind the bin. Ronan protested, but it was too late.

"Hey you," she yelled at the guards. "I'm over here!"

What the hell are you doing? she scolded herself, but to her surprise, her plan actually worked. The guards turned their guns from the cowering kids back in her direction.

What now? Camryn did the only thing she knew to do.

She ran.

Camryn flinched with every ping of gunfire that ricocheted off the ground behind her. She had no real plan. *Don't die*. That was the plan.

Finding herself facing death for the third time in as many days, Camryn wanted to laugh. She would have if all the breath in her lungs wasn't being used to run for her life.

But she wasn't running for *her* life. She was running for the lives of a group of kids she didn't even know.

She realized something in that moment, something that should have been obvious the first time she faced death in the endless abyss of the gorge that had almost swallowed her back in Kentucky: She wasn't afraid to die...

But she sure as hell didn't want to.

The dust flew around her as she zigzagged a path from her assailant, just as the hours of dodging paintballs in her backyard as a kid had taught her. *These guys need some target practice,*

Camryn was thinking just as something slammed into her from behind so violently that it lifted her feet from the ground.

The next thing she knew, her face smacked the pavement, and she skidded a few inches, the loose pebbles raking into her skin.

Get up! her brain screamed. The gunfire has stopped—for the moment—but she knew the guards were still behind her. They weren't leaving this alley empty handed.

No thought.

Only instinct.

Her brain in pure survival mode now—synapsis firing a thousand a second, sending adrenaline to her limbs, overwhelming her senses. The sun too bright. The voices too loud. The garbage wafting from the bins too rancid.

I must have tripped. That's what she was thinking when fire exploded between her shoulder blades. She opened her mouth to call for help, but no sound would come. *I can't breathe.* She opened her mouth wider, gasping, as if that would allow her to pull air into her paralyzed lungs.

It didn't.

I've been shot, Camryn realized as she forced her hands underneath her and strained to lift herself off the road. The effort was a thousand knives stabbing her spine, but she had to keep moving.

She pulled herself to her knees, preparing to run, when something in her periphery turned her blood to ice.

Someone lay in the alley behind her.

TWELVE

Camryn coughed as she scrambled back to the figure lying in the road, realizing…she hadn't been shot.

"Ethan!" Camryn screamed, the remnants of his pain fading from her back.

"I–I don't know what happened!" Ronan rushed up to them, glancing back at the guards who continued their cautious approach. "I didn't realize what he was doing until it was too late!"

Beside Ethan now, Ronan lifted him from the ground. Blood had already soaked through what remained of his shirt and ran like a scarlet river into the road.

"Put him down!" Camryn screamed. "I can do it!" Tears blurred her vision as she took Ethan's lifeless body from Ronan. "Don't touch him!" An animalistic protectiveness had taken over. She would rip anyone to shreds with her teeth if they tried. "Let me do it!"

"The guards are coming," Ronan protested. "We don't have time for heroics right now. Damn it, Camryn, let me help you!"

But his words came to her distorted. She was underwater. Submerged. She was drowning.

"Let me do it," she repeated as she struggled to pull Ethan from view of the guards.

The men were drawing closer now, approaching at a very human pace. Why they wasted time with such restraint, Camryn didn't care. Ronan relinquished Ethan to her and did the only thing he could to protect his two charges. He stepped in between them and the resuming gunfire.

I can do it.

They'd reached the end of the alley, and Camryn pulled Ethan around the corner onto the sidewalk of a busier street. She didn't care about the cars speeding past or who might see them. She only cared about getting away from the flying bullets.

Camryn lay Ethan down on the pavement, her eyes searching over his body. His lips were blue, his face an ashen gray.

No. No, no, no, no… You can't leave me again.

I just found you.

Since finding out about her celestial past, Camryn really hadn't had time to wonder what would happen to them when their time on this earth was over. Would they experience death as the humans did or be transported back to their celestial bodies to carry on with their existence as if this little eighteen-year detour into 'the real life of humans' had been nothing more than a stint on a bad reality TV show?

Akira had warned her back on the ship when she'd so stupidly tried to off herself with a kitchen knife that the same rules didn't apply to them now, but no one really knew for sure. No precedent existed for this.

She'd lain awake many-a-night pondering the mortal afterlife, but that was when she'd thought herself one of them. She'd never worked out any answers, but now she was even more desperate to know… Would she be able to find him again?

Ronan's words became more and more frantic as the gunshots drew closer. The men were shouting again.

With a snap, her ears finally opened to the sound. Camryn forced her attention away from Ethan long enough to spin toward the guards and sling a flaming bolt of lightning from her hand, not caring who saw.

The approaching guards didn't have time to react before they were hit by Camryn's electric current, the power sending them flying back, landing in a convulsing heap in the road. Smoke rose from their bodies as Camryn shouted to Ronan. "Will you please shut *up*?"

With the guards incapacitated, the group of teenagers ran past, stopping to gawk as the two celestial guards disintegrated into black smoke. When the boys finally reached Camryn at the end of the alley, the tallest of the group gaped down at the bleeding Ethan on the ground in front of her.

"Is he dead?"

"No!" Camryn shouted. "He's not dead!" She placed a finger to Ethan's neck, but her hands shook too violently to feel a pulse even if one had been there.

Ronan put a hand on her arm. "Camryn. He *is* dead. You're not helping."

I just need to stop the bleeding.

"Does anyone have any bandages?" The words came out hollow and rasping, her voice not her own. "Anything I can wrap him with?"

"Listen to me! Bandages aren't going to help him," Ronan continued to plead with her.

Camryn had never seen Ronan look so defeated. And she didn't have time to coddle him.

"Ronan."

"Yes?"

"*Shut. Up.*"

Ronan sat back on his knees, wiping his tears with the collar of his dusty polo.

Camryn looked around for someone—anyone—who could help her but every pair of eyes staring back at her were filled with the same vile sentiment—pity.

She lifted Ethan's head and pulled it to her, foolish hope still gnawing from every cell of her body.

This isn't happening. He's going to be fine.

But she knew Ronan's words rang true. Ethan was gone. She'd felt his departure like a knife stripping away her sanity, as paralyzing and traumatic as the first time their souls had been ripped apart. Thunder rumbled in the distance, echoing her quiet weeping.

The anguish grew inside her like a tumor, crushing her throat, her lungs, her heart. When she could stand it no longer, she threw her head back and expelled her anger, fear, and sorrow in one soul-splitting scream.

Her throat burned and the veins pulsed in her neck, the pool of her agony draining, only to be refilled once more—her soul harboring a never-ending supply. The lightning cracked so close that she felt its heat on her face.

The gawking boys fled to the other side of the street where more people had gathered, no doubt drawn by her screams.

She should be careful. She should control herself, but control was a word that no longer existed. Harriet Kaya would pay for this. *I'll kill her. Kill Apollyon. Kill them all.* Camryn wouldn't allow the thought to enter her mind, but she would kill Ronan,

Akira, Michael...anyone who tried to stop her. One way or another, Harriet would pay.

Her sobs racked her body so violently that she didn't feel the tugging at her shirt at first.

Not until Ethan let out a frantic gasp and squirmed in her grasp.

The gathered crowd gave a collective shriek and backed away from them.

What the—

Camryn's mind couldn't process what her eyes were telling her. Dead people don't move. Don't moan. Don't *breathe*. Had she imagined it? She pulled back to look down at a blinking Ethan hitching in breaths and trying to sit up.

When he'd succeeded, Camryn actually laughed at the impossibility of the situation. She twisted him around to look at his wound. A large portion of his shirt had been ripped to shreds, revealing the burns covering the majority of his back, but the skin around the jagged bullet hole was closing before her eyes.

This...cannot be real. But she looked up to see that she wasn't the only one who'd seen it. As a matter of fact, there were at least three cameras pointed directly at them.

"Are you okay?" Ethan managed to get out from between his swollen lips.

Camryn barked out another laugh. "Are you seriously asking if *I'm* okay?" She wiped at her eyes. "You were just shot."

Ethan's eyebrows shot up, his grin a smidge inappropriate for the given situation. Camryn had never seen him look more childlike.

"I was shot?" His eyelids drifted closed again. "Cool."

"Oh my *God*," the group of boys erupted at once.

"That was awesome!"

"Did you see what she did?"

"Did those guys really just disappear?"

"Are you, like, superheroes or something?"

Ronan passed a nervous glance left and then right. At least a dozen people had gathered around them now, more than half holding cell phones, documenting the whole scene.

"Okay, I have no idea what's just happened here," he said, "but we need to leave. I don't think President Kaya will show her face in front of this many people, but we can't take any chances."

"Hey," called the smallest boy in the group as Camryn pulled herself from the ground. He wore a sweat-stained, striped t-shirt and held an actual video camera. Camryn didn't think she'd ever seen a machine like that except on television.

"You're the Americans they're looking for, aren't you?"

Camryn exchanged a look with Ronan as they hefted Ethan to his feet. There would be no denying it, especially with what these people had just witnessed. "Um..." Camryn struggled to come up with some reasonable explanation.

"It's okay," another one of the boys said. This one taller and wearing a blue faded baseball cap. "You saved our lives. They were shooting at us, too."

The other boys were sharing their own videos with the gathering crowd, and suddenly their expressions of fear changed to something more like awe.

"Come on," said the boy with the ball cap. "We can get you out of here."

THIRTEEN

Camryn was fairly certain that Ronan didn't need the boys' help to get where they needed to go, but the fact that he allowed the group of enthusiastic teens to lead them down side streets and creepy alleys was a testament to Ronan's patience. Especially since the youngest one never stopped yapping the entire time.

"I'm Ravi," he said. "And this is David." He gestured to the boy in the blue baseball cap. Sweat Stains was Omer, and the quiet one, they all called Jaz.

"So, if you guys are angels—" Ravi hopped up and down, unable to contain his excitement, "—then were those men that shot at us angels, too?"

Ronan nodded while Camryn's eyes swept their surroundings. Again.

"Those guys were angels?" Omer exclaimed. "I thought angels were only supposed to help people."

Flashes of torrential rain and rumbling thunder shot across Camryn's memory—visions of the Great Flood, the agonized cries of women offering up their babies, extending them toward the heavens, pleading for God to spare the children…

"Angels are supposed to carry out God's will," she said. "That's not always…beneficial to humans."

The group slowed, and the boys grew quiet. Camryn thought she'd finally stumped them, but Omer reached for a decrepit handle and squeaked open the large, metal door in front of them. Camryn hadn't even realized it, but they'd reached the end of the alley.

Following the boys through the darkened doorway, Camryn was taken aback by the smell—the musty, stale odor of a building fraught with unuse, a building that, once Camryn's eyes adjusted to the darkness, she could only hope had once been a butcher shop.

Large, menacing hooks hung from the ceiling, and a row of what Camryn imagined were large coolers lined one wall. Even Ronan grimaced at the dried blood crusted around the many drains in the cement floor, but the boys appeared unmoved.

Jaz whispered something to Ravi, who turned to Ronan. "Jaz wants to know what happened to your wings?"

Camryn and Ronan both eyed the boy, unsure what he meant.

"We saw your wings." Ravi pointed at Ronan's back. "But now they're gone. And those other guys—poof. Poof. No wings." The boy moved his hands, illustrating how the men had transported from the window, using the manipulation of interdimensional particles to move through space instead of flying like Ronan had. "Not all angels have them?"

"Ah," Ronan opened his mouth in understanding. "My wings are still there," he said, turning to peer over his shoulder at his empty back. "And those other guys had wings, too. You just can't see them all the time."

The boys exchanged a look that said they didn't completely understand but weren't sure what further questions to ask.

"What those other angels did back there," Ronan tried to explain, "that's called transporting. It's the easiest way to travel within a realm. Harder to do when you have humans in tow, though." He winked at Camryn.

Omer shook his head. "No way these two are human," he said, shoving his thumb toward Camryn and Ethan. "Not after what we just saw her do back there."

Ronan's chuckle did little to dispel Camryn's grimace.

"So, if you were going to take us somewhere," Ravi asked, "we'd have to fly?"

"If there was more than one of you."

The boys' eyes widened at the prospect, and Camryn grew the tiniest bit annoyed at Ronan's amusement. Ethan was dying. Or had died. Or…

She still wasn't sure what had happened, but it certainly wasn't something to be laughed at.

"Some angels can even use portals," Ronan continued, "but those are mostly used to travel between realms, like from here to Eden or here to the Void."

Ravi stopped and whirled on them. From the look on his face, Camryn thought his head might explode. He actually put his hands on his head before he exclaimed, "Portals and realms and Voids… It's like D&D come to life!"

"Dungeons and Dragons," Ronan whispered to Camryn as if this were somehow privileged information.

Camryn opened her mouth to ask how Ronan had become so familiar with a human board game but then shook her head, deciding she didn't want to know.

"Are you sure it's okay to be telling them all this?" she asked instead.

No law forbade humans from celestial knowledge. In fact, angels had revealed themselves to humans throughout history, but revealing such existential truths wasn't common practice.

Ronan's face turned somber. "I'm afraid most of this information won't remain secret for much longer anyway."

Making their way through the building and exiting onto the street on the opposite block, the boys pointed in the direction that would lead them away from the embassy. "Thanks for saving our lives back there," David said.

"Uh, anytime." Camryn didn't know what else to say. This had been the most bizarre fifteen minutes of her life. "You really shouldn't get in the habit of taunting guards with guns, though. You won't always have someone around willing to get shot for you."

The boys looked as if they wanted to ask more questions, but Ronan dismissed them curtly. "We have to get some help for our friend here, so we can't stick around. We do thank you for the escort, though. And you should probably stay out of the city for the next few days. Er—you never know what might happen."

The boys looked excited at the prospect but thankfully didn't follow when they departed.

Camryn shook her head. "Boys."

Ronan grinned. "My sentiments exactly."

FOURTEEN

Camryn flinched as a car squealed past, making her long for the cover of night. At least with the protection of darkness, she and Ronan might have remained a bit more inconspicuous as they practically dragged their unconscious friend down the sidewalk.

After a few minutes of largely being ignored, however, Camryn began to relax. Maybe they looked like a group of drunk friends trying to make it home after a long night out. Maybe such a sight wasn't unusual for an early morning in Tel Aviv. Or maybe people only see what they want to see.

They'd traveled only a few blocks when Ronan looked around, his eyes searching, then pointed to a tall building with the street view consisting entirely of windows. "Akira's in there."

Picking up the pace, they reached their destination and pushed through a set of double doors into the dim foyer of a modest apartment complex. In front of them lay a narrow set of carpeted stairs leading up to the floors above. On each side of the stairs stood a single door, leading to what Camryn could only assume were two ground-floor apartments.

Camryn didn't even have time to ask where they were before one of the apartment doors burst open and Akira rushed out. The relief on her face vanished when she spotted Ethan. "Holy shit, what happened to him?"

Before either of them had a chance to answer, a quite perturbed-looking woman poked her head out of the apartment behind Akira, muttering angrily under her breath.

To Camryn, the woman didn't look to be much older than herself—probably late twenties—with long dark hair twisted on top of her head. The woman's matching eyes remained narrowed at the intruders of her domain as she spoke to them in a language Camryn didn't understand. If Camryn could guess from her expression and shushing gestures, she was telling them to *keep it down!*

Akira's head jerked toward the open door. "Take him in there."

"Do you know this woman?" Camryn mouthed.

Akira raised one shoulder. "I told her we needed to use her apartment for a bit, and she agreed."

But it didn't look to Camryn like the woman had agreed at all. She stood in the doorway with her arms across her chest, looking as if she would object, but one sharp glance from Akira and the woman stepped aside, watching with ever-widening eyes as Ronan dragged the bloody and battered Ethan into her home.

"Lay him down here." Akira pointed to a long sofa as they elbowed their way into the apartment, the woman whispering harshly all the while.

"I'm really sorry about this," Camryn apologized as she squeezed past the woman into the apartment, but the woman only glared at her.

"Lay him face-down. We need to get something on those burns."

Just then, a door on the other side of the apartment squeaked open and the woman darted toward it.

All eyes jerked toward the door, ready for danger.

The room breathed a collective sigh of relief when a little girl emerged from the room, rubbing her eyes as if she'd just woken from a nap. Everyone except the woman, of course, who continued to cast flustered glances their way.

Camryn chewed her lip and paced the length of the couch where Ethan lay. She apologized to the woman again but didn't think the young mother understood a word of it.

Akira ran her hands methodically over Ethan's body like a celestial scanner.

"Have we heard from Raphael?" Camryn asked.

"No, but—" Akira's hands hovered over Ethan's face for just a beat longer than necessary—not long enough for anyone else to notice. No one except Camryn. "He doesn't have any internal injuries. We can bandage him up," she said. "With time, he'll be fine."

With everything they'd been through in the past half hour, Camryn hadn't been able to get a good look at Ethan's wounds until now. Dark, angry streaks of open flesh covered his back as if he'd been whipped with a belt of flames. Though she couldn't feel the sting of the burns as she'd felt the deep, aching pain of the bullet when it entered his back, she could still imagine the level of agony he must be in now—enough to render him unconscious.

Camryn's eyes made the trek up to meet the woman's glare, daring to ask for favors after trespassing into her home. "Do you have some salve for his burns? Anything for the pain?" As if any over-the-counter medication would touch such injuries.

The woman pointed to the television on the console, rattling off more words Camryn didn't understand.

"What's she saying?" Camryn asked Akira.

"She wants to know if you're as dangerous as they say."

Camryn hadn't even noticed the television in the room, much less the news broadcasting from it. She looked at the screen now, as a smartly-dressed woman spoke more unfamiliar words, but the pictures over the news anchor's left shoulder, Camryn recognized.

Thankfully, they were the same still shots of Camryn and Ethan that President Kaya had used during her press conference. At least no new, incriminating footage played there—like a shot of her blasting two guards with a bolt of purple lightning.

"You can't believe everything you see on TV." Camryn's voice didn't sound as confident as she would like. "Tell her that." She swung her arm from Akira toward the woman.

Akira offered an annoyed smirk. "I think you just did."

Camryn stopped her pacing, her gaze flitting to the woman whose eyes were wide with surprise.

"You speak Hebrew?" the woman asked, looking at Camryn as if her head had begun spinning around on her neck.

"No. I—" Camryn shook her head, but as she focused her ears on the low volume of the television, she found that she understood the news being reported from the woman on the screen.

Camryn held up her hands. "I don't— I don't speak Hebrew. That was… That was a mistake. I—"

Ronan, who'd seemed too preoccupied with Ethan to pay attention to Camryn's conversation with the woman chose that moment to speak up. "In case you've forgotten, you speak every language," he said. "You were around when they were created. You just have to open your mind to remember."

Camryn's hands clenched at her sides. "That's literally all I've been trying to do for the past three days. Obviously, I'm not doing something right."

Ronan's face was thoughtful for a moment while Camryn battled her growing agitation.

"Maybe," Ronan began, "you're just trying too hard."

Camryn let out an annoyed laugh and collapsed into the plush purple chair beside her. She scrubbed her hands down her face, stopping to rub her temples for a long moment. "Thanks, Ronan. I'll keep that in mind."

Ronan exhaled and turned to the woman, muttering in her native tongue the question Camryn had been struggling to ask.

Camryn risked a peek up through her eyelashes to witness the woman's response. But before anyone could move, the apartment door burst open and a rather large, intimidating man rushed through. His narrowed eyes scanned the room before landing on Camryn and her companions.

He wore a fitted suit and shiny shoes, but something about the man—perhaps the vengeance burning in his eyes—gave Camryn the distinct impression that he was more likely a mobster than an accountant.

The woman rushed to his side, little girl in tow.

This must be the husband.

The man began speaking—threatening commands— but Camryn couldn't allow herself to be afraid of his words.

Because she *understood* them.

"I'm sorry," Camryn cut off his tirade. "I know this looks bad." She gestured to the television. "But I swear to you…we are not the bad guys here." From the look on the man's face, she could tell he understood her English, at least in part.

"President Kaya kidnapped him and tried to kill us." Her excitement at being able to communicate deflated as she realized…there was no way they would believe her. The whole world adored the leader of the SEF and what she symbolized. Accusing her of such things would sound ludicrous.

"I know that sounds crazy, but we're just a couple of kids." She gestured back to Ethan, still unconscious on the couch. "We just need to get him better, then we can leave." She glanced between the two adults. They seemed to be contemplating her words, eyeing all four of them suspiciously.

Akira and Ronan did what they always did when trying to explain things to unsuspecting humans. They kept their mouths shut, their presence otherworldly as it was. It would be a far stretch for anyone to believe they were just regular teenagers, especially when they spoke.

"Please…" Camryn begged. "Do you have anything for his burns?"

The man whispered to his wife, who reluctantly handed the little girl to her husband and disappeared from the room. She returned a moment later with a small, metal container. She gave the container to her husband, who stepped forward and handed it to Camryn.

"I believe you," he said in thick English. "I never trusted that woman much."

FIFTEEN

Up until that moment, Camryn's insides had been jumbled into a knotted mass of panic and uncertainty, completely out of her element in a foreign country with what she felt were four lives in her hands. Now they were at the mercy of this young couple, and things could have gone south quickly.

If these people refused to help them, what could they do? Go to the next apartment? And the next? Surely President Kaya would still have soldiers scouring the streets looking for them, and every passing minute was precious.

Camryn managed a ghost of a smile. "Thank you," she said through the tears in her throat.

Camryn plopped like a stone onto the couch beside Ethan and moved his shredded shirt out of the way. Silent tears flowed down her face as she gently massaged the cream into the burns, knowing it would do nothing for his pain.

Her hands traveled mindlessly, her eyes never leaving the spot between his shoulder blades where the bullet wound had vanished from, the skin as smooth and perfect as it had ever been.

Despite her careful pressure and his unconsciousness, Ethan let out a tortured moan at her touch. His breaths came in uneven spurts, his pain evident in every gasp. Camryn's chin quivered, and she swiped at her eyes.

Shit!

She would take any amount of his pain, all of it if she were able. She would give him her blood, her heart, her very life…if she could.

When they were still young angels in training, their *qanima* bond like a channel, she had been able to send thoughts or feelings as easily as breathing. She'd had the ability to push her strength into him by sheer will and receive his pain in return. Could she do that now? Perhaps not—she hadn't been successful at much lately. But she could try.

Camryn found Ethan's hand as it hung limply to the floor, his fingers resting lightly on the floral rug. She wrapped her fingers around his and studied his swollen face, his eye surrounded by a purple bruise and his lip crusted with blood.

What must the two humans be thinking right now?

It didn't matter. Nothing else mattered but this one task.

Camryn closed her eyes as the rest of the world vanished. She concentrated on the warmth of Ethan's skin, the heat traveling from his hand into hers, willing it to stop its flow. When—by some miracle—that worked, she went one step further. She pushed it back toward him, adding her own heat to his.

Her energy coursed from her hand into his, replaced by a torturous fire, reminding her of her time with Michael in the New York City church, right before the Heavenly Fire had nearly driven her to madness. She let out an agonized scream as the pain overwhelmed her senses, setting not only her back but her whole body in flames.

From somewhere far off, she heard the faint cries of a child, but it was miles away. When Ethan's moaning stopped, the fire around her subsided, and she collapsed into the sofa, panting with relief. She'd done it, but she was spent.

Sleep.

With no energy to hold open her eyes, Camryn rested her head on the sofa beside Ethan.

Just for a minute.

Cool moisture on Camryn's forehead yanked her back into the room. When she opened her eyes, she expected to see Ronan standing beside her, but the woman looked down at her instead—the same woman who, just moments before, had been screeching at them. Now, she wiped Camryn's hair from her face, cooing and *tsk*ing in a motherly tone.

The man and the little girl were nowhere to be seen, having retreated into another room at her screams, Camryn suspected.

Letting the woman wipe her brow, Camryn couldn't help thinking of her own mother. She hoped her parents were faring well…and not scheming plans to come help her. She could see her father showing up with nothing but a kitchen knife to defend himself and smiled at the thought.

When the woman crossed the living room to the kitchen area to rewet the towel, Camryn glanced up at Ronan. "Why isn't he healing?"

Ronan didn't seem to hear her at first. He was too busy staring down into the bloody mess of Ethan's face. He blinked himself out of his trance and peeled his eyes away. "What?"

"He was shot, and the wound just healed right up. Why aren't these wounds healing?"

"He was *shot*?" Akira took a step toward them. "Why didn't you tell me?"

Ronan's gaze darted between the two sets of curious eyes. He gave Akira a look that Camryn couldn't interpret.

"Yes, he was shot. And…he died," Ronan looked at Akira with trepidation. "He was dead, Akira. And yet…" He waved his hand in Ethan's direction. "He's alive."

Akira froze, her body turning to marble at Ronan's words.

"I don't think he has super healing powers—not immediate anyway," Ronan said in answer to Camryn's question. "I just don't think he can die."

Akira shook her head as if this was somehow bad news, but any attempt at an argument was interrupted by the click of the door behind them. They all turned to see the man, his hand still glued to the doorknob of the child's room, staring at them with wide eyes. He mumbled something that sounded like a curse, then straightened his jacket and joined his wife by the sink.

"And Camryn was able to dispose of two of Apollyon's soldiers with her Tempest powers," Ronan continued as if two human strangers weren't watching *and listening* to everything they said. "They are gaining power. That can only mean one thing—"

"It can mean more than one thing, Ronan," Akira cut him off.

"I don't think so—"

"Well, no one asked what you think!" Akira pushed past them and stomped to the large glass window, crossing her arms in front of her.

Ronan started after her, but Camryn latched onto his arm.

"Wait, what's going on?" Camryn spun him back to face her. "What do you think it means?"

Ronan put his hands on his hips and stared at the floor. "There have been rumors. Uh, a prophecy, you might say."

Camryn almost laughed. "A prophecy? What is this, a bad movie or something?"

"Don't say it like that." Ronan rolled his eyes. "It's written word, so take care not to be disrespectful."

Camryn straightened. The written word had been around for nearly two thousand years—much longer than Camryn had been a human—so she'd been privy to the continuous debate surrounding its validity. And even though its contents had likely brought about more death and destruction than Apollyon ever could, there was no denying the power of its words, or that the world would have been better off at times if even some of its warnings had been heeded.

"Old Testament. Isaiah." Ronan stared at Camryn's feet as he recited, "I have commanded those I prepared for battle; I have summoned my warriors to carry out my wrath…"

Camryn rubbed her hands over her face. "Sounds like a nightmare."

"Yeah," he affirmed, the look on his face denoting that he understood how grim it sounded. "There's more."

Strong arguments existed on both sides of the biblical debate, but even as a Fallen angel, she'd secretly hoped the words within the pages of this holy book could at least at some point be useful, if not wholly true.

"Go on."

Ronan looked her straight in the eye as he continued. "It's been surmised that this is connected to the two messengers who come into their powers at the end of Apollyon's reign…" he hesitated. "And, for a short time…" he paused again with a grimace as if the next words might get him into trouble, "These warriors cannot be killed."

Camryn chewed her lip. "That was one isolated incident. I don't think—"

"They have the power of rain and fire in their hands."

Camryn shook her head.

"They come from the west to Persia to defeat Apollyon in his last days."

Camryn closed her eyes with a sigh, accepting only the minute possibility that this maybe, possibly, perhaps, might apply to them. "If you think this is us," she said, waving a hand in the air, "why are we just now hearing about it?"

"Because Akira didn't want to tell you. She doesn't believe it." He gestured to Ethan. "But this confirms it, don't you think? It has to be."

Camryn closed her eyes and released a steady breath. "Warriors of Wrath. That sounds great." She turned back to face him. "Can't wait to get started on *that*."

"Well, I think you already have."

Camryn stared at him, questioning.

"The soldiers," Ronan said, as if that should be obvious.

"That wasn't God's wrath. It was mine."

"Eh…" Ronan shrugged as if there might not be a difference.

Camryn's glance flitted to Akira still sulking on the other side of the large window. "So, if that's us and we can't be killed. Why is that such a bad thing?"

"Well," Ronan cleared his throat. "According to the prophecy, you are eventually destined to die a horrible death." The words came out through a pained smile as if he were revealing a terrible punchline to an inappropriate joke.

Camryn gulped. "Eventually?" She looked at Ethan lying motionless on the couch. "And how long is this time of protection supposed to last?"

Ronan shook his head with a slight shrug. "As long as it takes to complete the mission, but… It will be over quickly."

The open apartment suddenly felt too small, the walls closing in. Akira's reasons for denying this prophecy were pretty clear. It was no secret, the feelings she had for Ethan—feelings she'd always had. Camryn had been able to ignore them during her life as an angel because such attachments were inconsequential to celestial beings, but here, in this human body, with its very human urges and proclivities, she understood it well.

And while Akira's flirtations irked her, at least she and Akira could agree on one thing. Neither of them wanted Ethan to die.

Ethan's stirring caught Camryn's attention. His eyes fluttered violently, and he struggled to sit up. Akira darted over from the window, and Camryn came to sit on the carpet in front of him.

"Don't move," Camryn urged. "You're hurt pretty bad. Just lie still, okay?"

Ethan nodded but did manage to lift his head enough to pass a glance around the grim faces staring down at him. "Damn, who died?" he asked in a groggy voice.

A round of nervous laughter circled the room.

Ethan took two ragged breaths, gathering his strength. "Camryn," he said finally. "There's something I need to tell you." His voice sounded pained, as if every word clawed at his burns.

"Shh… Whatever it is, it can wait till you're stronger."

"No," he gritted out, and everyone hovered on the words that hadn't yet been uttered. But before any profound proclamation could escape his lips, his body went limp again, and he drifted back into unconsciousness.

"It's okay," Camryn rubbed his hair. "You'll tell me later, alright?"

"He's going to be okay," Akira assured her. "He just needs time to heal."

Unfortunately, time was one thing they didn't have.

SIXTEEN

After a half-hour of excruciating silence, Camryn could no longer stand the stares boring into her from the narrow breakfast table in the middle of the kitchen. The couple hadn't said much since giving Camryn the salve, so she had no idea what they thought of their new houseguests. It couldn't be anything good, from the looks they were shooting her way.

Camryn returned their stare for a moment before wiping her palms down her pants, striding over, and extending her hand to whoever would accept it.

"My name's Camryn. And these are my friends, Akira and Ronan…and Ethan." Camryn glanced back to Ethan lying unconscious on the couch as the man reluctantly took her hand and shook it.

"I'm Yon," the man said. "This is my wife, Levana."

Camryn nodded to the woman with an apologetic smile. "Look, I'm really sorry about all this—" she began, but Yon didn't seem interested in her apology.

"Who are you?" he demanded.

"Uh...my name is Camryn," she repeated as if the man hadn't understood her the first time.

"I don't want to know your name. You and your friends—where did you come from? Why are you here?"

Camryn coughed out a robotic laugh. "*Here* is such a relative term." She twisted her hands in front of her. "Why are any of us here, really?"

Yon's eyes narrowed as he contemplated her words—or maybe he was just trying to make her squirm.

The couple had heard all their talk about prophecies, healing wounds, coming back from the dead, and had witnessed her little display of taking Ethan's pain. Of course, they would have questions.

But could she tell them the truth? Ronan hadn't had a problem with spilling all their secrets.

Camryn continued to fidget with the hem of her shirt. "You wouldn't believe me if I told you."

"You'd be surprised—" the man started, but his interest quickly shifted to the front of the room.

Camryn swung around just in time to see Akira and Ronan darting back to the window. As Akira leaned in and peered down the street, Camryn and the couple rushed to join them.

"Bloody hell..." Akira cursed as a battalion of soldiers came into view over the hill, their hands gripped tightly to long rifles strapped around their necks.

"Those aren't Israeli troops," the man stated. "Those are Turkish uniforms."

Ronan shook his head. "What is she doing sending troops into Tel Aviv after bombing Jerusalem last night? Is she trying to start World War III?"

"She did say she and the Prime Minister were working together. Maybe she's convinced him that someone else was responsible, or maybe—" Akira stopped, a look of abject horror crossing her face. "Maybe the Prime Minister is dead."

Levana brought her hands to her mouth and began what sounded like a mumbled prayer.

"We need a diversion." Ronan looked too excited at the prospect. "I'm thinking an explosion of some kind."

"We're not blowing anything up, dingus." Akira didn't take her eyes from the window. "We just have to stay out of their way."

Camryn turned, looking for an escape. "We need to hide, right?"

"We are hiding," Akira hissed.

"No, I mean like, get away from here. We can transport anywhere. Why are we still here?"

Akira's head swiveled toward her, jerking her chin in Ethan's direction. "A transport like that would likely kill him. Besides, I have us covered. They're going to walk past this building like it isn't even here."

"Oh, like you had us covered at the church? What was I thinking? I feel so safe now."

Akira scowled. "Alright. Everyone away from the windows." She directed everyone to the center of the room, never breaking her glare.

The soldiers had advanced a few more buildings, and their shouted instructions could be heard through the window that faced the street. From what Camryn could tell, the soldiers were sweeping every building, looking for the two "American terrorists." It would be mere minutes before they reached the building where they'd taken refuge.

Then what?

Camryn's eyes darted from the window to the still-unconscious Ethan to the door and back again. If she thought she could put Ethan on her back and make a run for it, she would.

With everyone's nerves wound as tight as the spot they were in, it was really the most inopportune time for the little girl to make an entrance once again. Everyone jerked as if on a synchronized timer when she squeaked open her bedroom door, a blanket clutched in her arms. The woman darted over and snatched up her daughter as if by simple proximity to the otherworldly beings, the little girl might contract some incurable disease.

Camryn immediately drew the layout of the building in her mind, almost like a blueprint. She found it strange now, the things that she just *knew*—like how there were tunnels under the church or that there were basement shelters in almost every apartment complex near the West Bank. Arael's memories were there, and they seemed to burst forth at just the right time.

"Is there somewhere you and your family can go?" she whispered to Yon. "Someplace safer than this?"

Yon considered this for a moment before uttering quick words to his wife, who snapped into immediate action. Looking relieved, she passed the little girl to her husband again before scurrying off into the adjoining room.

With his wife off gathering their things, Yon touched the little girl's chin. "This is Myria."

Camryn smiled at the little girl. "Hi, Myria. I'm Camryn."

Myria smiled back as she leaned her head into her father's shoulder, her brown curls falling into her pudgy face.

They watched Levana for a moment, flitting from room to room, stuffing things into a large black duffle before Yon turned to Camryn. "God has sent you here," he said.

Camryn coughed. "Excuse me?"

"Do you know what I do for a living?"

"Wait. Can we go back to what you just said—"

"I work for Prime Minister Gaba."

Camryn took a step back. Was this some kind of a trap?

"In a…" Yon hesitated. "A contractual sort of way."

"Okay." Maybe Camryn's hunch about him being a mobster hadn't been completely off base.

"There are many like me, unofficial employees, I guess you would say. We've all received the same instructions regarding you two." He gestured between her and Ethan. "Approach with caution. May require extreme force… You get the idea."

Camryn froze, her eyes darting. *What the hell is going on?*

"What are the chances that you would end up in my home today?"

Camryn's glance flicked to Akira. "Very slim."

"Yes. That is why I believe God sent you here—for protection."

"Protection?" Camryn mulled that over, unsure Yon understood the meaning of the word.

The fear must have been apparent on Camryn's face because Yon continued. "Don't worry. You are safe. No one will know you're here."

Camryn swallowed hard, still not trusting him entirely. "Why would you do that for us?"

"Your friend may have been right," he said, nodding toward Akira. "The Prime Minister hasn't been heard from since the bombings. It's all very hush-hush on the inside. No one in my circle really knows what's happening. And like I said, I don't trust Harriet Kaya."

Camryn shuddered at the implications if Yon and Akira's intuition about the Prime Minister were correct.

"In my job…I hear things," Yon continued. "You had family with you, no?"

Camryn gulped down the knot that instantly appeared in her throat. "We did."

Yon looked at his daughter, content in his arms. "I would only hope someone would do the same for my daughter if the time ever came."

Camryn cleared her throat. "Well…thank you," she managed to say.

Yon jerked his head toward the back of the kitchen and led Camryn to a small door almost hidden in the wall. With his daughter in one arm, he opened the pantry and nimbly pulled out several bags of onions, potatoes, and yams. With the vegetables out of the way, Yon lifted the pantry shelf, and Camryn gasped.

Inside was a stockpile of weapons—mostly guns. Camryn's heart groaned at the sight. Her father had a similar assortment in their basement back home.

"That's a nice collection." She nodded toward the arsenal.

Ronan joined them then, poking his head over Camryn's shoulder. "Nice!" he said with a nod.

Camryn picked up a small handgun, rubbing the grip reverently.

"You take." Yon nodded at the weapon. "Please." He lifted a few more, offering them to Ronan and Akira.

Akira huffed, turning away. "I'll keep my useful weapons, thank you very much," she said, putting an emphasis on the word *useful*.

True, the weapons in front of her would be useless against spiritual forces, but thinking of the guards still patrolling outside the apartment and the guns that even Apollyon's soldiers had wielded against them, Camryn understood that spiritual threats weren't the only ones they had to worry about.

"Oh, I couldn't." Camryn backed away. "Don't you need these?"

Yon opened his jacket to reveal the black object in a holster at his side. "I have what I need. And Levana as well."

Camryn let a small smile form on her lips as, for some reason, she didn't feel so homesick anymore.

Returning to Yon's side, Levana took Myria and glanced longingly toward the door. Yon nodded to the exit and spoke swiftly to his wife. "You go. I will join you later."

"No, Yon. You come now," his wife insisted. "This is not your fight."

"But this is my home. I won't leave it in the hands of strangers."

Levana stared at Myria, who happily chewed on the corner of her blanket. Levana exhaled a heavy sigh as she released the bag, letting it thud to the floor. "This is my home as well," she said. "And you are my family. I will not leave here without you."

Yon nodded to his wife as if this was expected, then poked his chin toward the window and the sound of the approaching soldiers. "We can help."

Camryn pondered the implications of pulling this family into their fight. She looked at the little girl. How jaded she'd already become to the weapons around her. And were those soldiers even human? Or would this turn into a supernatural battle of powers?

"Let's hope it doesn't come to that," Camryn said.

From her post at the window, Akira waved the room into silence. Four soldiers entered the building across the street. Several remained in the street, keeping watch.

Yon took position beside the apartment's only exit and unholstered his weapon. Camryn released the magazine of the gun in her hand to find eight 9mm bullets. She slammed it back into place, pulling back the slide to chamber a round. She snapped the safety off and nestled the grip in her hands.

Akira and Ronan extended their hands, producing glowing red and orange daggers with a flick of their wrists.

When the four soldiers emerged from the facing building no more than two minutes after they'd entered, everyone in the room seemed to hold their breath—even Akira, deflating Camryn's confidence even more.

The soldiers returned to formation in the street, and the leader shouted directions again, gesturing with two fingers at the building to their right. They marched in practiced formation, past their window and on to the next doorway without so much as a glance their way.

Camryn's legs trembled underneath her, and she collapsed back against the wall with relief.

"See," Akira said. "I told you I had us covered."

SEVENTEEN

Threatening gray clouds loomed in the distance, advancing on the city like a serpent. Camryn had become so accustomed to the sight that she wondered if she'd ever see blue skies again.

Her fingers gripped the cement railing in front of her as her eyes scanned the Tel Aviv skyline. Akira had reluctantly agreed to let her venture up to the roof alone, but what was the worst that could happen? She couldn't die, right?

Camryn realized with a ghost of a smile that this was the first time she'd been alone in over a week. Her parents would be proud.

They always seemed disappointed by her hermit-like tendencies, but they had developed out of necessity, not necessarily desire.

Camryn lived in a small town and attended an even smaller high school. Once the popular girls had turned on her, there weren't many friends to be had. But Camryn had come to the conclusion that she didn't need friends. It had always been just her and her horses, and that's the way she'd liked it.

But standing alone on the roof now, she realized why her parents had always discouraged her seclusion.

Solitude was where the dark thoughts found her.

Camryn closed her eyes and tried what her mother called "being intentional with her thoughts." Simple, yes. But if she caught it in time, Camryn could usually find a memory bright enough to cut through the darkness. But the one thing she could usually count on to bring her happiness—her horses—now brought her even more grief.

She pictured their round, dark eyes as she'd said goodbye to them back in Kentucky. Rebel had pressed his nose against her cheek, and Romeo had nuzzled her neck…as if they knew she had to go. Did they miss her? Did they understand why she'd had to do it?

Oh man, wrong direction. She'd somehow managed to make herself feel even worse.

Camryn bent over and gripped her knees, grasping for the reigns of her runaway emotions. But her fingers found nothing but more heartache. For the loss of her horses, her town, and everything else she'd ever known. *This is too much.*

Too much.

I'm so tired.

Tired of running. Tired of living in constant panic. Tired of being scared.

She'd spent her whole life in some form of anxious paralysis, and she didn't want to feel that way anymore. Fear did nothing for her. She just wanted to feel…nothing. She wanted to lie down on this rooftop and just not *be* anymore. There was no point to it—no point to any of it. She couldn't help Ethan. She couldn't stop Apollyon. She couldn't do anything that was expected of her. This mission—it wasn't for her.

"Let someone else do it!" she screamed at the darkening sky.

The clouds kept their meandering pace, ignoring her cries. Camryn ground her teeth to keep from screaming, her usual fear morphing into something more dangerous.

Her pulse thrummed but the stomach knot that usually accompanied her nerves was mysteriously absent.

Suddenly. Camryn was furious. Fuming. Boiling with the heat of a thousand hellfires.

She paced the length of the roof, feeling the heat rise in her ears.

I'm a human girl with limited powers. Ethan is wounded and unconscious. Michael is gone. And we're supposed to wage a war against the Prince of Darkness?

More pacing.

Even if they were only up against Harriet Kaya, how could they win? She was the president of a country. She had weapons, guards, a whole military at her disposal.

Camryn stopped, only noticing she'd begun to cry when a hot droplet of moisture slid down her cheek. She reached to wipe it away, and pulling her hand back, Camryn was horrified to find her finger crimson red.

Blood.

A moment later, another tear fell, then another. And another.

Camryn blinked away the tears that now covered her face only to realize the drops weren't coming from her eyes.

She turned her face up to the heavens as blood began pouring over the city, the heavens hemorrhaging onto the earth.

EIGHTEEN

Harriet sat behind her desk, her fingers steepled in front of her face. She'd been back in Turkey less than an hour and already had a room full of angry faces staring back at her.

Fahri, her national security advisor sat on the edge of his seat, his hands fisted in his lap. Two presidential counselors, Saban and Melik, were trying to present a more casual front, but their crossed arms and stiff posture gave away their unease.

"This was a grave miscalculation," Fahri said.

"We warned you of such an outcome," Melik followed.

"And *I* told *you,*" Harriet countered, "that sacrifices would have to be made for the greater good."

"And what exactly is the greater good?" Saban demanded. "Making our country look ridiculous? We attacked Jerusalem without due cause when they were trying to help us. And now we have Turkish troops patrolling their streets. Prime Minister Gaba isn't going to let this go unchecked. And we still don't even know where this mysterious terrorist intel came from. We've heard no talk of such things. The pictures you showed at the press conference looked like children, for God's sake."

"We're not having this conversation again." Harriet ran a hand over the smooth oak finish of her desk. She knew Gaba was no longer a concern, but she couldn't tell them that—not just yet.

"Do you realize what you have done by not honoring your agreement?" Melik swallowed hard. "There have been murmurings of nuclear activity."

Harriet stood and strolled to the corner window, looking out over the city. She was growing tired of their chatter. "We have nuclear weapons of our own," she said noncommittally.

An eerie silence fell over the room. The tension swelled like a balloon in the air behind her.

"You can't be serious," Saban said. "That's suicide."

Harriet turned away from the window to face them. "I think our allies will disagree."

Fahri grunted to his feet. "You're thinking of dragging the Alliance into this? You—you can't."

Their words buzzed past her ears; she didn't care what they had to say. They were ignorant and uninformed. But not for much longer.

Where is Apollyon?

The buzz of the phone interrupted her thoughts. She leaned forward and pressed a button.

Reggie's voice came through the speakers, distant and distorted. "Your guest is here," he reported.

Finally.

"Send him in."

Harriet noted the startled looks on the three men's faces when Apollyon strode through the door a few moments later. It wasn't customary to have commoners present during official presidential meetings. As a matter of fact, it was unheard of. But they didn't know how extraordinarily *un*common this man was.

Dressed in a navy suit, perfectly tailored for his chiseled physique, Apollyon's white hair had been perfectly styled to his head, not a hair out of place. He approached with the air of a man who knew too many secrets.

"Hello, gentlemen," Apollyon said with a wide smile. "I hear we'll be working together soon."

Malik and Saban joined Fahri in standing. "What is he talking about?"

"You haven't told them?" Apollyon appeared genuinely surprised.

Harriet waved him into the room. "I was waiting for you to join us."

"Mrs. Kaya, what is going on?" Saban demanded.

"Gentlemen, this is Apollyon," Harriet explained. "He is going to be taking the lead role in my advisory staff, effective immediately."

Their responses were equally shrill and exclamatory, all some version of:

"What?"

"Are you out of your mind?"

"That's preposterous!"

"Eh, eh, eh," Apollyon waggled a finger at the men. "Gentlemen, please." His voice escaped his mouth and coated the room like honey, the walls dripping with its sugary sweetness. "I am only here to help. We all trust our President's judgement, don't we?" He didn't wait for a response. "I know my place here, and I'm sure my expertise will prove invaluable." He spread his hands wide. "This is a good thing, don't you think?"

The men stood motionless for a moment, all the indignation seeming to drain from their bodies. Then one by one, they nodded their heads robotically.

"Very good," Apollyon nodded. "Now, you all are dismissed."

Fahri, Melik, and Saban shuffled out of the room like obedient children.

"I never grow tired of that," Apollyon said, gazing after them with a satisfied glint in his eye.

"It's quite unsettling," Harriet noted, taking a seat at her desk.

"Doesn't last nearly long enough, I admit. Otherwise, I would have the whole world under my rule by now."

With the others gone, Harriet grew uneasy in Apollyon's presence, but not for the same reasons as the first time they were in her office together. No longer a simple, ignorant mortal, she now had the accumulation of all his memories, all his future plans. Now she had the privilege of working with the most powerful angel in the heavens to bring to fruition his life's work, his magnum opus, so to speak.

Still, she wasn't looking forward to the impending conversation.

Apollyon walked with purpose to the chair across from her. He pursed his lips as if pondering his words.

Harriet's bubble of panic turned to a knot of impatience as he picked at an imaginary spot on the arm of the chair. *Just get on with it.*

Responding to her unspoken words, Apollyon cut his eyes toward her. "Very well," he said.

He straightened his jacket and leaned forward to burn into her soul with his ice-black eyes. "How?" His nostrils flared with forced calm. "How could you let them get away?"

Harriet stared into Apollyon's marble face. She'd expected the question and had her defense at the ready, meager as it was. "They had help."

Apollyon huffed. "I took care of the Archangels for you. You couldn't handle a little Dominion?"

"Don't forget about the Tracker. She was there as well."

Apollyon waved his hand in the air. "Akira is of no consequence. She should not have proven too much of an obstacle for the soldiers I gave you."

"Perhaps she is more of a problem than you give her credit for. My army has yet to locate them in the city. Her shield is strong. Even when we had an exact location, we almost didn't acquire the girl at all. If she hadn't come for him…" Harriet averted her eyes, not daring to finish the sentence.

"But you *did* have them. You had them in a building wrapped in layers or celestial protections and guarded by angels. And yet," Apollyon spread his hands, "they still managed to get away."

"One of the little bastards stabbed me!" Harriet exclaimed, rising in her chair.

Apollyon chuckled. "A minor inconvenience, I'm sure."

"Inconvenience?" Harriet sat back, a crack of a smile breaching her face. "You should have told me what would happen. I thought I was about to spontaneously combust." She found herself almost laughing, something she had never imagined possible in the presence of this man.

Apollyon surprised her then by offering her a small smile in return. A smile of comradery. Of solidarity.

Ever since Harriet had known him, she'd sensed the otherworldliness of this man. His hands wielded so much power, his eyes so much wisdom.

And now, she shared all of it. His touch in her office two days prior had opened her mind, enlightening her to the infinite wonders of the universe. She understood everything now—the meaning of it all, how every event in history had led up to the completion of his divine plan. She understood that plan now, too, and how it would benefit both realms.

She'd always longed for his love, but now she had something better.

She had his respect.

Even though she'd failed, he still trusted her. She could feel it in his smile.

"I'm sorry," Harriet settled back in her chair. "I won't disappoint you again."

"I hope you're right. But we do have our work cut out for us now. They know you are more than just one of my human puppets and that they are impervious to human weapons. That will provide them too much confidence. We're going to have to employ more…creative tactics."

"It doesn't concern you at all?"

"That he didn't die? Not necessarily. He *is* an angel, after all."

"He *was* an angel," Harriet amended. "I was there. I touched him, saw him. He may have been an angel once, but right now, he's very much human."

Harriet paused, a silence passing between them. "They could be the ones."

Apollyon scoffed. "Two incompetent children?"

"You just called him an angel. Now they're children? You know just as well as I do; they are not your average teenagers, even if they aren't fully angels."

"They may as well be. They're immature and impulsive, and I've never known them to complete any mission efficiently in their existence, even in their celestial state." Apollyon rose and strolled to the window to take the position Harriet held moments earlier.

"They're not the ones."

"If they aren't," Harriet asked, "why are you wasting so many precious resources on them? It's a huge distraction from the larger plan."

"You know why." Apollyon's voice remained calm, but Harriet noticed his whitening knuckles as he gripped the window sill in front of him.

Of course, Harriet understood his hatred of them. He'd shown her the offenses they'd committed against him, starting with their treason during his first attempt to take Elohim's throne.

But he had a second chance now at the heavenly seat. It would be disastrous if his obsession with these two humans were his downfall.

"They've made a fool of me time after time," Apollyon went on. "There are punishments for the crimes they have committed, and they must face them." He turned to face Harriet, his eyes flaming.

"Well." Harriet let out a sigh of understanding. "What's our next play? How are we going to find them?"

Apollyon turned back to the city view just as a red droplet dotted the glass in front of him. His eyes narrowed as more red liquid hit the building and streamed down the window, leaving a sickly trail in its wake.

"We stick to the plans with the Alliance. That seems to be going smoothly. As far as the two teenagers…" He raised his fingers to trace the droplets of blood creeping down the other side of the glass. "It looks like they will be their own undoing."

NINETEEN

Akira, Ronan, Yon, and Levana had gathered to gawk at the horrific sight unfolding outside the window. They all turned when Camryn slid back into the room, looking like a child who'd been caught with a crayon against a freshly painted wall.

Everyone gaped at the sight of her—hair fixed to her face by the crimson liquid oozing down her body and collecting in a bloody pool at her feet.

"Did you do that?" Akira pointed out the window.

"I—" The words froze in Camryn's throat. There would be no explaining this.

Akira took a step toward her. "Well, make it stop!"

"I can't," Camryn mumbled, her gaze falling on Ethan who remained prostrate on the couch, his shallow breaths his only movement. She needed him to wake up. She needed him to reassure her. She needed him to help her figure out what the hell was happening. She needed him...

"What do you mean? Look at this?" Akira demanded. "Do you have any idea the ramifications this is going to have? For—for the wildlife, the water supply, the–the—" she stammered. "Just make it stop!"

"I can't make it stop!" Camryn shouted, her words crashing through the room like an errant hurricane. She thought she'd left her fury on the rooftop, but it erupted inside her again, and Akira would suffice as an adequate target for her ire.

"But you knew that, right?" Camryn stalked toward Akira, fists tight at her side. "You probably get some kind of sick enjoyment out of watching me fail—over and over again. Does that make you feel better about your pathetic existence?"

"*Wow.*" Akira blanched, planting her fists on her hips. "You have some nerve, you know that? I am getting really tired of your insolence. If it wasn't for him," Akira motioned toward Ethan lying on the couch, "I'd be out of here so fast—"

"Oh, I bet you would. I bet you *would*." Camryn lunged at Akira, but Akira didn't retreat. She planted her feet and raised her hands in defense, ready for a fight.

Before they collided, though, another body slid between them, catching Camryn by the shoulders.

Levana.

Turning Camryn in the opposite direction, Levana directed the blood-soaked girl toward the bathroom. "Come now. You're dripping all over my rugs."

Camryn resisted only a little because, even in her agitated state, she was still semi-aware that her every move was making a crime scene out of someone else's home. She held Akira's glare, though, until the Tracker was out of sight.

Not until minutes later, safely in the shower, with the hot water running in red rivulets down the drain, did her wrath begin to dissipate, leaking out of her in hot tears down her cheeks.

Camryn's eyelids drooped from the flood of adrenaline leaving her veins. Unable to hold herself up any longer, she slid down to the shower floor, put her head on her knees and let the water wash her misery away.

"Eh, eh," Levana tutted when Camryn winced away from her.

"That hurts," Camryn complained of the alcohol pad Levana had just wiped over Camryn's forehead. Her injuries from the morning's blast had been bumped to the bottom of her priority list until she'd exited the shower a few minutes earlier and stared at her battered body in the bathroom mirror. A large purple bruise covered her left ribcage. A nasty gash gaped at her from her forehead and a kiwi-sized swatch of skin had been scraped from her elbow—just bloody, raw flesh.

She sat at the table now in a more comfortable gray t-shirt and patterned leggings—the only pants Levana had that fit the much shorter girl—but Camryn wouldn't complain. Clean clothes were a rare commodity as of late.

Finishing up with Camryn's bandages, Levana gathered the used alcohol pads, bandage packaging, and ointments before darting into the kitchen, mumbling something about soup and onions and loudly vocalizing her concerns about the amount of milk in her refrigerator.

How long had it been since Camryn had eaten? Just the mention of food made her stomach rumble.

A good ten minutes of chopping and stirring ensued, and soon, the savory aroma of what Camryn had to guess was some kind of lintel soup filled the apartment.

As Levana stirred the sizzling meat on the stove, Camryn stared out the large front window at the building on the other side of the street. The rain had stopped but the evidence of the bloody downpour was tattooed all over the city—and possibly beyond. Out the window now, it looked as if someone had taken a dump truck full of rust-colored paint and overturned it directly onto the row of buildings, streaking down their sides and running in scarlet rivers into the gutters.

The television had remained on the same channel all day, the volume low enough to be ignored, but now, the anchor's words caught Camryn's ear:

"From the bombing of one of Israel's holiest cities to blood rain, it really is turning into a week of apocalyptic proportions. We have yet to learn what caused the discoloration of the precipitation, or what it will mean for our ecosystem. It's sure to be inconvenient at best, but will likely have much more devastating effects..."

Camryn planted her face in her hands, groaning. Everything she did turned into such a mess.

Levana snapped off the television and went about placing bowls of steaming soup around the tiny table, motioning for everyone to join her and Camryn there.

Camryn's heart clenched when she counted only six bowls. She peeked over the back of the couch at Ethan, still asleep, and wondered if having some nourishment in his body would help him heal. Even if he couldn't die, he still needed food and water. If he didn't wake up soon...

Yon and Myria took their place obediently beside Levana, but Akira and Ronan remained on watch by the window. "Oh, no, thank you," Ronan tried a polite refusal, but Levana was having none of it.

"Come. Now." She snapped her fingers and pointed to the two empty chairs she'd drug from the hall closet. "Eat."

Akira shrugged to Ronan as they slowly meandered toward the table. Akira cleared her throat as she scooted her chair in beside Camryn, and Camryn pointedly avoided her glare.

The soup was thick and just hot enough to warm the chill that had crept its way into Camryn's bones. With every bite, her irritation dissolved bit by bit, and Camryn decided that Levana must have laced her recipe with some sort of pixie dust.

"Got any of that for me?" a voice grunted from the couch.

Spoons clanked against glass bowls and a small squeal escaped someone's mouth. Ethan's head popped into view over the back of the velvet sofa.

Levana jumped up and ran to him, a first aid kit at the ready, prepped for that very occasion.

Camryn, on the other hand, remained glued to her spot, afraid to let herself feel relief… *Not yet.* She could only stare as Levana took Ethan's face gently in her hands and examined it with disapproving murmurs. The woman had doctored and bandaged his visible injuries earlier, but her eyes scoured over him now like a lioness who'd just birthed a cub.

"Nice to meet you, too," Ethan grunted in obvious pain. He ran his tongue over the freshly bleeding split in his lip. Levana picked up a wet hand towel and pressed it to the wound.

"Well, you still look like shit," Akira said. "But you aren't as hideous as you were a few hours ago."

The swelling in his face had gone down noticeably and the burns weren't as fiery-red.

"I should be okay…" Ethan's voice was hoarse with pain. "By morning."

"You can barely move," Ronan said. "How are you going to be okay by morning?"

"Hey, aren't you supposed to be my hype man?" Ethan managed a tight smile.

Ronan smiled back, stuffing another spoonful of soup in his mouth. "Sorry."

Camryn finally broke herself from her paralysis and stood from the table. Grabbing a fresh bottle of water, she lowered herself onto the couch beside Ethan, handing him the container which he dispensed of in three long gulps.

"You think you can eat?" she asked, thankful for the late hour. If Ethan could see the horror show on the street outside, he would surely have more questions than Camryn could answer.

"I can sure try. Whatever that is, it smells great."

Levana brought over a bowl of soup and two small pills. Ethan didn't even ask what they were before tossing them in his mouth and washing them down with the rest of the water.

Camryn watched as he picked up the bowl and struggled to swallow a few spoonfuls of soup before finally giving up and dropping it back onto the table in front of him.

"Do you want me to—" Camryn offered to help, but he waved her away.

"I'm just going to lie back down." He lowered himself back down onto the sofa, looking spent, as if that little activity had zapped the hours-worth of energy he'd accumulated in his unconsciousness.

Seconds later, he was asleep again.

TWENTY

Myria yawned as Levana dropped a pile of blankets and pillows in the chair beside Camryn. Akira leaned against the door, arms crossed over her chest, eyes closed, pretending to sleep. Ronan reclined against the window, knees drawn to his chest, tapping feverishly on the Halo that had gone silent hours ago.

Camryn looked up from the small chair beside the couch where Ethan lay. "Thank you," she mumbled. Levana nodded and reached for her daughter's hand, but Myria seemed to have other ideas.

Her tiny, round face broke into Camryn's line of sight as she stared down at the burns on Ethan's back. Camryn smiled at the little girl in her mermaid pajamas.

"Is he going to be okay?" Myria asked.

"Yeah." Camryn nodded, unsure of how much of her English the child understood. "Yeah, he's going to be okay."

She pointed to the purple bruise around Ethan's eye. "Ouchie."

Levana called to the girl from across the room, but Camryn waved to her. "It's okay," Camryn assured her.

Camryn looked back into the little girl's worried eyes. "Are you scared?"

Myria nodded.

"Yeah, some scary stuff happened today," Camryn said, leaning forward and planting her elbows on her knees. "So, what do you do when you're scared?"

The little girl gave the smallest shrug. "I hold my papa's hand."

Camryn smiled at Yon, who regarded them intently. "That sounds like a good plan." Camryn yawned and took a pillow from the pile. "I think I'm going to try to sleep now, okay?"

Myria nodded, but she didn't move away. Instead, she put her head down on the cushion beside Ethan and placed a tiny hand on his arm. She spoke several words in Hebrew before Camryn realized what was happening. The little girl was praying for him.

Myria finished her prayer and stood, blinking at Camryn with her big, brown eyes. Camryn stared after the girl as Myria turned and skipped to her parents, never looking back.

Camryn woke with a start, blinking up at the ceiling and wondering what had woken her. She couldn't put her finger on anything out of the ordinary until…

Boom!

There it was again. This time, though, Camryn didn't have any problem identifying the sound.

No. Not again.

She scrambled to join Akira and Ronan by the window. "They're coming from the north," Akira pointed.

Another blast, closer this time but from the opposite direction, caused Camryn to turn. She lifted her hand against the blinding brightness of the light shining in from under the door.

That's strange.

She didn't remember a light being there when she'd fallen asleep.

Camryn turned slowly and crept toward the light, stalking it deliberately, drawn like a cat to the hunt.

"What are you doing?" Akira hissed, but Camryn didn't hear.

Another rumbling shake brought Yon and Levana out of their bedroom. "What is going on?" Yon demanded just as Camryn placed a hand on the doorknob. Everyone in the room rushed at her, pulling her back. "You can't go out there!"

Even Ethan sat up and called to her, but she couldn't turn away.

Camryn felt hands on her arms, trying to stop her, but they were powerless against the light that compelled her.

Opening the door, Camryn took a step back, finding the light had dimmed, revealing only the empty street and the orange glow of dawn in the city.

Looking closer, though, Camryn realized…the street wasn't empty. And the blood that now ran down the sidewalks and gutters wasn't the same blood that had poured from the sky hours before. The blood flowed from the bursting boils that covered the dozens of bodies lying in the street, their eyes protruding from their skulls, tongues rotten in their mouths. Camryn screamed and recoiled from the horrific scene.

Backing away, her foot brushed against something hard. Camryn gasped and looked down into the face of a woman about her mother's age, her skin a sickly gray. Camryn bent down to help her, but nothing could be done. The woman was dead. They all were.

Camryn stood, her heart racing, her breath coming in too-short bursts.

"I'm sorry." She spun around, taking in the whole scene. "I'm so sorry."

Camryn wrapped her arms around herself as her body shook, out of her control.

Then the light returned, shining like an indomitable sun, growing larger—filling, consuming. From inside the glow, a voice reverberated around her, the brilliance vibrating with its power.

"The sword of the Lord is bathed in blood."

"What?" Camryn called into the yellow void. *What the hell is that supposed to mean?* But the voice had gone silent.

Responding to the light, or possibly the dreadfully ominous words of the fiery luminescence, her body shook harder, as if someone had her by the shoulders, jerking her back and forth.

Even when the glow began to diminish, her nerves remained on full current. Her sight returning, Camryn blinked through the fading light and into Akira's scowling face.

"What the hell is your problem?" Akira demanded.

Camryn's head swiveled from side to side. She found Ronan beside her, looking more concerned than angry, and a soft carpet underneath her. She was back in the apartment, lying on the floor under the fuzzy, red blanket, all eyes staring at her.

Relief swallowed her. *It was just a dream.*

"I—I saw something," she stammered.

"A memory?" Ronan asked.

"No, more like a vision. I've had them before, back home, before the..."

Before the flood.

The same flood that had destroyed her home—she'd seen the scene play out in her mind, over and over before it had actually happened. What had Ethan called them? Premonitions?

The sword of the Lord is bathed in blood.

Camryn's relief disappeared, replaced by harrowing dread. The scene that was now burned into her eternal memory might not have happened yet, but sometime soon…it would.

DAY THREE

TWENTY-ONE

Camryn opened the bathroom door with a yelp. Stumbling backward, she almost tumbled over the toilet and into the bathtub. Ethan reached out and caught her, wincing with the effort of pulling her back to her feet.

"Oh, God, I'm so sorry! Are you okay?" Camryn exclaimed.

"Yeah, just a bit sore." He lifted his arms, moving them in small circles. "Are *you* okay?"

"Yeah, I'm—" she started, but stopped short when her eyes landed on his face. "Wow. How do you look so good?" She was elated to find his injuries almost completely healed. Granted, he still looked terrible, but so much better—a black eye and split lip the only evidence of the beating he'd taken the day before.

A playful smirk caught Camryn off guard. "Well, I'm told I get it from my father, but I don't know. I've never met the guy."

Camryn's chest expanded with a sort of joy that forced her lips into a wide smile. "You know what I mean. You're swelling is gone and—" she whirled him around to look at his back. "Your burns are mostly scabbed over."

"Well, I'm not a hundred percent, that's for sure, but I don't know. I've always kind of been a fast healer. Another one of those things that kind of made sense after we found out about our past. Is it not the same for you?"

"Not that I've ever noticed, but…" Camryn lifted her shirt high enough to see the fading bruise on her ribs, now a nasty pale green instead of the bright purple it had been hours before. She peeled back the bandage on her elbow to find a completely scabbed over wound.

Camryn's mouth gaped open. How had she never noticed that before?

Ethan leaned a shoulder into the wall and crossed his arms in front of him, giving her time to process this new revelation. "So, listen," he said when she finally looked up from her wounds, pushing the door shut behind him, "something kind of weird happened to me last night."

"Last night? While you were unconscious?"

"Yeah, I heard something…in a dream?" He said the last part like a question, as if not entirely sure he could trust himself.

"Join the club."

"Huh?"

Camryn waved him on.

"Well, I know you're kind of the expert in the area and I just wondered what you might make of it."

Camryn grinned. "Well, you have to tell me what it is first."

Ethan looked hesitant. "Yeah, well. I heard…just a few words. I don't know who was speaking. It was just a voice."

Camryn grew still, suspecting she knew what his next words would be.

"'The sword of the Lord is bathed in blood.'" Ethan grimaced, as if he understood how horrific it sounded. "That's what the voice said. What do you think it means?"

Camryn's face must have shown her trepidation, or maybe it was her silence, but Ethan pulled himself from the wall and straightened. "Camryn?"

"I heard it, too."

"You—"

"Yeah, I heard the same thing."

Camryn reached and yanked open the door beside him. "We need to talk to Ronan."

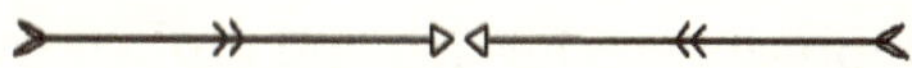

"So, this prophecy," Ethan asked after hearing Ronan's theory as they sat huddled in a corner of the living room. "Are we sure it's about us?"

"Not entirely," Ronan replied in a hushed tone. "It's just an educated guess."

"So we *could* go out and be shot dead in the street? No do-overs?"

"Potentially."

"But probably not," Camryn added.

Akira scoffed. "Look at you being the optimist."

"I just know it's all we have to go on right now."

"Well it's pretty useless as far as prophecies go," Ethan said. "All it tells us is the ending—a horrible ending honestly. It doesn't tell us the most important thing—what's supposed to happen next."

"Maybe the mysterious voice has some better clues."

"'The sword of the Lord is bathed in blood?'" Akira questioned. "What the hell is that supposed to tell us? Other than you two are morbid as hell?"

"Those aren't our words," Camryn countered. "And you know it means something. Both of us heard it. That's never happened before."

"That's true," Ronan said. "But like she said, we still don't know where to go from here. I think it was just some kind of warning."

"Where does that leave us then?"

I say we start at the Turkish Embassy," Ronan offered. "Everything seems to center around that building. That's where Sam, Jay, and Raphael were headed and probably where Michael started his search for them. Maybe we can find something there."

Camryn tapped her foot lightly against the tile floor. "Yeah, except they all disappeared from there, never to be heard from again—" She did a double-take at the figure in the hallway. "Excuse me, what the hell are you doing?"

Ethan stood from his hunched position inside a small closet in the hall. He held up a black t-shirt as if he'd just found buried treasure. "Laundry closet. Found a shirt."

"Congratulations, but you can't just take that. We've already broken into these people's home and made a huge mess. We're not stealing their clothes, too."

"Levana gave you an outfit. I'm sure the guy—"

"Yon," Camryn corrected.

"I'm sure Yon won't mind."

Camryn sighed as Ethan pulled the shirt over his head with obvious effort. It took everything in her not to rush over and aid him in his thievery.

As everyone headed to the door, Camryn hesitated. There wasn't much else to do, but she didn't feel right just leaving while they slept. Camryn touched the gun holstered at her side—the gun that Yon had insisted that she take. These people had done so much for them. And they were just going to leave without saying goodbye?

"Come on," Akira beckoned from the open door, but Camryn was still unsure. Doing the only thing she could think to do, she went to the refrigerator and wrote a quick note on the grocery pad stuck to its front. Finishing the scratchy note, she read over the message again.

That'll have to do.

Standing in the same spot where she'd held a dying Ethan the day before, Camryn could still make out the circle of his blood staining the concrete, even amid the streaks of crimson rain drying in the street.

"That's disturbing," Ethan said, looking down at the spot. To his credit, he hadn't blanched when she'd explained to him, as best she could, about what she had done. He didn't even wrinkle his nose at the smell, and Camryn loved him even more for it.

"Imagine being conscious for it," she said.

"That's odd," Ronan said, cutting into their grim banter. "The building is still empty. Shouldn't people be back to work today?"

"It was really easy to get into yesterday, too," Camryn recalled. "This might be another trap."

Akira studied the tops of the surrounding buildings. "Or maybe there was a tragic shooting here yesterday and the building is still a crime scene. Do you people not listen to the news?

"Come on," she said when no one answered.

Following her lead, the group advanced up the alley, careful to stay in the shadows. Approaching the building, they found the back door unlocked…again. Following the same path Camryn and Ronan had taken the day before, they entered and made their way up the stairs to the office where she and Ronan had found Ethan.

The room looked the same—furniture pushed to the perimeter of the room, one chair in the middle with yellowed marks in the dark oak where the handcuffs had marred the wood.

Ethan's hands remained deep in his pockets as he surveyed the space with a hard glare.

Camryn put a hand on his arm. "Are you okay?"

"Yeah. Fine."

But he didn't look fine. He looked like he wanted to punch someone in the face. Camryn backed away, afraid to press him further.

While Camryn and Ethan opened drawers and peeked under chairs, Ronan began tapping away at the keyboard and Akira hovered over his shoulder.

"What do you think you're going to find in there?" Camryn inquired.

"Probably more than you're going to find in those cabinets." Ronan grinned.

Camryn raised an eyebrow. *Okay*, she thought. *Go off, I guess.*

"These machines are fascinating," Ronan said to no one in particular. "It's amazing how far human technology has advanced—almost caught up to us, haven't they?" He grinned with true appreciation.

"Only a few hundred more years," Akira muttered.

"Come look at this," Ronan called a few moments later. "There isn't much on this computer, but I was able to trace the IP address of her desktop in Turkey from this one and hack into her hard drive. Most of her files are encrypted, but there's something here." Ronan pointed at the screen.

Ethan and Camryn came to stand behind him. Over his shoulder, multiple searches were pulled up, each looking very different from the others; some memos, some emails, some formal-looking legal documents…

"What are we looking at?"

"Look here." Ronan moved his finger around the screen. "And here. And here. All these documents have one thing in common."

Camryn quickly skimmed the pages.

"What is *White Horse*? What does that mean?" Ethan asked.

Camryn's vision from the night before flashed across her memory—the woman with her skin as pale as ash. She hadn't explained what she'd seen to the others. The whole "sword of the Lord" thing had occupied the morning's conversation. But somehow Camryn knew that whatever *White Horse* was code for, it had something to do with her premonition.

"Give me a few more minutes and I can get into these encrypted files."

Akira groaned. "Come on, Ronan. We don't have all day."

Ronan twisted to face Akira. "I'm hacking into the computer of one of the most powerful leaders in the western world. And I have to do that without anyone noticing. It might take a moment."

Akira threw up her hands and turned away, mumbling under her breath.

Camryn was rubbing her stomach, trying to calm the knot roiling inside when Ronan pulled his hands from the keyboard and froze. "Oh my God," he said.

"What? What is it?" Everyone raced around to see what had startled him so. On the screen was an image of President Kaya at her desk, her mouth moving in conversation.

"Is that—" Akira pointed.

"I got into the camera," Ronan whispered as if he were afraid Harriet Kaya and her guest might hear him through the screen.

"This is live?" Ethan asked.

"The mic. The mic," Camryn waved her hand at the keyboard. "Turn on the mic."

Ronan jumped into action, pressing a few more keys and Apollyon's voice came through the speaker, slightly distorted, but clear enough to make out his words.

"Kale is already at Lanister's for the pickup," he said. "He's ready to carry out his duties, so I would say everything is coming together nicely on my end. How are things progressing for you?"

President Kaya lowered her gaze as if the question had been intended to shame her. "We'll find them," she said. "We have the others, so one way or the other…" She ended with a shrug.

The others?

"Well, I'll let you get to it then," Apollyon said, and the woman on the screen stood.

Camryn didn't hear a door shut, but a moment later President Kaya collapsed back into her chair, dropping her face into her hands.

Camryn's mind went immediately to the Archangels. Sam, Jay, Raphael, and Michael hadn't been heard from in over twenty-four hours.

"What do you think she meant by 'the others'?" Camryn asked. "Do you think they have them?"

"I don't know," Ronan considered. "It's possible."

"And that doesn't concern you? I mean, if he's managed to capture the collective group of Archangels, things aren't looking very good for us."

Ronan peered up from the screen with a look that dropped Camryn's stomach to her feet. "If you think that's bad, I'm afraid things are about to get a whole lot worse."

TWENTY-TWO

"It's a biochemical research facility," Ronan explained after concluding his internet search for the Lannister's that Harriet Kaya had mentioned. "They house everything from anthrax to smallpox to chemical weapons like hydrogen cyanide and mustard gas."

"Mustard gas..." Ethan repeated. "I remember reading about that in history class. It was used in World War I, wasn't it? It's the stuff that makes crazy blisters on your skin when it touches you?"

Ronan nodded. "Yes, I believe so."

"It's a gas?" Camryn asked. "So it spreads through the air?"

"It can be a liquid or a gas," Ronan explained. "Why do you ask?"

Camryn leaned on the desk and watched the alarm unfurl on the faces gaping back at her as she described the horror she'd seen in her vision the night before and her fear that the two might be connected.

"Oh, God," Akira grimaced at the visual.

"And you're sure this wasn't just a bad dream?" Ronan asked.

"I've had nightmares all my life. This was nothing like that."

"But if they do have a chemical weapon like that, we don't even know how they're planning to release it—through the air, the water?"

"Well, whoever this Kale is, he was at Lannister's fifteen minutes ago. He's sure to already have what he went for."

"So how are we going to stop him? We don't even know who he is."

"I know who he is," Akira said.

"You do?" Ronan turned with an inquisitive look.

She shrugged. "I've worked with him before. He's one of Apollyon's lackeys. Been trying to climb the ranks for a while now. He's just in the past few years started taking on more important jobs."

Camryn studied Akira from the corner of her eye. It was easy to forget how close Akira was to Apollyon and how recently she'd worked side-by-side with him.

"Any idea where he might be going?"

Akira plopped down into the chair Ethan had been tied to, tapping her red fingernail on her teeth. "I've never worked with him in Israel, but I do know he's not the biggest fan of the mortal world, so if he's on the surface, it's only under direct orders."

Camryn rolled her eyes. "I don't really see how that's helpful at all."

"I'm just providing information, Camryn." Akira leaned her head into her hand, pressing her red curls into her palm. "I didn't say it was helpful."

Camryn bit her lip, feeling somehow stricken by Akira's bland response. If Akira could be relied on for anything, it was a snarky comeback.

“Wait.” Ronan blurted, clicking more keys until he found what he was looking for. “That might actually be helpful. Look at this.” Ronan pointed to the computer screen again.

“What am I looking at?” Ethan asked.

“It’s an underground aquifer that feeds most of the fresh water to the country. Do you think he could have been picked for the job because of his subterranean knowledge of the area?”

Akira straightened so quickly that Camryn thought the Tracker had heard something she and the others hadn’t. “Forget what I said before. I know exactly where he is.”

Camryn was pleased to find her body becoming accustomed to the kaleidoscope of color swirling around her as she transported through space—Ethan, not so much. Once they were firmly on solid ground, he leaned forward and heaved, but managed to hold on to the few crackers he’d eaten for breakfast.

Steadying herself, Camryn gazed around at a lush, green forest that had somehow managed to escape the downpour of bloody proportions the day before.

At her feet, the sound of running water gurgled by—a small mountain stream flowing in a rocky bed.

“Is this it?” Camryn couldn’t imagine such a scrawny stream being any kind of water source for an entire country.

“No,” Ronan answered. “The aquifer is underground. This is just a tiny tributary.”

“Underground. Sounds great.” Camryn said. “So how do we get there?”

Ronan squinted up the mountain. “We don’t—”

“This way,” Akira said as she took off up the hill, following the stream toward its origin.

“You’ve been here before?” Ethan inquired, pushing a thick bramble to the side so Camryn could pass through.

"Uh…" Akira shrugged. "This is Kale's territory. I've been here with him once or twice."

"And you didn't think that was important to tell us?"

"I'm telling you now. Besides, how was I supposed to know he'd bring a chemical weapon back to his own sector? And I had no idea there was an aquifer here."

As they walked, the stone bed grew into a sharp embankment rising up on either side of them, growing steeper with every foot of altitude.

"How could you not know something like that?" Ethan pressed.

"The few times I've been here, we weren't talking about work, okay? It never came up."

Ethan's eyebrows shot up, finally understanding what Akira wasn't saying.

Camryn watched the irritation cross Ethan's face and realized just how much of Ethan and Akira's relationship than she didn't understand. They'd had thirty years together that Camryn knew nothing about. That was her own doing; she'd been the one to abandon him in Syria, after all. She understood that. But it still annoyed her.

After a few more minutes of walking, Camryn noticed the large slabs of limestone on either side of them shrinking and the embankment turning to a grassier terrain. They pulled themselves over a particularly large boulder, and a lush oasis emerged in front of them. The clouds still grayed the sky, but Camryn could imagine the meadow in its full beauty, full of blooming color and warm from the sun.

"Wow, this is gorgeous," she said.

"Yeah," Akira looked around with a pleased grin. "It's most beautiful here at night."

Camryn glanced around trying to picture it.

"Anyway, I've never used a physical entrance like a cave or anything," Akira went on. "But I do remember that there is one around here somewhere."

"I still say we just blow it up," Ronan said. "If there isn't a way in, we make one."

"Ronan." Akira pinned him with an annoyed glare. "Stop with the explosions, okay? We aren't blowing anything up. Ever."

Ronan frowned. "Well, you sure know how to suck the fun out of everything."

Akira rolled her eyes and turned back to her search.

Camryn turned in a circle but saw nothing but a grassy bank to a mountain stream and a tree-covered embankment leading up to an even greener mountain. "I don't think there are any caves around here—" she said right before the ground opened beneath them and swallowed them up.

TWENTY-THREE

Camryn's scream was extinguished by an explosion of pain in her right shoulder as the jagged surface of rock broke her fall. Her body rolled from the impact and she felt herself falling into a blur of rushing blackness.

A hand reached out and caught her by the arm, pulling her back onto the rock. "Thanks," she exhaled, trying to catch her breath.

Regaining her footing, Camryn finally stood to take in the cavern that they'd dropped into. Not a big space, no bigger than her quaint farm house back home, with a hole in the middle about the size of her bedroom.

The sound of rushing water echoed from the opening, fast and dangerous. The walls of untouched limestone encircled them, and the hole they'd just fallen through provided the only light to see by.

"Damn it to bloody hell," Akira cursed, rising from the ground. "I don't know why any self-respecting angel would ever *choose* these worthless bodies. Shit, that hurt."

"I can think of one reason," a male voice echoed from the shadows. Camryn peered around Ronan to lay her eyes on the magnificent specimen who must be Kale. Tall and lean with a long jaw and golden curls that fell to his shoulders, the image left Camryn so mesmerized that she didn't even feel Ronan grasping for her, firmly gripping her upper arm.

Akira didn't seem affected by Kale's charms, though, laughing in response to his joke. "Well, yes. There is that."

Kale's bright smile never faltered and his eyes remained trained on Akira as he pulled a short sword from the sheath on his back and pointed it directly at Ronan's face.

"Why have you brought him here?"

"Oh no." Akira raised her hands in front of her and slid between Ronan and the blade. "He's with us."

Kale's eyes narrowed at Ronan. "I've heard of Righteous spies, but a Dominion?" Kale gave his sword one grand twirl before sliding it back into place on his back.

"Some courage you must have, my brother." He nodded to Camryn and Ethan. "That makes him kind of like a dirty cop in human terms," he said by way of explanation but did a double-take, examining them more closely. "But you knew that already, didn't you?"

A lock of blonde hair had fallen into Camryn's face, but she was too entranced to move it— by his beauty or from fear, she couldn't be sure.

Kale reached to brush the hair from her face, but an almost imperceptible movement from beside her stopped him. Kale's gaze flitted to Ethan's face and stayed there for several moments.

Whatever Kale saw in Ethan's eyes caused him to pull his hand away from Camryn, regarding Ethan warily.

"These must be the two fugitives Apollyon has been on about. I haven't seen a *qanima* bond that bright in ages."

Only then did Camryn realize Ronan had a hand on Ethan's arm as well, holding them like prisoners. She wished someone had clued her in on the game because she had no idea what was happening.

"A pretty penny you'll get for these two, ay? Might even get your own legion out of this one."

"That's the plan," Akira gloated, eliciting the beginnings of a protest from Camryn.

Her objection was cut short, though, by a reprimanding pinch from Ronan. She looked questioning at him but his gaze remained straight ahead.

"You know I always look forward to a visit from you," Kale said. "But I'm afraid you've caught me at quite the most inopportune time." He held up an orange canister with a metal lid, similar to a small soda can. "I'm in the middle of something, you see."

"Yes. About that—" Akira began.

Kale shook his head. "Please don't tell me Apollyon sent you to amend our agreement. You can go back and tell him that the job was already done when you got here and I expect my payment, as we discussed."

"Don't be so hasty." Akira grinned. "I think you might like to hear what I have to say."

"Oh?" Camryn watched Kale's posture turn from defensive to cautiously interested.

"Yes," she purred. "Because Apollyon didn't send me. I came of my own accord."

Kale gave a devilish grin. "Normally that would excite me, but it seems we're both alternately obligated at the moment."

He held up the canister. "I have this..." Then he nodded to Camryn and Ethan. "And you have them. You do see how things could get messy?"

Akira batted her long, dark eyelashes and sauntered toward Kale, her boots scraping a seductive song against the wet stone. "Just hear me out," she said, twirling her index finger in one of his golden curls.

"You let me in on this mission," she nodded toward the canister. "And you can accompany me when I collect my reward for these two." She nodded toward Ronan and his captives. "We'll say you helped capture them. Split the reward."

Camryn imagined that Akira's voice would sound flirtatious to anyone else, but to Camryn, she heard a spider, slowly seducing her prey.

"I'm listening..."

"It's very simple, really..." Akira's words slithered down the cave walls, slow and deliberate. "All you have to do is take that big thing you have there..." Her fingernails raked from his wrist, coming to rest on his chest.

Akira's lips were at Kale's ear now. "And put it in my hand..."

Kale's body went slack. Camryn could almost feel him unraveling in Akira's web.

"I don't see how—"

"And we do it together." Akira spoke slow and soft, her hand traveling down the length of his torso, stopping at his belt and giving it a gentle tug. "Would you like that?"

Camryn looked away then. Of all the items on her list of things she hoped to never see, Akira in full-on seduction mode was number one on that list.

Camryn's eyes were occupied with more appealing things—like tracing the cracks in the cave wall, when a raging fury tightened in her core. But the reaction didn't belong to her. She glanced at Ethan and saw the muscle twitch in his jaw and his fists tight at his sides as he scowled at Akira practically making out with Kale in front of them.

Camryn tried to take a deep breath, struggling to keep her focus on the task at hand. *Now is not the time,* she reminded herself, but the air caught in her throat, thick with Ethan's animosity and Kale's silent calculations.

"I suppose that could work..." Kale said as he allowed Akira to slide the canister from his hand.

"That's good," she breathed, running her tongue over his earlobe even as she extended her hand toward Ronan, handing the canister off to him.

"What—" Kale blinked as if coming out of a trance.

"Sorry for the deception, friend." Ronan shrugged as he jammed the canister into the pocket of his khakis. "Nothing personal, I assure you."

Kale backed away, putting some distance between himself and Akira. "Oh, darling." He laughed, coming back to himself again. "What good do you think that's going to do? You don't think that's the only canister, do you?"

Akira flicked a glance to Ronan then back to Kale, looking unsure. "I did, actually."

"Oh, that is too precious." Kale laughed again. "What good is a plague when it only affects a few thousand people? Most of the world would never even hear about it." He lowered himself into a fighting stance. "There's a team of angels just like me all over the globe—in London and Cairo and Moscow—with canisters of their own." His fingers twitched in front of him.

"It's quite unfortunate that I have to kill you all, and you won't be around to see the results." His grin became sinister. "It's going to be *biblical.*"

Akira crouched to mirror his posture. "I'm afraid I can't let that happen."

"The thing is, darling, I don't think you can stop me."

Akira smirked. "Who are you kidding? There are four of us and only one of you."

Kale didn't take his eyes from Akira as he extended a hand outward, an invisible force sending Ethan sailing as if a cannon ball had slammed into his stomach.

"Hmm..." Kale cocked his head. "I don't think I really have to worry about those two."

Camryn and Ronan both rushed back to where Ethan lay moaning on the ground.

"I'm fine," Ethan said between his teeth. "Stop him."

Ronan nodded and slipped the canister into Ethan's hand before rushing to Akira's aid.

"You really shouldn't have done that," Akira growled with a lunge. Kale ducked, but not fast enough. Akira sailed toward him, latching one hand around his neck and swinging around, attaching herself to his back like a scorpion.

Ronan took the opportunity to join the fight, launching a high kick directly into Kale's chin. If Kale had been human, it would have killed him.

Kale slammed himself backward into the cave wall, dropping Akira to the ground. He reached for his sword again, but extending his hand over his shoulder, found only air.

"Looking for this?" Akira asked, raising his weapon in front of her. Akira tossed the sword to Ronan.

Swordless and outnumbered, Kale seemed to weigh his options. "You're protecting them." He cocked his head. "Why?"

"I told you, I'm turning them in. Can't have you killing them before I collect my reward."

Kale narrowed his eyes. "They aren't your prisoners. They aren't restrained." He motioned toward Camryn and Ethan crouching against the farthest wall. "In fact, the grungy one almost shit his pants when you kissed me. What the hell is going on here?"

Akira sighed as if she were bored with the conversation. "It's a long story, Kale, but it would simplify things immensely if you would stop fighting this."

Kale shook his head. "You know I can't do that. It would be quite a terrible look for me if I allowed you to thwart this mission when we're so close to seeing it to completion."

With another swish of his wrist, Camryn and Ethan left the ground, rising toward the cave ceiling, Kale's invisible hand gripped tightly around them. His other hand stretched toward Akira and Ronan, freezing them in their place. "Did you think I wouldn't destroy you, darling? Did you think I cared for you that much?"

"Think about what you're doing." Akira struggled against his invisible grip. "Apollyon clearly specified that she is to be brought to him *alive*. If you kill her, there will be hell to pay. Literally."

"Not if there's no one around to tell him." Kale moved his arm toward the pool of rushing water, carrying Camryn and Ethan with the motion.

Akira laughed. "If you believe that, you're more stupid than I thought. Apollyon will smell your lies as soon as they're out of your mouth."

"Speaking of mouths," Kale lifted his chin. "I will miss those red lips of yours."

"Don't look down," Ethan murmured, but it was too late. Camryn stared into the hole below them and the black water flowing just beyond. Every breath echoed in her throat, as if even the air in her lungs knew it could be her last.

Kale's gaze strained toward Ronan even as Camryn and Ethan hovered over the hole. "I'm going to need that back."

With a grunting effort from Kale, Ronan's grip loosened and Kale's sword dropped to the ground. "Now, what am I going to do with the two of you?"

Camryn knew that Kale couldn't dispose of Akira and Ronan without a weapon. Dropping them in the water would do no good as they didn't need oxygen or even physical bodies to survive—something that couldn't be said for herself and Ethan. But once the weak humans were out of the way, Kale would be free to pick up the sword and slaughter Ronan and Akira with little effort.

"We have to do something," Camryn mumbled.

"Got any ideas because I'm fresh out," Ethan said as he struggled against Kale's power.

"I can't—" Camryn strained to rouse anything from inside herself—even a few degrees of heat—but nothing stirred.

"Camryn, come on," Ethan urged. "My fire isn't going to do us any good if I can't throw it. You have to do something."

"I'm trying!" Camryn shouted, the force of her words blowing the hair from Ethan's eyes. He turned his head away from the wind as a slow grin spread across his face.

"Do that again. Yell at me."

"You want me to—"

"Just yell at me!" Ethan screamed.

"Okay!" Camryn screamed right back, bringing a gale-force wind crashing through the cave.

Akira's hair whipped around her face and Kale clenched his eyes against the dust that swirled in the air.

"You want to fight?" Camryn shouted. "Why don't you tell me what the hell is going on between you and Akira? Want to talk about *that*?"

"Nothing!" Ethan called over the wind. "Nothing is going on between us anymore."

Camryn's mouth dropped open. "Anymore?" she shouted. "When were you two hooking up? While I was in New York City running for my life, crying myself to sleep every night? And you were with *her*?"

Camryn felt Kale's hold on them weakening, but that would not do. If he let go now, they would drop straight into the water. Camryn glanced down at the canister still in Ethan's hand where Ronan had left it.

"You left me!" Ethan replied. "I waited for you every day. And you never came back. You weren't there. You weren't there, but *she was*!"

The wind blew harder then, fighting even Kale's supernatural grip. Camryn felt his hold break just as the wind reached its peak, slamming Camryn and Ethan into the cave wall a safe distance from the crashing water. A crack of thunder was the icing on her whirlwind cake, but Camryn wasn't finished.

"I had no choice!" Her hair swirled in the air around her and she squinted to see Ethan as she continued to scream at him over the howling wind.

"I left to protect you! And you just forgot about me that easily?"

"Forgot about you? Are you serious? I heard nothing from you for thirty years—and I'm the one who forgot about *you*?"

Camryn was furious now. A large boulder on the opposite side of the cavern began to totter against the force of the wind. "I was waiting for you! You know that!"

"Guys!" Akira called, breaking Camryn from her fury-filled tirade. "Sorry to interrupt your lover's quarrel, but we could use some help here."

The wind died down, but it had done its job. Akira and Ronan had broken free from Kale's hold and each had one of his arms pinned to the cave wall.

Camryn glared at Akira and opened her palms at her sides. She released her wrath in two currents of electric lightning, shooting straight from her splintering soul.

Kale stiffened when the current hit him, then collapsed to the ground. But his armor had taken the brunt of Camryn's energy, and he was up again in a blink. Before Camryn knew it, Ethan was hit again with Kale's power. But this time, it had a more direct target.

The canister left Ethan's hand and sailed through the air. Camryn watched it fly over her head, out of her reach. The only way she could catch it…

Camryn didn't even think before she took two running steps and launched herself into the air toward the canister. The water loomed black as ice below her, but if she could just hit it, maybe she could bat it away.

The orange stripes of the canister drew closer to her fingertips. *I'm going to do it. This is actually going to work!*

Then a white wing burst into her periphery and an arm hitched around her waist and the canister landed in the water with an almost imperceptible splash.

Ronan and Camryn rolled onto the rock on the other side of the pit, Ronan's wings disappearing on impact.

"Are you crazy?" Camryn screamed. "I could have saved them!"

Ronan sat up, glaring down at her with eyes of flame, panting at what had almost happened. "Are *you* crazy? You almost killed yourself."

Camryn raised up on her elbows. "I could have caught it!"

"No, you couldn't have," Ronan said. "But I could have if I hadn't been trying to save you!"

The words were barely out of his mouth when Ronan left the ground, sailing through the air and into the boulder beside them, and Kale's face replaced Ronan's in the space above her.

Why am I still lying on the ground? Camryn could hear her dad yelling for her to "*Get up!*" and his repeated warnings that "*You're most vulnerable on your back.*"

Camryn rolled to her side, but not before Kale planted a booted foot on her shoulder, pinning her to the stone floor.

Camryn strained against his foot but to no avail. His hand extended toward her and she braced herself for the stiffening paralysis just as a small blue ball of flame slammed into him, sending Kale skidding across the cave floor.

On her feet then, Camryn stood her ground in front of Kale, her mind racing, unsure what more she could do against his angelic powers.

Kale lurched toward her, but instead of grabbing Camryn, he stumbled face-first into the stone floor, a flame of fiery hair coming to land in a crouch over his exposed back.

"Not today, *darling*," Akira said, standing and yanking her dagger from between Kale's shoulder blades.

Kale disintegrated into a pile of ash and disappeared before Camryn could catch her breath.

They all stood for a moment, staring at each other. Then staring at the water rushing beneath the cave floor.

No one said a word.

The canister had hit its mark. They'd come so close to death today and had nothing to show for it. But even if they had been successful, what good would it have done in the grand scheme of things? There were others just like Kale all over the world. If the other canisters of plague-like poison hadn't been released already, they would be soon.

"Is there anything we can do?" Camryn asked.

"Warn them?" Ronan said with a shrug. "But would anyone believe us?"

"Not likely," Akira answered.

"I'll check in with Zephaniah," Ronan said, pulling Michael's Halo from his pocket. "Maybe there's been word on the others." He turned away from the group, clicking away at the device, leaving Camryn, Ethan, and Akira to avoid each other's eyes.

TWENTY-FOUR

Ethan would have preferred to stay in the relative safety of the mountain, but a very mortal need for food and medical supplies drew them back to the city.

Camryn had refused to go back to the apartment. "We've put those people in enough danger," she'd said, shooting down the suggestion immediately. So, Akira had found an abandoned office complex with all the amenities they needed—functioning plumbing and an interior room without windows.

Within an hour, Camryn's foraging skills had reaped a flashlight, a first-aid kit, a half-full case of bottled water and a few other random items no one else thought would ever be useful but Camryn insisted were essentials.

For the past hour, she'd sat silently picking through her pile of treasures, not even acknowledging the food Ronan had brought back with the medical supplies he'd procured.

In Camryn's eyes, they had suffered a huge loss. But to Ethan, the mere fact that they were still alive was a massive win.

"Here, let me," Camryn murmured as Ethan struggled to rewrap the bandage Levana had squeezed around his bruised ribs the day before. Ethan resigned himself to her hands but still couldn't look her in the eye. Of the two conversations he had coming this evening, this was the one he dreaded the most.

"All that stuff I said back there—" Ethan started.

"Don't worry about it," Camryn interrupted, keeping her eyes on her work. "I know what you were doing."

"Anger is a really good motivator." Ethan fingered his Lakota token—something he found himself doing more often these days. "I knew you needed it."

"I know."

Ethan finally turned his head to look into her eyes. "I didn't mean any of it."

Camryn handed Ethan his shirt and gathered up the old bandages. "Well, you should have. I deserved it."

Ronan sat perched atop a dust-covered desk, twirling a discarded ruler between his fingers. "I sent our coordinates to the Archangels and Zephaniah—just in case he changes his mind."

"At least we can say we've done all we can do," Akira replied. She shifted her weight, even though she didn't need to.

"Well, we could have blown the whole cave to bits—"

"Stop."

"I'm just saying."

"You're an idiot, you know that?"

"How could I forget when you're constantly reminding me?" Ronan teased, turning his attention to Ethan and Camryn talking quietly on the other side of the room.

"So, are you going to talk to him?"

"Who, Ethan? About what?"

"About how you feel."

Akira grimaced. "I don't feel any kind of way."

"Okay," Ronan smirked.

"What was that?"

"What?"

"That look. That was *oozing* with sarcasm. What was that for?"

"Akira, the only reason you're in the predicament you're in right now is because of your feelings for him."

"Oh, I'm in a predicament now, am I?"

"You know what I mean. You voluntarily relinquished your Righteousness, allowed yourself to be exiled so you could come here and watch out for him—something he doesn't even know, by the way." Ronan looked over at Ethan. "As much as I love him, I didn't even do that."

"First of all, I accepted exile as a favor to Michael…to watch out for the both of them."

Ronan shook his head. "Michael would *never* have asked that of you."

"He didn't have to ask. You saw how distraught he was after what happened with her at the battle," she said, nodding toward Camryn. "He needed someone. And I had nowhere else to be for a few thousand years." Akira strained to keep a straight face.

"Okay, I realize how absurd that sounds, but look at them." She gestured to Ethan and Camryn whispering in the corner. "I can't compete with that."

Ronan smiled and nodded. "So that means you want to," he said in a singsong voice.

"Shut up." Akira punched him in the shoulder. Ronan laughed, gripping his arm in feigned pain.

"I don't like this," Camryn blurted as she stared up at the ceiling from her makeshift bed in the middle of the office floor. The room was quiet and dark, Akira and Ronan opting to patrol the building to allow the humans some much-needed rest.

But Camryn wasn't sleeping.

"Me either," Ethan agreed. "What are we talking about?"

"I feel like we're being used. Kind of like...before, and I don't like it."

Ethan raised himself up on his elbow to look at her. "You mean the Flood?"

"Yeah, I mean, warriors of wrath...the sword of the Lord? I don't want to be either of those things. Just like I didn't want to cause a flood that would destroy every living creature on the earth."

"You didn't cause that flood. You were just protecting our home. Would you have done anything differently?"

Camryn chewed her lip. "What do you mean?"

"If you'd known beforehand what was going to happen, would you have just let those Nephilim make camp on our mountain? Or would you have fought back?"

"You know the answer to that."

"Yeah, I do. And I think that's why He chose you. And why He's chosen you again."

"Us," she reminded him.

"Why He's chosen *us*," Ethan agreed.

"Look, I can agree—putting all that Flood business on you was a pretty shitty thing to do. But this is a different situation. We already knew God sent us here for a reason. We just didn't know what that reason was. Well, now we do. It doesn't change anything."

Camryn groaned. She hated that his words made sense.

"And anyway, what else can we do? Just forget about Apollyon and not try to stop him?"

Camryn exhaled. "I keep trying to think of this through Arael's eyes, but… The teenager in me just wants to go home and forget all about angels and demons and celestial wars. I just want to feed my horses while we listen to Taylor Swift. I want my cell phone," she whined. "I want to go to school." Camryn laughed at the absurdity of the thought. High school had always been her own personal hell…before she remembered what Hell was actually like.

"You know it'll never be that simple again."

"Yeah," Camryn answered in a wistful tone. "I know."

DAY FOUR

TWENTY-FIVE

With no windows to gauge the time by, Ethan was getting pretty good at judging it in other ways. A few hours had passed since Camryn's last nightmare, so Ethan guessed that dawn was fast approaching.

He counted the ceiling tiles for the umpteenth time—seventy-three tiles if you count the seven missing ones—but between the pain in his back and the impossible nature of their situation, Ethan was unable to shut off his mind. There would be no rest for him until Apollyon had been stopped and Camryn could live in a world safe from the fear of him.

Ethan's gaze flitted to the door where Akira and Ronan had taken up their usual post. He caught Akira staring in their direction, but she quickly looked away. Camryn's deep, even breathing told him that she was sleeping soundly, so he eased himself off the floor beside her and trudged over to the door.

Ronan stood, as if Ethan's arrival was his cue for dismissal, and left Ethan with a weary slap on the back that seemed to say, "Good luck." Ethan rubbed his palms on his jeans before lowering himself down the door frame to face Akira.

"So, you and Kale, huh?"

Akira's eyebrows knit together. "Excuse me?"

Ethan rubbed his knuckles across his nose. "Just doesn't seem like your type, is all."

"Let me stop you right there because you forfeited your right to have this conversation with me a long time ago."

"You're right." Ethan shoved his hair back out of his eyes. "That's not really what I wanted to talk to you about anyway."

Crossing his legs on the floor beside hers, Ethan took a moment to really look at Akira, something he'd strategically avoided since she'd shown up on that Navy ship a few days ago. Even in the shadows, he recognized the hints of vulnerability—the pained smile, the slumped shoulders—that she reserved only for him.

"So," Ethan began, waving his hand in the air, "how did Michael talk you into this mess?" Ethan motioned toward Ronan reclined on a plastic-covered sofa. "And how did you two end up working together?"

Akira leaned her head back against the wall. "You boys and your toxic masculinity."

"Sorry?"

"Michael didn't talk me into anything. I made a decision and I followed through. I knew you two needed me, so…" She raised a hand noncommittally. "Here I am."

Then she looked over at Ronan with his eyelids plastered shut, offering them what little privacy he could. "And I haven't been able to get rid of this doof since you two vanished eighteen years ago. He had so many theories, had me chasing down so many bogus leads." The look on her face was reminiscent, as if Ronan were a mischievous child that she just couldn't be mad at.

Ethan chuckled. The mental image of Ronan following Akira around like a pesky little brother was one he'd have to keep in his pocket for a rainy day.

"So you guys didn't know where we were? I just assumed you two were part of Michael's guardian troop all those years."

Akira rolled her head from side to side on the wall behind her. "We didn't know. No one did. Not even Raphael. Only Michael and whoever he had guarding you."

Ethan stared at the floor. No wonder Michael had treated him the way he had in New York.

"We looked for you the whole time. He wouldn't let me give up," she said, throwing a glance at Ronan. "Even when I was super pissed about it."

They shared a quiet laugh.

"He really admires you," Akira said after a moment.

Ethan nodded. "Yeah…I know." Ethan swallowed hard, trying to force out the words he'd been dreading.

"Just so you know…" He cleared his throat. "We appreciate all you're doing—all you have done to help us."

"We?" Akira cocked an eyebrow.

"I know it's hard for you to believe, but Camryn doesn't hate you. I think she's finally allowing herself to trust you, but she doesn't want to let her guard down just yet."

Akira rolled her eyes.

"What?" Ethan threw his hands in the air.

"It's truly disgusting how you defend her. No matter how she treats you or anyone else, you have an excuse for her."

"That's not fair."

I know, I know. She's your *qanima*. I got it."

Ethan fought to keep his voice low. "There are two sides to every relationship, Akira. Most of the time, she's just defending herself against you."

Akira's open expression slammed shut. "Okay, are we done here?" she asked, standing.

Ethan rose with her. "No, actually we're not."

He reached out and grasped her wrist but quickly dropped it. "I also wanted to say…for what it's worth… I'm sorry about what happened between us."

Akira wrapped her arms around herself and looked away. "You know I don't care about any of that. We had fun, and I only ever wanted you to be happy."

"Then what are you so pissy about? I *am* happy—as happy as I can be under the circumstances."

"Really?" Akira asked as if she didn't believe it. "She treats you like shit and that makes you happy?"

Heat rushed into Ethan's cheeks like an erupting volcano. "Watch it," he warned.

"What exactly are you apologizing for, anyway? That it happened at all? Or that you left me in Miami with no explanation and no idea what the hell happened to you?"

"Left you?" Ethan's voice was strained. "What are you talking about?"

Akira's face fell and she spun away. But not before Ethan saw the tears that had sprung into her eyes.

He grabbed her by the elbow and pulled her back. "What are we fighting about right now?"

Akira glared down at his hand. "Let me go or I will rip your arm off and beat you with it."

Ethan dropped her arm.

"Thirty years," she said, her voice a harsh whisper. "Thirty years I was by your side, picking you up, keeping you going.

Thirty years and then one day, you were just gone. No explanation. No warning. You abandoned me on a mission and I was left to wonder if you were even still alive."

Ethan swallowed. When he'd deserted his Miami mission to search for Arael in New York City, it had been spontaneous, a last-minute decision. But he wouldn't have told Akira even if it had been a well thought out plan."

"Until I found out from *her* that you'd been thrown in prison."

Ethan's voice was dangerously quiet. "You know why I couldn't tell you."

Akira arched her brows. "Do I?"

"If I hadn't been captured, you would have been the first one Apollyon would have come to when he realized I was gone. He would have tortured it out of you. I couldn't—it would have been too dangerous for you."

"And what about this time?" Her eyes traveled up and down his human body. "You'd just come back into my life, just to vanish again."

"You know I don't remember anything about how I got here. I don't even know that this was a choice," he hissed. "You can't be mad at me about—" Ethan began, but Akira shushed him with a raised finger, her eyes darting toward the front of the building. Ronan stood from the sofa, alert to something imperceptible to Ethan's human ears. Ethan followed their intense glare as the commotion roused Camryn from sleep.

Akira dashed toward the sound, the others following close behind. She raised a red-nailed finger to her mouth and directed them to spread out on either side of the door that led out onto the street.

Ethan pulsed his fingers, bringing the heat into his hands, his only defense at the ready, burning just under his skin.

Akira removed her daggers from her belt, listening for a moment longer before swinging the door wide.

Ethan couldn't see who stood on the other side of the door, but he felt the tension leave Akira's arms. Her daggers dropped to her side as she exhaled. "Where the *hell* have you been?"

TWENTY-SIX

Raphael practically fell into Akira's arms. Scratches marred his otherwise ethereal face, the evidence of such violence as offensive as a coffee stain on the Mona Lisa. He hadn't taken the time or had the forethought to change out of his warrior armor, but whatever hell he'd been through had left it battered and buckled.

His wings, still partially extended and feathers askew were the only thing preventing him from falling onto Akira and crushing her into the floor.

Ronan moved to Raphael's side, slinging an arm over his shoulder for support. Smoothing down his wings, Ronan helped Raphael into the building. Ethan joined Ronan at Raphael's other side, and together they dragged the Archangel through the foyer toward the conference room.

"Where is Michael?" Raphael grunted as Ethan and Ronan led him to their inner refuge. "When I got his message, I thought it was too good to be true."

They lowered Raphael down on the sofa as Camryn ran to retrieve the first aid kit from the desk where Ethan had left it.

"We're here," Ronan assured him. "But Michael didn't send that message. I did." He held up Michael's Halo for Raphael to see.

Raphael's long eyelashes fluttered rapidly. "So…" He gulped. "Michael's not with you?"

"No," Ronan explained. "Michael gave us his Halo before he went looking for you. He hasn't been with us since—" He paused. "Since your separation."

Raphael's face fell, the granule of hope in his eyes vanishing. "I have to go." He struggled to sit up. "I have to find him."

"Wait just a damn minute!" Akira shot forward. "Where the hell have you been? Who did this to you?" She pointed to his face, covered in deep, red gashes.

Raphael stared at the floor, taking a few breaths before muttering, "Dagon. In the dungeons."

Even Akira inhaled sharply at the prospect. The dungeons were Dagon's special place of torture. Angels who entered there never came out.

Akira widened her stance. "Pardon?"

"The embassy was a trap, as you all have likely figured out by now." He glanced around the group. "We were ambushed and dragged into his lair. Locked up for most of the time, only taken from our cells for…interrogations."

"Oh my God…" Camryn mumbled, almost dropping the first aid kit in her hands.

"He wanted information on you two: How you got here, things like that. I gave him nothing, but I don't know about the others. Sam and Jay..." Raphael's head dropped into his hands.

"And they just let you out?" Ronan asked.

Raphael shook his head and sniffed. "The last time they took me from my cell, I was able to overpower them and make it past their protections in enough time to portal out—the quickest portal I've ever made." Raphael managed a chuckle.

"If Michael isn't with you," Ethan said, "we can only assume they have him there, too."

Akira nodded. "Sure. I mean, that's where Apollyon kept him before."

Camryn glanced around at the faces in the room. *Before*—after she'd betrayed him to Dagon in the valley of the Alborz, and he'd been dragged into the Void as a bloody, mangled mess.

Akira continued as if she hadn't noticed Camryn looking like she might hurl on the linoleum. "Ronan and I can transport to the perimeter," she said to Raphael. "See if we can get in without a portal."

Ethan grasped Akira's elbow. "You two can't just show up down there together. How would you explain it if you get caught?"

Akira stared at Ethan's hand on her arm for a moment before raising her eyes to his. "We won't get caught."

"All the entrances are heavily guarded," Raphael said. "Your only chance would be where I just came from. Near the northern border."

Akira nodded and looked pointedly at Camryn. "You two, do not leave this room together." She reminded them of the aura that they couldn't see. "Without my shield, you'll alert all the Nephilim in the city that you're here." She thumbed a hand toward Raphael. "And he's going to be useless to defend you."

With Ronan and Akira gone, Ethan took up post by the door. He may not have superhuman hearing or the ability to sense a spiritual presence, but he had *some* skills. He'd caught sight of the yellow mist of Michael's nervousness—if only for a second—back at the church, and he could throw a fiery curveball if necessary, so...he had to believe he could be of some use in protecting Camryn while Ronan and Akira were away.

While Ethan stood watch, Camryn opened the first aid kit and examined its contents. "Uh..." She flicked a glance at Raphael. "Will any of this stuff help you?"

Raphael smiled wearily. "Well, the disinfectant is probably useless, but we can clean some of the blood off, at least."

"Yeah, okay." Camryn closed the kit and searched the section of cabinets against the back wall. "Have you seen anything around here I could wipe his wounds with?" she called to Ethan.

Ethan stepped into the hall. "I'll look in the bathroom. I think I saw some paper towels in there."

In the bathroom, Ethan found the towels in question and wet them in the sink.

Ethan rounded the corner into the conference room a few minutes later. "They're not the cleanest, but they're cleaner than—" Ethan began, but the words withered like melting snow as his eyes scanned the room.

An empty chasm opened inside him, threatening to suck him into its vacuum—the same hollowness that had consumed him in Eden in those first moments after waking in exile. Ethan dropped the towels on the ground.

The room was empty.

TWENTY-SEVEN

Camryn's stomach clinched as the colors churned, bright and swirling, all around her. She'd become accustomed to the disorientation that happened every time her human body traveled through space at a rate at which it was not designed, but being in the midst of a transport without any warning or preparation made it as nauseating as the first time.

She had never been drunk in all her seventeen years of life, but she imagined this must be what it would feel like.

Even when solid ground materialized under her feet, the earth continued to spin, and she flung her hands out on either side to keep from face-planting into the dirt.

I need to lie down. She began to lower herself to the ground, but the hand around her wrist pulled her upward.

The queasiness eased, and the earth slowed its spinning—gradually, gradually, until the vertigo was all but gone.

Camryn blinked several times, bringing the world around her into focus. Below her feet lay a dust-covered limestone path with tall, thin evergreens providing cool shade on either side. The path led to an ancient-looking stairway, with a three-arch gate leading up to a place she recognized as the Temple Mount, the only site in the Old City of Jerusalem that hadn't been completely destroyed by the bombs a few days earlier.

"What's going on?" Camryn looked up at her escort. A second ago, she'd been examining his wounds in an office building in Tel Aviv. Now she was here.

No warning.

No explanation.

"Raphael, what is it? Is something wrong?" He must have detected a threat—that was the only explanation that made sense. Camryn cursed her human brain as it once again left her lacking.

"We left Ethan. You have to go back for him."

"I can't go just yet." Raphael gripped her elbow, urging her forward. "There's someone who wants to see you."

Camryn's stomach clenched at the hardness of his eyes. "Wants to see *me*? Who?"

Raphael started toward the stairs, his gait much steadier than it'd appeared back at the office. With her arm still in his grasp, Camryn had no choice but to follow.

They reached the top of the steps and arrived onto a flat plaza surrounded by what was left of a beautiful old retaining wall. The two smaller-domed structures had been damaged in the bombing, but the marble, mosaic-tiled Dome of the Rock stood as a testament of resilience.

Normally this area would be teeming with people—local residents and tourists alike—but after yesterday's events, it was deserted. Except for Camryn and Raphael.

And three people on their knees in front of her.

In the plaza with the golden-domed temple providing a glorious backdrop, Lindsay, James, and Elizabeth knelt before her with their hands secured behind their backs. Some invisible binding locked their tongues in place as they struggled to speak, but couldn't. A nasty bruise adorned her mother's cheek. They knelt stoically, all except Elizabeth, whose quiet sobs gave away her reticent terror.

Camryn's eyes darted from one to the other. *Mom. Dad. Elizabeth. Dad. Mom.* They each seemed to plead with her, their own silent petitions.

Kill these bastards, said her father's eyes.

Be strong, said her mother's.

Please help me, Elizabeth's echoed.

What the hell is happening?

"Camryn!" President Kaya stepped out from the western entrance of the temple looking as professional as ever. "I'm so glad you could join us today." She pulled three syringes from the pocket of her blazer. "It would be a shame for you to have missed this."

At the sight of the vials in the woman's hand, Camryn's world came to a crashing halt. What could they possibly contain? *Nothing good*, she thought as visions of bloody boils and rotting skin darted through her mind.

Camryn measured her words carefully. "Please. You don't have to do this. Look, I'm right here." She stepped forward, raising her hands in surrender. "I'm the one you want."

President Kaya looked regretful. "That isn't my call, I'm afraid. And even if it were, I would never grant you such mercy. Not after all you've done to us."

Us? This woman was growing increasingly delusional and Camryn increasingly confused.

"I'm—I'm sorry. Look, Apollyon can do whatever he wants with me. Just let them go."

The woman's laughter hit Camryn like a slap in the face. "Oh, Apollyon will do what he wants with you. You can rest assured of that. And watching your loved ones die… That's just the beginning."

Camryn's eyes darted to her father's face. Her fingers twitched with electric current. He didn't move his head, but his message was clear. The look in his eyes urged her to "*Do it!*"

Not even listening to President Kaya's chatter, Camryn studied the woman's movements, her slow pacing. Camryn knew if she timed it just right, she could take her out with one purple strike of lightning. She would only need to—

A surge of heat shot from her wrist up the length of her arm, interrupting her silent calculations. Her arms felt suddenly heavy, and she looked down to find both hands handcuffed in front of her. The strange material didn't burn her skin, but the electricity drained from her fingers as quickly as she had conjured it.

Camryn raised her eyes in what seemed like slow motion, swiveling her head up to stare into Raphael's expressionless face. He grabbed her forearm and shoved her forward.

"Raphael?" Camryn wasn't even sure she'd spoken his name or if the question remained only in her mind. In any case, Raphael didn't answer.

"What— What are you doing?" Camryn managed to choke out.

A look, unrecognizable, crossed Raphael's face. His jaw tightened and his eyes narrowed. He lifted his chin and glared down at her.

"How could you do this? To them?" She raised her cuffed hands to her parents. "To Michael?"

Raphael's face twitched in anger. "I'm not doing anything to Michael. I'm doing this *for* him."

Camryn's mouth opened then closed again when words refused to come.

"These human lives mean nothing to me. They are here for an instant," he said with a snap of his fingers, "then they die. That's what you mortals are born to do—to die."

"But this?" Michael had fought so hard to defend the mortal world against Apollyon's schemes. Camryn couldn't believe Raphael would disregard Michael's life work in such a way. "After Michael fought so hard against this?"

"You think I care about Apollyon's plan?" he scoffed. "I've had no hand in any of that. I only care about you. And apparently, so does Apollyon. And you know what they say—nothing brings two rivals together like a common enemy."

"I'm..." Camryn stumbled over her words, "not your enemy."

Raphael's eyes narrowed. "Aren't you, though?"

Camryn desperately wanted to follow this conversation through to the end, but Harriet Kaya was on the move.

"President Kaya, please," Camryn begged as the woman approached her mother.

Harriet stopped behind Lindsay, stroking the woman's hair and running a manicured hand down her face. Harriet pulled one of the syringes from her pocket and held it up for Camryn to see.

The needle was long, the vile filled with a dull green liquid.

"This," she said, looking at the syringe, "is a tranquilizer—a very high dose." She pulled Lindsay's chin up, exposing the soft skin of her neck. "It will paralyze her muscles slowly, making it impossible for her to breathe."

Camryn strained to expand her own chest as if she had been injected with the liquid herself.

"It will take roughly five minutes for her to die—an excruciating way to go. And you'll be here to witness it all."

Camryn grunted and struggled against Raphael's grip.

"Unless you can answer one question for me. Then I might be persuaded to release them."

Relief stilled her. "Anything. What do you want to know?"

"How did you get here?"

Camryn pursed her lips, unsure what the woman was asking.

"How were you and your friend, both Fallen angels, born to earthly parents? That's all Apollyon wants to know. Tell me how you did it, and they all go free."

Camryn sank to her knees with a splintering exhale of breath. It had to be that question—the question she'd been asking herself since she'd found out about her past, the one question she couldn't answer.

"Ask me something else. Anything else. I don't know how we got here. I don't remember!"

"Well, that's unfortunate." Harriet raised the syringe to Lindsay's neck.

"Stop! Please!"

Until that moment, Lindsay had remained quiet, staring straight ahead, not even daring to blink. She occupied her space on the ground with stoic dignity, her head held high as she did with everything in her life, and mouthed three words, slow and deliberate.

Camryn's chin sank.

It was over. Whatever was going to happen, Camryn would be powerless to stop it. This would be part of her story. Her legacy. Her parents—the two people she loved most in this world—would die because of her. Her mind traveled back to that last meeting at the Conclave Hall before the Flood. Finding out about the Founders and losing Jacob and Salome.

History did have a way of repeating itself.

"I love you, too, Mom," Camryn said with no emotion in her voice.

President Kaya frowned. "Well, that was beautiful but pointless." With no further preamble or ceremony, Harriet stabbed the syringe into Lindsay's neck and pressed the plunger.

Lindsay's eyes grew wide and her body rigid before she slowly slumped to the ground.

With the thud of her mother's body against the limestone plaza, Camryn was no longer in hers. She was someone else. Somewhere else. She was watching this from above with clinical precision.

Her eyes traveled robotically to her father, who flailed about, trying to get to his wife. Camryn thought he would kill himself struggling against his restraints. He might have done it if Harriet Kaya hadn't done the job for him with a quick jab of a second syringe into his neck.

A few seconds later, James was quiet.

Only then did Camryn hear the hysterical sobs of Ethan's mother.

Camryn knew what would come next for Elizabeth, and the slightest twinge of regret worked its way into her walled-off mind, knowing that Ethan wouldn't get the chance to say goodbye.

As Harriet approached, Elizabeth grew more hysterical, leaning away from her impending death. Her face was red and wet from the tears that ran from her eyes and dripped from her nose. Blood trickled down her fingers from the broken skin on her wrists, torn by her struggles.

"One more chance." Harriet eyed Camryn. "You wouldn't save your own parents. What about Ethan's?"

"Elizabeth," Camryn heard herself say in what sounded like someone else's voice.

The woman didn't appear to hear her.

"Elizabeth!" Camryn shouted.

Elizabeth finally looked at her, sobs still hiccupping through her body.

"Stop crying."

Elizabeth quieted but appeared confused by Camryn's words.

"Stop. Crying," Camryn reiterated. "Ethan loves you, and he is *so* proud of you." She stepped toward the woman, and, mercifully, Raphael didn't stop her. "Think of your last few days with him. That is how he will remember you." Elizabeth did stop crying then and a resolve formed on her face.

"I will tell him..." Camryn continued. "I will tell him you were brave."

Elizabeth sniffed and stared at Camryn through swollen eyes. But she didn't pull away as President Kaya came to stand behind her.

"I don't know why you insist on being so stubborn," Harriet sighed.

Camryn locked eyes with Elizabeth and held the woman's stare as tightly as if she were holding her hand.

Camryn forced herself to watch Harriet plunge the needle into the side of Elizabeth's neck. Watched Elizabeth draw her last, gasping breath. Forced herself to take in every image—her mother lying in a heap, her father with his eyes still open, Elizabeth, her frozen face wet with tears—she would remember it all like a snapshot in her mind.

Camryn stood, numb, taking it all in. But she felt nothing. All the emotions she should be feeling—her rage and anguish and sorrow—she would bottle that up and stick it in a safe spot in the back of her mind. She would need it later.

But right now, she had to be a blank, unreadable canvas.

Raphael stared down at the nearly catatonic girl at his side. She was doing that thing again. That thing that she did any time something remotely traumatic happened in her life. Raphael struggled to keep his eyes from rolling back in irritation.

Camryn stumbled, and he reached to catch her. "Coward." He shook his head in disgust. "And you're the one Elohim chose to save Creation? As if that were possible." He jerked Camryn by the arm and led her toward the domed building beyond.

She might be unaware now, Raphael thought, *but soon…so soon, she'll be free of this body and this weak human mind and I can tell her all the reasons I have to hate her.*

He would tell her again and again—as many times as it took to break her.

Because she had broken him.

He stopped in the doorway and spun Camryn to face him. He leaned down to look into her vacant eyes.

"Did you really think that after all those years of war against Michael—against the one angel in existence that means anything to me—that I would just forget it all?" He studied her face for any sign of comprehension.

"I thought when you first saw me on that boat that you would see right through me. You have a *qanima* yourself, after all. Imagine if the roles were reversed—if it had been I who had tried for centuries to kill him. And what you did to Michael on that mountain…" Raphael trembled with rage. "Would you do anything less?"

Camryn stared, not even a twitch of a frown on her face. "Can you even hear me, you little shit?"

Blink. Blink.

"Yes," he said, standing and taking her by the arm once again. "I think you can."

Arriving at the cell they'd prepared for her in the small storage closet, Raphael shoved Camryn in and slammed the door. The bars weren't supernatural, but did they need to be for such a useless human? She was as powerless against iron as the Fallen were against Heavenly Fire.

Harriet's heels clicked on the stone floor as she breezed into the storage room. "What's wrong with her?" she demanded.

Raphael's eyes flickered with an eternity of animosity. "Don't worry. She'll come around."

"Well, I should hope so. Apollyon will be here soon. He won't be pleased to find her like this."

"What difference will it make? Her mind isn't impenetrable, even in this state."

Harriet looked at the girl with distaste then checked her watch. "We should go. Do you think it's safe to leave her like this?"

Raphael scoffed, turning his back to Camryn. "There are a dozen soldiers guarding the building. She's not going anywhere."

TWENTY-EIGHT

Ethan scurried around the conference room, stuffing items into the bag Akira had borrowed from Yon's apartment: a few bottles of water, the flashlight, Camryn's gun she'd hidden with the rest of her loot, a legal pad of paper. *What the hell do I need that for? Too late now. It's already in the bag.*

Camryn and Raphael had vanished all of ten minutes ago, but the few minutes Ethan had stood, wondering what the hell to do next, had felt like an hour.

I'm sure they'll be back, he tried to reason with himself as he'd paced around the cluttered space.

But they hadn't returned, and Ethan couldn't think of any good reason they would have left him there alone.

His chest ached with the physical absence of her. Now that he and Camryn had been reunited, the emptiness that he'd dealt with all his life had grown suddenly unbearable. He had to get back to her.

He had no plan. No idea where to even start looking, but somehow Ethan knew he would find her. She would lead him.

He shouldered the backpack and had just pushed open the side exit door when Akira and Ronan appeared on the stoop in front of him.

"Where the hell do you think you're going?" Akira demanded, pushing him back into the building and closing the door behind them.

Ethan almost collapsed with relief. Akira would find them. She'd know what to do.

"We have to go. We have to find them."

"Find who?" Ronan put a calming hand on Ethan's shoulder.

"Raphael and Camryn." Ethan struggled to put the words together in the right order. "They're gone."

"Gone? Gone where?"

"That's what we have to find out. You—you have to track them. You can do that, right?"

Akira drew in a breath, but before she could answer, the back door crashed open, and a woman in a well-tailored suit stepped through.

"You'll be reunited with your friend soon enough," the female voice said. The three stood staring as Harriet Kaya smiled at them like an old friend.

It took Ethan's brain a few beats to translate the message his eyes were sending. The president of Turkey was standing in the doorway of this old abandoned office building. *No, that can't be right.*

His racing mind almost short-circuited at what he saw next.

Raphael stepped through the door behind her. Confusion spread through the room like a bad rash.

"Raphael?"

Harriet placed an approving hand on Raphael's arm. "Raphael has proven invaluable to our plans the past few days. From getting Michael away from you at the church to finding you here."

Ethan glared at the Archangel. "You've been working for her this whole time?"

"You've been the one leaking information to her!" Akira practically shouted. "Where we were, what we were doing. She's been one step ahead of us this whole time. Because of you!"

"How could you?" Ethan spat.

"You know, that's not the first time I've been asked that today," Raphael said.

"Where's Camryn?" Ethan demanded. "What have you done with her?"

"Not so fast," President Kaya said. "You'll see her again, but there's really no rush. You two have proven very difficult to separate." Her face tightened with irritation. "Especially with Michael always in the way."

Michael.

"What have you done?" Ronan finally spoke up.

"Only what is demanded according to the *qanima* bond," Raphael replied. "Do not misunderstand. Michael is and always will be my priority. He is safe for now, as long as you all do what you're told. And I have provisions in place to ensure Apollyon keeps his word."

Ethan tried to keep up with the conversation, tried to figure out what the hell was going on. But it was no use.

They have Camryn.

Where? He didn't know.

What was happening to her? He didn't know that either. Ethan flexed his hands.

"I wouldn't do that if I were you." President Kaya pinned him with her stare. And before Ethan could tell her where she could shove her opinions, Raphael sprang at them.

A flurry of activity whirled around Ethan, activity too fast for his human eyes to follow. But when the action slowed and the other angels came into view, President Kaya and Raphael stared down at him and his two celestial friends, their hands bound in chains.

TWENTY-NINE

The chill of the unyielding stone sent a shiver through Camryn's bones. She lay prostrate on the floor of the cell where Raphael had deposited her—how long ago? She wasn't sure. But the sunlight that had greeted her from the window across the room had now morphed into a stream of moonlight.

There's no time for this.

No time….

She lifted her head, but a vision of her mother—lifeless, lying on the sun-scorched earth—knocked her back to the ground.

When she drifted back into the darkness this time, someone was there to greet her.

An angel. A vision of radiance and light sliced through the shadows of her mind, rousing her—if only slightly.

"Get up," said an opulent voice from all around her.

"I can't."

"Yes, you can," the voice came again, gentle, but firm. "Get up."

Camryn listened to her own breathing.

Inhale.

Exhale.

Focusing on one limb at a time, Camryn drew one leg underneath her. Then two. Then with one arm, she pushed herself upward. Then the other. She bent her knees, lifted her head. Slowly. Robotically. Until she was standing.

The angel extended a hand through the bars and into the cell, and when Camryn took it, the bars around her vanished.

No, they were still there, but she was outside them, standing beside Clarion, her Guardian counterpart of her assigned territory in Persia before the Flood.

The angel turned slowly and swept her hand toward the wall—a blank slab of limestone blocks—as if something important was plastered there.

"What?" Camryn squinted. "It's just a wall."

"Run," Clarion said.

"Excuse me?"

Panic bloomed on Clarion's face. She leaned in and whispered, her words a secret. "Run," she said, more frantic this time.

Clarion's panic became her own, and a moment later, Camryn was running. She ran the short distance toward the wall, thinking she would run straight into it…until the wall disappeared, revealing a long, dark corridor beyond.

Camryn ran on, an unknown dread clawing at her chest. The strange déjà vu had become familiar by now as another memory of her celestial life dredged itself from the recesses of her mind.

She glanced back over her shoulder to find two unsettling things. First, the wall was gone, along with any resemblance of the storage closet she'd awakened in, now absorbed in a moment lived long ago. Second, her blonde hair had turned a raven-black and had been loosed from the knot on top of her head. It now hung freely, flowing behind her as she fled.

Her head swiveled forward as she crashed into another angel coming up the corridor in the opposite direction.

"Arael?" the angel said. "Is it really you?"

She'd been on the helicopter traveling from the Navy ship to the air force base in Beersheba the last time a memory had hit her like this. The memory that haunted her still. The memory of Michael portaling them to the valley of the Alborz, offering her a choice between two impossible outcomes. Michael bleeding, screaming, being dragged away by Dagon's demon dogs.

Dagon had approached her in the heat of the most impossible decision she'd ever had to make, his words illuminating another path, a third option, a possibility she never would have dreamed.

She'd been so torn by Michael's proposition, so desperate, so terrified, that she'd accepted Dagon's offer the instant he'd offered her another way.

Now, staring up into the face of the angel in the corridor before her, she knew exactly where she was. She'd been thrust into the aftermath of that decision.

In the time she'd been transported to, barely an hour had passed since Dagon had lured her down from the summit as she'd sparred with herself over Michael's offer. Dagon had made a lot of promises in exchange for her assistance, but would he follow through?

The word of a Fallen Angel wasn't worth much. She'd been stupid to trust him so quickly. Then again, desperation usually lends to stupidity.

She'd yet to see Apollyon since her valiant return to his court, but that was to be expected. Michael's capture had been a pipe dream of his for so many centuries that many wondered if it would ever really happen. And now that it had, all of Hell would be celebrating. Or torturing him. Or celebrating by torturing him.

And it had been her actions that had turned the tide, not only for the Fallen and the Nephilim but for humanity.

Now, with Michael out of the picture, the army of Heaven would be powerless in defending the mortal world from Apollyon's attack. They would fight, sure…for a while. But without a leader, eventually, they would fall apart. And Apollyon would finally have what he wanted. He would finally be able to implement the next stage of destruction with little or no interference from Heaven.

"Where's Michael?" she panted. "Do you know where they're keeping him?"

"In the dungeon," the angel reported. "But he's—"

She didn't wait to hear the rest. She was already moving.

One of the angels who'd escorted her back to the Void after Michael's capture had congratulated her on her victory. She'd only managed to stare back at him. Had it really been a victory? Capturing Michael had been her life's mission, what she had worked for millennia to achieve. The motivation for everything she had done as a Fallen angel had finally been realized.

So why did it feel so *wrong*? She tried to exhume the loathing she'd felt as she'd lain on the battlefield during the First War. She thought of everything Michael had taken from her—and from Uriah—trying, *trying* to hate Michael again.

When Arael reached the lower quadrant, she slowed. She'd never had reason to venture this far into the depths of the Void and wasn't as familiar with the terrain. Listening, her celestial ears heard not a sound—had the angel in the corridor been wrong?

She inched around one corner. Then two. Until she reached the final corridor. Most of the chambers were dark—all except one. One doorway glowed with a dim lamplight, casting flickering shadows into the darkened hall.

Fighting her urge to hide, Arael had to remind herself again that she had a right to be there. Thirty years of running—that habit would be a hard one to break.

She made her way closer, listening for tortured screams but heard none. Nothing but ragged breathing and the shuffling of feet.

She detected only two energies in the room. One belonged to Michael, but who was the other? Did it matter? Michael was the one she needed to see. If she could see his face, look into the eyes of her banisher, maybe then she could live with what she'd done to him.

She drew back her shoulders and stepped into the room.

THIRTY

There he was.

Michael. Unrecognizable, save for the slashes left in his skin from the demon attack.

Chains dangled from hooks in the ceiling, mossy and thick. Chains leading down to Michael's wrists tied above his head—the only thing keeping the Archangel from collapsing to the floor. His legs certainly weren't doing the job.

Michael's head hung low to his chest, and his hair covered what little she might have seen of his face, the silvery strands dripping with sweat and blood. The damage done by the hellhounds evidenced by the slabs of flesh that hung from his back.

Her breath caught, and her eyes darted to the other occupant of the room. Akira stood just inside the door, red curls falling over wild eyes. A dagger trembled in her hand, glowing orange with Heavenly Fire.

Akira jabbed the weapon toward her. "Get back. You're not touching him."

Well, that was unexpected.

"She's not going to hurt me." Michael's voice seemed to claw its way out of his throat, but Akira didn't appear convinced.

Smart, Arael thought. *I'm not so sure of that myself.*

Michael had betrayed her in the most unspeakable ways, used her to kill innocent people, and imprisoned Uriah. She should be elated to see him suffering like this. She should be celebrating right along with the rest of them.

But intruding thoughts whispered to her from the far reaches of her mind. Michael had helped her. Unwarranted. Unsolicited. He'd rescued her from her New York City apartment and Dagon's army. He'd had no reason to do it. He hadn't been attempting to capture her for himself as she'd originally thought. He had actually offered her a way home. And he had acknowledged the mistake in her exile, something she had all but given up hope of.

"Why are you protecting him?" Arael asked Akira, backing away from her with a wary glare. "You were beside me in every battle I fought against his forces."

Akira moved to Michael's side, eyeing Arael with the same wariness. "Perhaps that's why we never won." She spoke the words as her attention turned to the chains that held Michael upright, all while keeping Arael in her sights.

"I hope you didn't come here to finish the job you started tonight because I really don't have time to kill you right now."

Arael glanced back and forth between the two for a moment, trying to decide if this could possibly be a horrifically timed joke. But no. Neither appeared to be in a joking mood.

"You've been helping him…all along?"

"Why is that so hard to believe?"

"Because you work for Apollyon, that's why," Arael said as she moved to Michael's other side, "And you're a Fallen angel." She kept a cautious eye on the Tracker as Akira worked her hands around the chains.

"Well I wouldn't be a very good spy if you suspected me, now would I?"

"They're not coming off," Michael groaned. "It's no use."

Arael watched Akira's hands a moment longer before she spoke. "What are you doing?"

"Trying to undo these protections. I've seen Apollyon cast them hundreds of times. I should be able to unravel them, but I don't know… These are," she grunted, "more difficult."

It took Arael's celestial mind mere seconds to process centuries of memories: Michael. Akira. Uriah. Battle after battle. Every snarky comment.

Yes, Akira had always been a bitch to her, but she'd been loyal to her as well. Protected her, or more specifically, protected Uriah, which, in Arael's eyes, was more important.

Within that tangle of history and memory, it did make some kind of sense. Michael's words on the mountain. Akira's annoying presence throughout the years.

Arael eyed the chains, could almost see the layers of protections around them, shimmering with a taunting effervescence. Someone wasn't taking any chances with this one.

"Try that," Arael said, pointing to the blade in Akira's belt.

Akira eyed the weapon with surprise as if she'd forgotten what it could do, then pulled the dagger from her waistband.

Not *her* dagger. This dagger had an intricately designed hilt and glowed with orange fire.

"That's a weapon of the Righteous. Where did you get it?"

"Raphael," Akira said, slashing the blade across Michael's chains, sending the Archangel crashing to the floor.

"Raphael is here?"

"He's gathering the others. They're coming," Akira said, struggling to lift Michael from the ground. "Are you going to help me with him or continue to be useless?"

"Wait," Arael said. "We can't leave without Uriah. Michael," she took his chin in her hands and raised his head to look into his eyes. "You have to tell me where he is. I have to get him out of here."

"Uriah's here?" The horror that darkened Akira's face was enough to chill Arael's blood.

Arael raised her eyebrows as if to say, "I know. Can you believe it?"

"Yes. As of a few hours ago when Michael found him with me in New York and decided that was deserving of a prison sentence."

Akira stared at her, blinking. "So," she swallowed, "he's been with you? Is—is he hurt? How did you find him?"

"He found me, actually. And he isn't hurt. At least," she turned her gaze back to Michael, "he wasn't the last time I saw him."

Michael shook his head, but his eyes remained closed. "Uriah must pay for his crime."

"What crime?" Arael protested. "Of turning me in to Dagon? We are far past that by now, Michael. Look at me. Apollyon is practically ready to hand me a crown. He isn't going to hurt me—not until he finds out I helped get you out of here." Arael sat back on her heels. "Which I'm less inclined to do if you refuse to let him go."

"As much as I hate to admit it," Akira cut in, "Arael is right. Uriah could never do such a thing to—" Akira cut her eyes to Arael but seemed to choke on the word—*qanima*. "—her," she said instead. "He would never dare."

Michael's eyes slowly moved between the two females as if weighing his chances of winning this fight.

Arael dropped Michael's hand and stared into his bloody face. "I know what I just did to you is beyond reprehensible. And I will spend the rest of my existence trying to make it up to you. But think about what you did to me on that battlefield so many years ago and the centuries I've dealt with that pain. *You owe me this.*"

Michael forced his eyes up to meet hers. "Fine," he groaned. "It is done."

Arael's chest loosened. Her head dropped in relief. Drawing in a breath, she took Michael's arms from Akira, raised him up with one hand, and leaned him on her shoulder. She jerked her head toward the door. "You should go," she said to Akira. "Find Uriah and get him out of here."

Akira's face held an expression of actual pain for the first time in Arael's memory. "They'll kill you," Akira whispered.

"They have to catch me first."

Akira stared for only a moment before nodding. When she reached the door, she turned back. She blinked once, then she was gone.

Arael steeled herself against Michael's weight. "Let's get you out of here."

THIRTY-ONE

Arael had barely made it to the door before Dagon's dark energy reached the cell ahead of him. She could almost see the shadow of his presence closing in. He was coming. And he wasn't alone.

Shit.

Arael backed into the room, surveying the walls of chains and torture devices and the floor speckled with dried blood.

"Sorry about this," she said to Michael, lowering him to the ground and placing his hands in another pair of handcuffs protruding from the wall. "These aren't locked, so don't move."

Michael grunted some kind of response. Arael just hoped he understood.

Because Apollyon had arrived.

She took her fear and shoved it to the far corner of her mind, reducing it to nothing but a speck. She filled her thoughts instead with praise and gratitude to Apollyon for sparing her life—things he would love to find there.

When the two newcomers finally stepped into the room, Apollyon, with his white hair and robes contrasting with Dagon's dark ones—the complete embodiment of light and dark—Arael greeted them coolly, stepping in front of the chains Akira had busted to free Michael just moments before.

Apollyon practically ignored her as he approached Michael, hands clasped behind his back.

Arael couldn't pull her eyes away from the creature who had forced her into hiding for three decades. His eyes were cool, unbothered. His mouth set in a perpetual smirk.

"I see the Nephilim got a little overzealous with our capture," he said, kneeling before Michael. Arael prayed that he wouldn't notice the unsecured cuffs around Michael's wrists.

Thankfully, Apollyon never took his eyes from Michael's face as he pulled a dagger from his robe and raked it down Michael's cheek. The hellfire left a sizzling trail of flesh in its wake. "They still haven't forgiven you for all that Flood business, it seems."

Michael grunted away from the weapon in his face.

"And though *they* may hold a bit of a grudge, I hope you understand that, to me, this isn't personal at all."

Arael had to commend Michael for the scowl he managed to produce as he grunted out, "It might not have been personal before, but it's sure as hell personal now."

"I can see how you would feel that way," Apollyon continued. "But I assure you, this is much bigger than any squabble between us. You are merely standing in my way."

Michael spat a mouthful of blood at Apollyon's feet. Apollyon backed away and raised his hand—a signal to Dagon, who stepped forward, staff in hand, his thick beard doing little to hide the permanent scowl on his face.

Without any forethought, Arael reached out and grabbed the staff, jerking it from Dagon's grasp.

Her eyes widened as they both stared at the weapon now in Arael's possession, each just as surprised as the other to find it there.

Dagon studied her with curiosity. "I would have given it to you. You only had to ask."

Apollyon honed in on her, his eyes darting to Michael's wrists in the unlocked chains. She could almost see his mind working, calculating. Did he know?

His arm twitched toward her. To warn her? To immobilize her? She didn't know, but now was not the time for taking chances.

With the slightest shift of Apollyon's arm, electric lightning shot from Arael's hand.

Don't think.

React.

There would be no chance for Apollyon to anticipate her moves if she didn't know before she did it.

Apollyon slammed into the wall, her electric current flowing through him. Even with her awakening power, it would have been enough to kill a lesser angel. But Apollyon resisted.

Grabbing for his staff, Dagon swept Arael's legs out from under her. She landed on her back with a thud, the weapon swinging up toward the ceiling. Dagon lurched toward her but stopped, hovering just over the gleaming point. He reached to grab it, but Arael was on her feet again, slashing the chains that held Michael's wrists.

He slumped to the floor—not the effect she'd hoped for.

Come on, Michael, I need your help here. But it was too late. Arael was frozen, pain coursing through her body as Apollyon immobilized her with his powerful grip. His face strained, and he squeezed the invisible hand around her.

Her power sparked inside her, countering Apollyon's that crushed her from the outside.

With no other weapon at her disposal, she unleashed the inner beast who'd lay dormant for decades. Using her mind to direct it, she imagined the power surging from every crevice of her body. She'd only ever expelled her energy from her hands but felt it now like a living creature slithering beneath her skin, begging to be released. With a scream of pain, her whole body became the conductor of all the energy she held inside.

It burst forth from within, expelling Apollyon's hold on her and blasting both him and Dagon into the opposite wall. The wall crumbled, depositing large chunks of stone on top of the two angels.

Arael retrieved the staff and wielded it as if it were her own.

"Michael, get up!" she commanded. He struggled but failed to heed her command.

It was no use anyway.

The stones tumbled away as two enraged angels emerged from the pile of rock. Dagon rushed at her while Apollyon held back, calculating. Dagon reached for the staff, but Arael twirled it out of his reach, spinning to position herself between her two attackers. She jabbed the staff, left then right, wounding both angels, but not nearly enough.

Michael lay on the ground. Useless. Arael leapt over him, the staff extended in front of her. "Don't move!" she shouted as Apollyon raised a hand toward her again.

"Kill her!" Dagon shouted, but Apollyon hesitated.

"Arael." He licked his lips. "Think about this."

Dagon protested. "What are you doing? Kill her!"

Ignoring him, Apollyon inched toward her. "I'm giving you one last chance to join me. I can make you a god, second in command to all that I possess," he said. "We can *rule the world* together."

"Apollyon—" Dagon spat.

"Silence," Apollyon shouted, surprising Dagon and Arael both.

Arael couldn't imagine why Apollyon had hesitated, but she wouldn't waste the opportunity. She slammed the staff into the wall behind her with a roar, shooting her energy into the weapon to mix with the Heavenly Fire coursing through it. A thin crack formed, traveling up the wall and over their heads. Arael's wings burst from her back. She jumped to cover Michael as the room collapsed around them.

When the last stone had fallen, she wrapped her arms around Michael and pulled him from the cell. Leaning most of his weight onto her shoulder, she dragged him from the dungeon.

Arael could only hope that Raphael would have tracked Michael's location by now. She could see him now, prowling the perimeter of the Void, looking for a way to get in despite its protections and wards.

"Can you call to Raph?"

"Mmm..." Michael groaned.

"Michael." She reached up and slapped the Archangel a few times on his cheek. "Michael, I need you to call Raphael. Let him know where you are."

"He knows."

"Okay." Arael looked around. "Okay, good. Keep sending that signal. We'll be to the outer perimeter soon."

"Arael." Michael struggled to speak.

"Shh, Michael, don't try to talk."

"Arael, you have to come with me."

"It's too late for that. They'll never let me anywhere near Heaven after what I've done to you."

"Apollyon will kill you."

Arael shrugged. "I don't know. He had the opportunity back there, and he didn't take it."

"That's because right now, you have something that he wants. Don't ever let him take it from you. Michael heaved a breath. "Without it, you are expendable."

Arriving at the end of one particularly long tunnel onto the edge of the deep mountain gorge, Arael almost smiled at the sight before her. Raphael, Samael, Japhael, and even Gabriel stood. They had never looked more menacing with their weapons drawn, an army of angels and an open portal behind them, prepared to storm the gates of Hell to get their brother back.

Michael's army.

Arael blinked back the tears that threatened in her eyes. *This is what loyalty looks like.* These angels had not gathered out of fear or obligation. They were there because they loved their leader and would follow him anywhere—even into Hell.

The impressive assembly froze at the sight of her, or more so the sight of a Fallen angel—sworn enemy of Heaven—carrying a limp and bloody Archangel out of the inner sanctum of the Void.

"Quickly," she called to them, and they snapped into action.

The Archangels surrounded her, taking the burden of Michael from her shoulders. They all came except Raphael. He stood back, immobile, staring at her with the fire of vengeance burning in his eyes.

Arael could hardly meet his glare but bore his wrath as she knew she deserved.

"I don't care how long it takes me," Raphael said with fiery hatred in his words. "You will pay for this."

He turned with Michael on his shoulder and stalked through the portal. The others filed behind. Most refused to look at her, but some offered her reluctant smiles as if they recognized her sacrifice.

Zephaniah was the last one through. He inclined his head and offered a soft warning. "Be careful."

Then the portal closed, and Michael was gone. She'd done it. She'd gotten him out.

And now she was all alone.

Arael closed her eyes and soaked in the blessed quiet. Quiet that didn't last nearly long enough. Only two breaths passed until harsh voices broke through her lonely cocoon of isolation. Apollyon and Dagon had escaped her trap. There was no use in running. No matter where she went, they would find her.

Still, her feet moved beneath her. She ran along the ledge of the gorge, feeling the heat of the lava flowing below her.

"Arael! This way!" she heard Akira call to her from down a darkened tunnel.

Emerging onto a jutting mass of rock that protruded from the cave walls, Arael looked to her right to see Akira on an adjacent cliff, her auburn hair matted with sweat and blood and a barely conscious Uriah leaning on her shoulder.

Uriah's eyes widened when he caught sight of Arael. He tried to raise his head, but it swiftly lolled back onto Akira's shoulder.

Akira nodded to Arael with a sad smile.

"Go! Get him out of here!" Arael shouted as voices grew closer from the tunnel behind her.

Akira gave Arael one last apologetic look before she and Uriah disappeared.

Arael turned to face the approaching assault. She contemplated giving herself up. They would catch her eventually. Dagon had blown her cover. She couldn't go back to her life of hiding.

But of course, she wouldn't make it easy for them either. She turned back to the chasm, opened her wings, and flew to the other side.

DAY FIVE

THIRTY-TWO

Blinking away the remnants of the memory, Camryn pried open her eyes. Once she'd accomplished that first feat of waking, like the first domino falling, the rest of her body followed suit. She raised herself up on her elbows to take in her surroundings for the first time.

Squinting through the darkness that blanketed every corner of the room, Camryn expected to find President Kaya or Raphael waiting there like a villain in a bad movie.

But she was alone. Camryn stood, examining every corner and exit, assessing her odds of escape.

Where she had been numb and groggy before, in the wake of this latest memory, Camryn's body trembled, humming with what felt like an eternal energy. She heard things she hadn't before, noticed things that had previously escaped her attention.

Her mind and body had never felt more connected—more *alive*.

Camryn ran her fingers over the aged limestone, thinking how much this room resembled the basement of the church, the size the only real difference. This space was small, a storage room of some kind. A few crates filled one corner, and three multi-colored rugs were rolled and standing against the opposite wall.

Camryn ran her hand down the bars that held her—solid iron that didn't budge when she shook them. She'd expected that, though. They wouldn't leave her here with shoddy restraints.

Raphael is working with Harriet Kaya.

Yesterday, Camryn couldn't have imagined ever speaking their names in the same sentence.

What would that union mean for their mission?

And Michael?

Camryn thought of Michael as she knew him now: Whole. Well. *Alive*. She remembered wondering, on the roof of the air force base in Beersheba, how he could have survived the demon attack. Now she knew the answer.

She may have been responsible for his near demise, but she was also the reason he—and the world—were still here today.

She had failed at so many things. But at that one thing—possibly the most important thing—she had succeeded.

And now she had another job to do. She had to get out of this cell.

Camryn had just knelt to brush away the layers of dust that coated the floor when the door swung open and two guards stepped into the room.

She didn't recognize either of them, but could feel their ethereal presence, despite their military garb. How Apollyon entrusted an army of Fallen angels to this very human woman, she would never understand.

Camryn rose slowly as one of the men approached the door to her cell and reached to unlock it.

Could she fight them off? Did she want to? She needed out, after all. One way or another.

As the guard opened the door and entered, Camryn stepped backward until her back hit limestone. She planted her hands against the wall, almost digging her fingers into the brick.

"What is she doing?" the other guard asked.

The guard before her narrowed his eyes as the building began to tremble under her palms. Softly at first, asking permission. Then more aggressive, like an animal loosed from a cage.

"Stop that," the guard commanded, pointing his rifle at her. She didn't think he would pull the trigger, but Camryn dove anyway. With both hands on the ground now, she commanded it to move.

And it did.

The ground shook. Camryn cried out as the guard brought the butt of his gun down hard against the back of her head, but he was too late. The stone walls cracked and jostled until the building split, sending rocks and debris falling all around her.

No wings sprang from her back this time. No bubble of protection surrounded her, but when the shaking stopped, she stood in the midst of it all. Safe. Unharmed.

The room lay in ruins around her, and two guards under her feet.

But they weren't dead. Not even unconscious. She had mere seconds before they would be free of the rocks and as furious as a pair of rabid dogs.

She looked around for something to use as a weapon.

And found nothing.

With no bars holding her in place and not even a roof over her anymore, Camryn could make her escape.

So close. She looked through the half-demolished wall of the temple to the outside world. How far would she make it before the guards were free of the rubble and on her again?

"You won't get far," a velvety voice said, seeming to read her mind.

Camryn spun to see Clarion step through the debris with Akira and Ronan at her flanks.

Akira raised both palms to her. "Before you ask, he's not with us, but we know where he is, and yes, we're going." Akira tossed Ethan's backpack at her. "Now."

A smile played on Camryn's face just as the stones under her feet began to rise. "Not yet," she said, stepping back as a dusty hand emerged from the rubble.

Before the guard could fully stand, though, Akira shot forward and slammed her dagger straight through his eye.

The angel roared, but his cry died with him. His mouth remained open in a ghastly howl, but no sound escaped.

Then, he vanished.

Ronan disposed of the other just as quickly. Camryn did smile then, despite everything.

Stepping out into the plaza with her friends a few moments later, the clouds immediately cleared. Light slowly crept over the city like a shy child emerging from behind her mother's leg. Basking in the sunlight, Camryn felt like a new person, a new creation born of so much grief and trauma.

She looked up into the sun, took a deep, cleansing breath, then said more to herself than anyone else, "Let's rock and roll."

THIRTY-THREE

The courtyard was crowded—more crowded than it should have been, considering the area had been bombed the day before and roads leading to the Old City were unpassable. Still, the reporters had come. Only a half dozen—three reporters and their respective camera operators, but even one would have been enough to spread her message to the world.

Ethan knew the plan, had heard President Kaya rattle on about it for hours: bring the reporters in, bring him and Camryn out for the public to see, list their crimes to the world, then have them carted away to rot in some Turkish prison for the rest of their lives. That's what the public would be told, anyway. Surely, they wouldn't get off that easily.

Ethan groaned as he tried to shift in his restraints. His shoulders ached. Having your hands cuffed behind you all night would do that to a person. He'd been confined to a chair similar to the one he'd been cuffed to at the embassy, locked overnight in a jewelry store on one of the more accessible streets of the city. Alone. What had happened to Akira and Ronan—if they were even still alive—he didn't know.

Four celestial guards stood at the entrance of the shop; all weapons trained on him as if he could kill them all with a flick of his hand.

Who knows? Maybe I could.

From where he sat, though, he had a perfect view of the courtyard and the impromptu news conference being held there. President Kaya had made sure of that.

Ethan flinched as the small shop radio crackled with another news alert. If Ethan could have wished for any super power in that moment, he would have wished for telekinesis so he could knock the radio off the counter with his mind. It taunted him, just out of his reach, and he'd bruised and scraped his wrists throughout the night trying to hook his foot into the cord to unplug the damn thing.

"Jared Shaste here with your news minute," the radio blared. *"As we continue our coverage this morning of the deadly disease striking multiple countries around the world, leaving hundreds dead seemingly overnight. Health officials in Israel, Turkey, Egypt, Russia, and most of Asia are reporting individuals presenting with flesh breakdown on the inside of the mouth and esophagus and boils on the skin from what investigators now believe to be a highly potent chemical weapon.*

Many questions remain, but investigations have determined that the contaminants have been spread through the water systems of these countries. And while the origin of the chemical attack is not yet known, officials in Israel are reporting a possible connection to the blood-like precipitation experienced two days ago in several of the affected countries.

Officials say more than nine hundred people have been stricken so far and four hundred are dead. The World Health Organization is holding an emergency meeting as we speak to determine what steps should be taken to combat this deadly attack.

All night it had droned on, rehashing the events of the last few days—from the bombing in Jerusalem to the "American terrorists" to the blood rain that still puddled in the streets. Now, thanks to Apollyon, they had a new story to saturate the airwaves with—though it appeared Camryn was to be the culprit there, too.

The sword of the Lord is bathed in blood.

The words rolled through Ethan's mind as he stared at his reflection in the inches of crimson liquid that stood in puddles around him in the half-demolished building—syrupy goop that didn't seem to be drying or evaporating like normal rain would. It remained, maybe as a reminder of Camryn's power. Maybe as a precursor to the horrors yet to come.

Akira had ranted about the ecological effects it would have. The media reported actual fatalities.

Ethan thought of his conversation with Camryn the night before. She carried the weight of every life lost in the Flood as if she'd personally slaughtered them herself. Now this. She'd blame herself for this, too.

The radio quieted just as President Kaya took the stage in front of the waiting cameras.

"Where is Prime Minister Gaba?" one of the reporters shouted before the president had even begun speaking. "No one has heard from him since the bombing. You and he were reportedly working together at the time. Is he alright?"

Ethan huffed. "I guess everyone thinks this is a little weird," he said to the silent guards.

President Kaya pressed her lips into a line and cast her eyes downward, the perfect image of someone about to deliver regretful news. "No. I'm sorry, he's not." She brought her eyes back up to meet theirs, confidence filling her voice. "Prime Minister Gaba and most of his cabinet were killed in the bombings."

Harriet waited until the murmuring died down before she continued. "As head of the Western Alliance, I will be taking charge until new elections can be held."

"The Western Alliance that you championed?" the female reporter asked. "Seems rather convenient, doesn't it?"

"Is that a question?" Harriet challenged.

The crowd quieted, out of shock or fear, Ethan wasn't sure. "All of Prime Minister Gaba's initiatives will be upheld," Harriet continued, "and his wishes and plans for the country will be considered." She scanned her eyes among the handful of reporters on the periphery of the courtyard. "Truly devastating news."

The reporters waited in unprecedented quiet.

"But that is not the reason I called you here today." She gestured to Ethan's guards, striking them into motion. Two of them flanked either side of the open door while the other two approached Ethan warily, their boots sliding in the slick blood.

"Time for your television debut," one of the guards sneered.

"Hey, why don't you go to hell?" Ethan glared at the men as they continued their slow approach, willing them with all his mental strength to burst into flames.

They didn't. But *something* happened.

Ethan felt the vibrations the same time the guards did—not too violent but strong enough to knock a glass display to the floor and shatter it into pieces. The tremor lasted only seconds, but the look on the guards' faces told Ethan that the earthquake had not been expected. Ethan struggled against his restraints, ignoring the pain in his shoulders.

The guards looked back to President Kaya, who had a finger pressed to the intercom in her ear, shouting to the guards in the courtyard and looking furious enough to snap their necks with her teeth.

Her guards scattered, leaving her alone on the platform while the soldiers guarding Ethan appeared unsure of how to proceed.

Did he even dare to hope?

President Kaya searched the distant horizon as if expecting to find something there. The cameras followed her gaze but found only empty streets.

As Ethan watched in anticipation, an oddly familiar sensation filled his chest, and that feeling…that magical euphoria erased every discomfort—his thirst, his weariness, the ache in his shoulders disappeared with the returning flicker of the *qanima* bond.

THIRTY-FOUR

Ethan stared in anticipation as the guards wobbled and slid on the now-frozen floor. The first two went down, feet flying into the air. The outside guards rushed to their aid, slipping down to join them on the frozen goop that their shoes had been stuck in just moments before.

With all four guards scrambling back to their feet, Camryn dashed into the shop, scanning the room for other threats. Akira and Ronan appeared beside her, their human clothes replaced by their more traditional battle armor.

"Personally, I would've gone for a more dramatic entrance," Akira said.

"An explosion would have been cool." Ronan shrugged.

The nearest guard made a move for his weapon, but Ronan was faster. He shoved his sword into the hollow of the guard's neck.

"Move and die," he said with a wink as Camryn and Akira rushed to Ethan, releasing him from his bindings.

With his hands free, Ethan pulled Camryn to him, crushing her in a desperate embrace. "I didn't know if I'd ever see you again…"

Camryn squeezed her arms around him, inhaling a deep breath like she always did when she was in his arms. "I probably smell like a garbage can."

"Smells like Heaven to me." Her words muffled into his chest.

Ronan gave a quick glance back to the courtyard—more than enough time for the guard on the floor to swipe at Ronan's sword at his throat, springing to his feet faster than Ethan's eyes could track.

In a flash, the other guards followed suit and faced off against them, one guard for each of them.

"We don't have time for this!" Camryn said. "She's getting away."

They all looked to see President Kaya being escorted from the stage, the reporters in quick pursuit.

"Sorry about this, guys." Akira shrugged as she threw out a small round bulb, emitting a glowing red gas.

Before Ethan could blink, Akira and Ronan had transported them to the courtyard, and they found themselves directly in front of Harriet Kaya and her entourage.

The hellfire mist had been only a brief distraction as Ethan's guards appeared on the courtyard before them, making a barrier between them and the fleeing woman.

"President Kaya, please," Camryn begged. "Please do something. You are the only one who can stop this."

Ethan could barely see the woman as she cowered behind her angelic escorts, but the cameras were close enough to hear every word.

"Why would I want to do that?"

"Your country," Camryn pleaded. "Think of the people you've fought so hard to protect. And all this death—this plague that you've spread. You can tell the media whatever you want, but we all know who is responsible. And your people are the ones suffering."

"My people?" Harriet scoffed. "Dear girl..." She waved her hand around at the city. "What we see here—this world—is like the jumbled mess of yarn on the backside of the seamstress's loom. What I've seen—what Apollyon has shown me—is the masterpiece that lies on the other side. This world...These people... They will soon be a distant memory of a life once lived."

Ethan glanced at the few reporters who lurked on the periphery of the conversation, making sure they'd captured the exchange.

President Kaya shouldered through her circle of guards to face them. "You," she said to Akira, taking the angel's red hair in her palm and letting it fall through her fingers. "You are the ones I will rule one day." She ran her eyes over the lot of them. "These worldly kingdoms will soon pass away. Them and everything in them will return to dust. Apollyon will take his rightful throne, and you will bow to us. Not Elohim. Not some worldly ruler. But us."

Ronan and Akira drew their daggers. "Not if we have anything to do with it."

President Kaya lowered her eyes to the celestial weapons. "Do you angels think you can harm me with those? I am human. Celestial Law forbids it."

Camryn raised her gun at the woman. "This isn't a celestial weapon." She placed her finger on the trigger. "And I'm no angel."

Harriet's jaw tensed, and her eyes narrowed, but what Ethan saw, just like the yellow mist wafting off of Michael back in the church, was not what he expected. Once again, Ethan only caught a glimpse, but he knew the color of anger—had it burned in his brain like a brand. And this wasn't it.

What is she trying to hide?

The emotion rolling off of her now tasted salty in his mouth.

Fear.

No. Not plain ole, every-day fear.

Terror.

But why? She had a gun pointed at her face, sure. But ten times that many weapons pointed right back at her aggressors. Surely she wasn't *that* afraid to die.

"You *stupid* children," Harriet seethed. "You think you can ruin this for me?" She shook her head vigorously and took a step back. "No. You won't." She turned to the guard on her left. "Bring them in." The guard on her right leaned in, whispering something in her ear.

"I know he isn't going to like it," she practically screamed, her hands balled into fists at the ends of the stiff arms she had plastered to her sides. "But I am not letting them get away again. He will like that even less."

Camryn lowered her gun just as four Israeli military vehicles appeared, slowly making their way over the piles of concrete and glass, the only remnants left of the Old City. Behind the vehicles, a battalion of Israeli and Turkish troops marched.

If the soldiers in the plaza were any indication, Ethan was willing to bet these new soldiers were not human. Not all of them anyway.

I guess the gig is up. No more pretending Camryn and Ethan were some illusive "American terrorists." Harriet had either forgotten she'd brought all these cameras here, or she didn't care.

What will this mean? Ethan wondered. *What will it mean for the world to witness a spiritual battle like what's about to go down?*

The Flood had ended the mutually beneficial relationship between the humans and angels. Now, all that existed of those relationships were legends and stories. Tales that most humans didn't even believe anymore.

Would they believe now?

"That's nice and all," Akira said. "But I think I forgot to mention…" She put a finger to her chin and pursed her lips. "We brought an army of our own."

Ethan glanced behind him at the empty courtyard. "We did?"

Camryn followed his gaze, and Akira and Ronan exchanged an uneasy glance. "Uh, yeah…*we did.*"

A small flame sparked from Ethan's fingers when Zephaniah materialized on the steps beside him.

"I'm sorry." Zephaniah inclined his head. "Did I miss my cue?"

Ethan exhaled, smiling with the corner of his mouth as he leaned over and whispered, "I thought they said you couldn't help us."

"Michael is still missing." He shrugged. "I made an executive decision."

The group kept their eyes trained on President Kaya as the rest of Michael's army appeared atop the ruined city behind them.

Where Ethan had only caught glimpses of random emotions before, he was almost blinded by the mixture of rage and terror exploding from Harriet Kaya now.

Akira laughed. "You didn't expect this to be easy, did you?"

A look of resignation joined the fury on the woman's face. "You little bastards are going to pay for this."

The guards grabbed Harriet by the arms. "Madame, we have to get you out of here."

President Kaya stepped back between the two angelic guards, and the three of them vanished from the plaza, transporting her away from the battle.

"Well," Akira said to Ronan, "Looks like you're finally going to get those explosions you were looking for."

Ronan exchanged his daggers for the sword at his side. "This isn't exactly what I had in mind."

Before the words were out of his mouth, a rocket blasted from one of the distant vehicles toward the group in the courtyard. Zephaniah shot into the air, crashing into the weapon, sending it careening off its original track just as the Fallen army attacked. The rocket veered to the right, exploding into the remains of a coffee shop on the other side of the courtyard.

Zephaniah made a flying loop through the air, then straight back down into the midst of the fighting.

Ethan put his back to Camryn's, giving them a complete view of the action while Akira and Ronan took a fighting stance on either side of them.

Ethan pulled the heat into his hands, ready to join in the fray when a pained shriek cut through the noises of battle.

"Help! Someone help me!"

Ethan felt Camryn stiffen behind him. They all looked around and noticed the woman at the same time—lying in the street in front of the coffee shop under a piece of debris that had been blown into the air by the explosion.

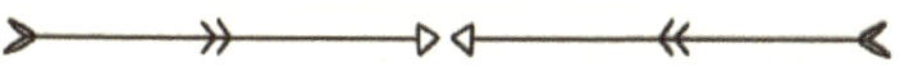

It may have been true that an angel couldn't harm a human with their weapons, but humans could definitely be harmed by the results of angelic actions. That had been evidenced throughout history. Camryn's mind went straight to her first human friends,

Jacob and Salome. Then to her parents and Elizabeth. Would she ever get the chance to tell Ethan about his mother? Did she even want to?

So much remained out of her control. It would be impossible to save everyone. So many had died already. But this one…maybe she could save this one.

"Get me to that woman," Camryn shouted.

Akira pointed at the still-approaching trucks. "Camryn, we don't have—"

"Get me—" Camryn said again, "—to that woman!"

Akira sighed as if she understood the futility in the argument even as four Fallen soldiers lunged for them. "You all go. I'll deal with these guys."

Camryn traced a path in her mind from where they stood to the injured woman, but too many Fallen stood in the way. There would be no getting through.

Ethan stepped in front of her, poking Ronan with his elbow. "Slash and burn?"

Camryn had no clue what that meant, but Ronan apparently did. A wicked grin spread across the angel's face. "Slash and burn," he said with an eager nod.

Ethan whipped two balls of flames into his hands. Ronan twirled his blade.

In a flash, they were off, slicing and blazing their way through the wall of celestial soldiers. When two larger-than-average angels stepped into their path, Ethan hurled two streaks of opaque flames into them, white daggers of fire. The guards convulsed and landed flat on their backs. Ronan darted forward, pausing between the two guards to bend and bury his blades in their chests.

Ethan didn't slow but looked down, watching the two angels disappear in a cloud of black smoke.

“Not gonna lie,” Ronan said with a nod. “I didn’t think that would work.”

“Me neither.” Ethan smiled.

Camryn, who had followed the males as they blazed a trail for her, looked back at their path of destruction. They had made it across the courtyard, thanks to her friends. She wanted to applaud them. Hug them. Thank them at the very least. But those things would have to wait. Right now, she had a job to do.

THIRTY-FIVE

Rockets continued to hurl their way, but were intercepted by Zephaniah and his forces while Ronan lifted the slab of concrete off the woman's leg. As the blood rushed to her now free appendage, the woman screamed in pain.

"It's okay," Camryn said to the woman. "I'm here to help you." The woman didn't even acknowledge her, just continued her painful wails. *So much for introductions.*

"You know what to do," her father's voice echoed in her mind. *"You've done this a hundred times."*

"Yeah, but not on a real person," she replied. The cameras were still rolling, mostly capturing the angelic battle taking place in the courtyard. But at least one remained focused on her.

"Don't think about them," her father soothed. *"Just focus on the job in front of you."*

Right.

What to do first?

She lifted the woman's pant leg to see a knot on the side of her calf and her leg bent at an unnatural angle "It looks like your leg is broken," Camryn explained. "I'm going to have to set it." The woman moaned again but nodded. Two of the woman's colleagues grasped her arms, bracing for the pain.

Within minutes, Camryn had the bone set and splinted and the woman's other injuries bandaged—the quickest work she'd ever done.

"Uh..." Camryn began. "You're gonna need to get that looked at by a doctor." She cleared her throat. "Right away."

"Thank you," the woman said in her native tongue.

Camryn pressed her lips together and began to stand.

"What's your name," one of the reporters asked.

"Who I am isn't important," she replied. "We need to get you guys out of here."

"We're live streaming," one man said. His name tag read Levi. "We aren't going anywhere."

"Your lives are in danger," Camryn insisted.

"Yeah, and what's new," the man replied.

Camryn blinked, glancing at the other reporters all staring back at her. Waiting.

"My name is Camryn Martin. This is Ethan Reyes." She said, pulling Ethan into the shot with her. "We aren't the monsters that Harriet Kaya has made us out to be. We were supposed to stop this—" she said, gesturing back at the fighting "—somehow." She closed her eyes, angry at the tears that threatened. "But we failed."

"Or maybe... Maybe we were supposed to tell you something..." Camryn's eyes popped open with a deep inhale of breath. "But the Big Man Upstairs has been pretty quiet lately, so...no messages from God today, I guess." Camryn turned to walk away.

"Whatever message you were meant to send to the world," Levi said from behind his camera, "I think you already did it."

Camryn looked down at the woman with the splint on her leg and around at the battle surrounding them. She saw the vantage point the cameras had had on President Kaya's escape and the role she'd played in it all.

Camryn cleared her throat and nodded. Maybe Levi was right. Maybe that was all they were supposed to do. Expose Harriet Kaya for who she really was.

She turned back to the camera and exhaled.

"I hope you all understand that what you're seeing here today and what is happening all over the world… This is only the beginning of the horror of what they have planned." Camryn tugged at the hem of her shirt.

"Harriet Kaya has had all of us fooled for a long time. But forget who we thought she was. Think about who you are—who you want to be. What you want your future to look like… Is this it?" She stepped aside to allow a better view of the plaza. "Today, it's us she wants to kill." She gestured around at her friends. "Tomorrow, it could be one of you. If you disagree with her. If you rebel…

"You've heard her words. She doesn't care about you. And you've seen what she's capable of. But you also saw something else here today. That alone, we might not be able to beat her. But together…we at least have a chance."

When she'd finished, Camryn pulled her gaze up to meet Levi's and found something unexpected. He worked his jaw and nodded in solidarity. In eyes that had been filled with fear and uncertainty just moments before, she now watched something else take shape—a resolve, a boldness that hadn't been there before.

Looking around at the rest of the crew, she saw the same thing in their eyes. She saw hope.

Camryn looked back to the camera.

"And Harriet, if you're listening to this—you and whoever you're working for—you can both mark my words. You will not win this fight. Humanity will prevail."

Camryn stepped back between her friends, taking each by the hand.

Ethan squeezed Camryn's fingers as Akira appeared in the street beside them, panting and covered in blood that didn't appear to be her own. "Hey." She planted her fists on her hips, breathless. "What did I miss?"

"Leave the equipment," Camryn commanded, her impromptu speech forgotten. She nodded to Akira and Ronan. "These two are going to get you to safety."

While Akira ran her eyes over the speechless group of humans, Ronan extended his hands. "Anyone with heart problems or motions sickness should not ride this ride."

They shrank back from him.

Camryn grimaced. "Just don't take them far," she said. "The closer the distance, the less it will suck."

While Akira and Ronan got to work transporting the humans to the hill overlooking the city, Camryn and Ethan surveyed the battle raging around them.

"What now?" Ethan asked her.

"Now," she said, electricity sparking from her fingertips, "I guess we fight."

And fight they did—with every weapon Elohim had blessed them with: fire and ice and wind and hail. They fought. It seemed like hours had passed, and the battle showed no signs of waning. Gunfire rang out from the military trucks that President

Kaya had summoned, though the bullets did little harm against the celestial horde.

But what else could be expected? Their leader had called them here. And soldiers were not trained to run. They would fight—just as she would—until they could fight no more.

"Camryn!" She heard over the din of battle, and looked up to see Ethan across the clearing. "Behind you!"

Camryn whirled to see Zephaniah and a dark-haired angel on the ground behind her. The Fallen soldier wriggled free of Zephaniah's grasp and was on his feet in a blur. Camryn sprang forward as the soldier swung around with his blade aimed at Zephaniah's back. Camryn's arm shot out, launching an ice dagger straight toward the angel.

And straight through his chest.

Zephaniah jumped up, glancing quickly from the disintegrating angel to Camryn and back again. He tipped his head in thanks just as a rocket came hurtling toward them. Camryn and Ethan dove in opposite directions as the projectile hit the jewelry store, exploding in a ball of fire.

Camryn crawled a few yards toward a delivery van that sat abandoned on the street. Covered in sweat and dust and gore, she pulled herself to a sitting position against the back tire.

Ethan dove behind the van just as Camryn dared to look down at the hand she had gripped under her rib cage. The hand that was covered in blood.

"Oh my God…" Ethan breathed.

"It's okay," Camryn assured him. "It's okay."

Ethan continued to stare at her hand, at the blood oozing through her fingers. "That doesn't look okay."

"I think—" Camryn struggled to suck in a breath. "I think it punctured my lung."

"Wh–what can I do?" Ethan's voice cracked. "Just tell me how to fix it."

But there was nothing to be done.

Camryn shook her head, gritting her teeth and hitching a breath through her nose. Stars were already forming across her vision.

"No," Ethan insisted. "We can't die, remember?"

She looked over Ethan's shoulder and saw the cameras the reporters had left, their battery lights still blinking red. *Oh, God…* How horrifying that they were capturing all this on live television. Suddenly she was glad her parents weren't alive to witness this. How would they react to her very public death?

They would be grief-stricken, just as she had been at losing them. Of course, they would be…at first.

But then, they would be livid. They would want justice. They wouldn't sleep until the culprit had paid the price.

Camryn smiled.

"I think," she said, her eyelids growing heavy. "I think we're done."

So heavy.

"No," Ethan said again, shaking her awake. "I'm not done. We're not done!" Camryn could hear the tears in his voice and latched onto his hand. *How to make him understand?*

But she couldn't explain it to him. *No energy. Need to sleep.*

"Go," Camryn whispered. He still had time to escape. "Please."

"You're crazy, you know that?" Ethan settled down on the road beside her and laced his grimy fingers with hers. "You think I'm going anywhere without you?"

He held out his free palm, igniting a small blue flame. "If we're going, we're going together."

Camryn squeezed his hand. She ground her teeth through the pain as the unmistakable sound of a rocket whistled overhead.

Akira screamed as the rocket hit its mark and the van Ethan had just dove behind erupted in a blue blaze. Ronan grabbed her, held her back.

"He's—he's gone," Ronan said, his voice tight.

No. He can't be.

"They're both gone," Ronan said, his voice so quiet he seemed to be talking only to himself.

Grief and anger wrestled inside Akira, melding into a lifeform of its own—a beast living and growing within. She couldn't control it. Couldn't contain it. Had to set it free.

Akira continued to scream.

THIRTY-SIX

*Oh, God…*Camryn groaned. But where she was, God would never hear her.

The air pressed in, heavy and hot.

So hot…

But worse than the heat was the oppressive darkness of the place—darker than anything her human mind could fathom—so crushing that she thought it would destroy her.

This isn't happening.

Not real.

Must be a dream. Yes, that had to be it. This was all in her head, like her chat with Samael before he opened her mind to receive her celestial memories.

Relief. Then terror, as she remembered that her consciousness could withstand horrors her body could not.

Camryn writhed on the ground. Clawed at her chest.

I have to get up.

It took a moment and a great deal of effort, but she finally pried herself from the ground, wiping sweat from her eyes. Under her hands, the sharp prickle of small black pebbles needled her skin. Pits of boiling lava hissed and spewed around her.

I have to get out.

She struggled to her knees, every movement a chore. Her throat parched. Her skin burned. *Have to move. Have to get out,* she repeated to herself…until she looked up.

Oh, God… It seemed the lava pits were the least of her worries.

A circle of flames surrounded her about fifty yards out in all directions—a prison of fire.

Turning her head, she followed the inferno in a complete circle then collapsed back on her hands, too weary to push herself from the ground again.

The soft whimper working its way up her throat was cut short when something scampered across her fingers, followed by a prick of pain. She jerked her hand back with a scream.

Spiders.

She raised her fist to see two angry red welts marring the thinly lined skin.

Oh no. Her panic amped up as her fingers began to throb. She clutched her hand to her chest and scrambled to her feet, her weariness quickly replaced by instinct. Fight or flight. But there would be no fighting these things.

So, she ran. Her brain sent fire to her limbs, propelling her forward, but where could she go? Spiders sprang at her from all directions. God, she hated spiders. *Disgusting. Vile.*

They crunched under her feet, jumped onto her legs. She screamed and swatted them away as she ran faster. Ran toward nothing, away from the dreadful monsters, until she spotted something in the distance—a large, flat rock just tall enough to be safe from these abominations. She just had to get there.

Her feet kicked through the blanket of spiders swarming around her.

Almost there.

As Camryn drew closer, she lunged for the rock but miscalculated the distance. She latched onto the ledge but fell backward, landing in a sea of arachnids. Spiders crawled into her hair, onto her face. She clamped her lips together to keep them out of her mouth, but her screams echoed in her throat.

She sprang up again, faster than she had ever moved, slinging her arms and mussing her hands wildly in her hair. Finally free of the hideous vermin, she jumped for the rock again. Eventually finding a foothold to propel herself upward, she clawed at the stone until her nails were bloody stumps.

Camryn cried out, thinking she would fall again, but finally, she pulled herself onto the surface.

Collapsing on the rock, her pulse thrumming even though her heart had long ago stopped beating, Camryn swiped at imaginary legs crawling over her skin. The relief was overwhelming, almost joyful, manifesting in tearful sobs.

I did it. I made it.

She was safe—for the moment.

So she let her tears flow. Why not? No one was here to see her, to stop her. And God knew she had plenty to cry about: Ethan. Her parents. Michael. All those she hadn't been able to save.

She gave herself over to anguish and let her body have its release. She cried until no more tears would come. Until she felt empty and hollow inside, carved out like a jack-o-lantern on Halloween.

Her mind slowed along with her tears, allowing a few errant thoughts to form in her head. Camryn tried to blink them away.

She wished for something...anything to help her escape. Why this? Why had death brought her *here*? Why couldn't she just...cease to exist.

But it didn't work that way.

She knew where she was and why she was there.

This is my punishment.

Even if she and Ethan had fulfilled the prophecy. Even if her death managed to inspire a rebellion and stop Harriet Kaya, she would never know about it, never know how it all ended—if it had all been worth it.

A bead of sweat rolled from her eye toward her ear. Or maybe it was a tear.

What would become of her? Was she destined to spend eternity in the sweltering heat of this inferno surrounded by these torturous abominations hellbent on sinking their dreadful fangs into her?

She blinked up at the blackness above and had almost found the sweet relief of unconsciousness again when a soft rustling sound made its way up to her ears—a sound she'd heard only once before.

You've got to be kidding me.

She looked down to see that the spiders had disappeared, only to be replaced by a tangle of slithering reptiles.

Rattle snakes.

She pulled her limbs up, too weary to even scream, but not before one of them struck, latching onto her ankle. She kicked and scrambled away from the edge, but that just drew more attention. All their beady eyes trained on her, moving closer, closing in.

Was this to be her punishment—what Apollyon planned to do to her for eternity? Attack her with all the darkest fears of her heart?

She looked at her wounds. Her hand, her ankle—two spider bites and one snake bite.

This isn't real, she told herself, trying to calm her irrational fears. *It's just an illusion.*

But it *felt* real. And what was horrifyingly worse—these wounds wouldn't kill her. No, her body could be consumed by snakes and spiders and any number of horrendous tortures, and her suffering would never end.

She wrapped her arms around her knees and lowered her head. Squeezed her eyes shut. Hoped that when she opened them again, she'd be back on her front porch and the past week would all have been a terrible nightmare.

How long she stayed like that, she couldn't be sure, but eventually, another sound intermixed with the hissing and rattling of the snakes.

Camryn…

It was a voice. Very faint, but someone was there!

Camryn turned in all directions but saw no one. She scrambled to the edge to peer over.

And what she saw would've stopped her heart—if it hadn't stopped beating already.

Camryn gasped as she went scrambling down the rock face, sliding the last portion, landing hard onto the ground. Snakes twisted around her ankles, but she didn't care. *They're not real. Not real,* she repeated to herself as she stumbled to get to him.

Ethan, lying lifeless on the ground with snakes slithering onto his chest, over his legs. Camryn kicked and screamed at them, picked them up, and hurled them into the distance.

Her fear suddenly extinguished, she just needed to reach him.

Her breath caught when she spotted the triangle of circular wounds decorating his chest—bullet holes. Her gaze returned to his ashen face, and she knew she was too late.

No, she whimpered. *Not this again. I can't do this again.* She shook him and screamed his name to the flames around her. She clutched his shirt and buried her face in his chest. His blood mixed with her sweat and tears into a gruesome mask on Camryn's face.

She cried and screamed and longed for the numbness that she knew would never come. "I can't do this, Ethan. I can't be caged in here with you like this for eternity. Anything else. I'll take literally anything else…"

She talked to him for what seemed like hours. She told him about his mother. About Elizabeth's last minutes, how brave she'd been, even though she knew he couldn't hear her. She talked to him as if he'd respond, and then…he did.

"Camryn…"

Camryn sniffed, tears still streaming from her eyes. It was the same voice she'd heard before—Ethan's voice. But it hadn't come from the body lying in front of her. It had come from inside her head.

She quieted and stared down at the body before her.

"Ethan?" She leaned over and traced the lines of his face, smudging the dirt and blood from the fight in the plaza. *This isn't real.*

But he looked real. Felt real.

Camryn wouldn't have had the strength to stand and walk away from him if the voice hadn't come again.

"Where are you?" the voice in her mind implored.

"I'm here," she answered, but her thoughts floated back to her, unheard.

She stood, kissed her fingers and pressed them to Ethan's lips. *Not Ethan.*

She trudged toward the wall of flames. Toward the voice. One step. Two. She had to find a way through.

The simple act of walking—putting one foot in front of the other—reminded Camryn of wading through waist high water. Her legs weighed a hundred pounds. She looked down at her feet, sure she would find something holding them back, but…no.

When her eyes drifted forward again, she screamed. Her mother stood in front of her, her face as gray as Ethan's with dark circles rounding her eyes. A single trail of blood ran from behind Lindsay's ear and disappeared under the collar of her shirt.

Camryn froze. *She's not real*, she repeated to herself. Lindsay stood still as a statue, staring straight ahead. Camryn wanted to hug her, to touch her. But *she's not real.*

Deep breath. *Okay.*

Camryn attempted to step around the woman when Lindsay's hand shot out and grabbed Camryn's wrist. Lindsay's head turned until she stared into Camryn's wide eyes.

Her chest heaved. *Can't breathe.*

"Why didn't you save me?" her mother whispered.

The words cut like a blade.

Camryn closed her eyes and pictured her mother's face—her real face. The face that had comforted her, scolded her, protected her for the last eighteen years. When she opened her eyes again, the mirage had disappeared. But her words lingered.

Why didn't you save me?

Camryn hadn't had time to grieve for her parents—to even tell Ethan about his own mother.

"I'm sorry, Mom."

And she *was* sorry. But she couldn't dwell on that now. She would say her goodbyes later. Now, she had to keep moving.

Camryn decided that time must be another illusion of the Void after walking toward the wall for what seemed like hours.

Losing hope and without Ethan's voice urging her on, Camryn collapsed.

Maybe this is what I deserve. Maybe this had been the deal. Maybe after she'd rescued Michael from the dungeons—the prison she'd put him in—Elohim had allowed her eighteen more years of ignorant bliss—no knowledge of heavenly battles or celestial grudges—and now this was to be her existence, to pay for all her grievances against Heaven.

She lay down on the hard, jagged rocks, pulled her knees to her chest, and stared at the distant flames holding her hostage in this hell. *Let the spiders and snakes take me.* The flames licked and flickered until the image doubled in her vision. Her eyes drifted down to the pool of water next to her.

Camryn shot up.

There was a *pool of water* next to her. She quickly dipped her hand into it, her thirst exploding in her throat, but it came out dry. *No*!

Another illusion.

"Don't do this to me!"

She didn't think she had any tears left until they sprang into her eyes again. Camryn let out a strangled cry. How cruel would it get?

She tried again because…she couldn't resist. But garnered the same result. Her hand went through the glassy surface of the puddle and touched dry rock. She pounded her fist into the ground, letting the rocks make tiny cuts in the side of her hand.

"Stop! Stop! Stop it!" she screamed into the air, knowing no one would hear her, then lowered her head between her fists, still balled against the ground. She sobbed and cursed and prepared to push herself to her feet. But where would she go? She had no idea. Still, she had to get away from this monumental torment.

Just as she turned her head to curse the puddle one more time, her words lodged in her throat.

She cocked her head. She squinted. She turned to look at the wall of flames, then back down at the pool. She lowered herself to the ground and performed the ritual again.

If Camryn hadn't been so miserable, she would have laughed.

She pushed herself to her feet and headed straight for the flames.

The closer Camryn drew to her prison wall, the hotter the air became around her, pushing her back, repelling her. She squinted against the heat and brightness of it. So close now—closer than she imagined possible. If she reached out, she could touch it.

And that's exactly what she planned to do. The pool had revealed its secret.

God, I hope I'm not wrong.

She extended her hand to the flame then jerked back at its stinging burn.

"Shit! Shit! Shit!" Camryn examined her fingers, fiery red from the touch. Disappointment crushed her. She'd been so sure. She shook her hand furiously then held it up to get a better look. The blisters were still there, but something was missing.

She examined the top of her hand where the red welts of the spider bites had been, the skin now smooth and unmarred. The pain that had accompanied the bites had faded as well.

An illusion.

Not real.

But they had seemed real. She may have left her physical body in the plaza behind that white, burned-out van, but her mind wasn't in on the joke.

The pain had been all too real to her and lasted for quite a while. But it was gone now.

Maybe she'd been right after all.

Or maybe not. But one thing was true. She wouldn't know until she was safe on the other side of the flames...or burning inside them.

Not giving herself time to change her mind, Camryn sucked in a breath, squeezed her eyes shut, and stepped into the flames.

THIRTY-SEVEN

Just keep moving.

The thick heat enveloped her like a blanket of flames.

Stinging.

Burning.

Pain.

She'd experienced such torment only once before—inside the church in New York City, a Fallen angel being incinerated inside the house of God. But this time, it wasn't unbearable. Scratch that. It *was* unbearable, but her tolerance had increased tenfold. She could now endure what, on earth, would have killed her.

Camryn kept her eyes pinched shut and raised her arms to shield her face from the licking flames. She coughed as the smoke filled her lungs. *You don't have lungs, idiot,* she tried to reason with herself, but in her desperation, there was no reason to be found.

Her chest burned, and her throat wheezed.

When she didn't immediately step through to the other side, it occurred to Camryn that this wall of fire might not have an end. She might trudge through the torment of it for months…or years…or forever.

No. I won't survive it. Turn back? Keep going? She hadn't yet decided when, with one last stumbling step, she was free. Camryn collapsed onto her hands and knees, gasping for fresh, clean air. But there was none to be had.

The heat was no less oppressive on the other side of the wall, but the pain had dissipated, at least. She didn't have time to revel in that small victory, though.

She had to find Ethan. The real Ethan.

The area on the other side of her prison was no different than the inside—black rock under her feet, lava pits spewing in the distance, a purple-black sky overhead. Maybe this side of the wall would be free of imaginary tortures, at least.

She could only hope.

The rocks crunched under her feet as she trudged along, looking for…what? Another wall of fire holding Ethan captive?

"Ethan!" she called. "Can you hear me?"

No response. How had he gotten through to her? How had she heard his voice?

"Ethan, damn it! Answer me!"

She tripped over a protruding rock and stumbled to her knees again, a quiet sob escaping her lips.

Don't cry, she sniffed. *Not now.*

Forcing herself to her feet again, something appeared in the distance—something that hadn't been there before.

Could it be?

Camryn stood.

Impossible. Too far. But she had to try.

She didn't dare let herself dream that it could be him. She couldn't take the devastation if this were just another cruel mirage. She focused on the ground under her feet instead. One foot in front of the other.

After what had to be hours of wading through the thick atmosphere of the Void, the figure finally came into view.

And there he was, sitting with his head in his hands. Camryn's heart practically jumped from her chest.

It was him—she could feel it. Feel *him*.

Her relief escaped in a strangled cry. Ecstasy washed over her. If she had to endure this place, at least they would be together.

"Ethan," she called, but he didn't move. She tried again but received no response. She trudged toward him. And slammed into an invisible barrier.

She looked left then right. Up. Down. She saw nothing.

Then Ethan's shoulder's shook. Just once. *He's crying.* Camryn placed a hand on the barrier between them—gently. She experienced a twinge of relief when her fingers didn't come away blistered. It wasn't hot. Just solid.

She backed away and stretched her palms toward him. If she couldn't push through, maybe she could try something else.

Camryn flexed her hands and hurled a lightning bolt straight toward him. Without the restrictions of her physical body, the energy shot from her hand with such force she almost fell backward. *Whoa…*

But the bolt had hit its mark, and Ethan stared at the smoking spot on the ground in front of him.

It worked!

Camryn's joy was short-lived, though, as the wall cracked and popped before her eyes, repairing itself from her attack.

"Camryn?" Ethan called. She saw his mouth form the word but didn't hear a thing.

"I'm here," she screamed, scrambling forward, clawing at the spot. *Stop. Stop. Stop.* This had to work. She had to get through.

But the hole continued to close, blocking her from Ethan once more.

Camryn screamed in frustration, but backed up, planted her feet, and blasted another hole through the barrier, again and again.

Blast. Repair. Blast. Repair.

But the small holes weren't nearly big enough for Camryn to crawl through, and they repaired themselves so quickly…

Ethan didn't move, just watched the electric currents blow through his prison wall. What must he be thinking?

Camryn kicked the barrier. Mere feet stood between her and Ethan, but it may as well have been a hundred miles. She tried pushing her thoughts to him with her mind, but they echoed back to her like an empty well.

Still.

He began making his way toward her—or the direction from which the lightning had come—his face curious.

Yes! Camryn coughed out a laugh. He was coming closer. He would surely feel her, wouldn't he?

He'd taken only a few steps when he stopped, his eyes focusing on something in front of him that Camryn couldn't see. The look of horror that crossed Ethan's face sent a chill down Camryn's spine that could combat even this oppressing heat. What was he seeing?

She pressed another shot of electricity from her hands, effortless, landing directly in front of him this time.

He blinked rapidly, snapping out of the grip of whatever nightmare had stood in front of him. He rushed toward her and pushed against the barrier when he drew close. He ran along the perimeter, trying to find a way through. Camryn called to him, beckoned him, coaxed him, but to no avail.

Ethan put his hands on his knees and roared. At least that's what it looked like from where Camryn stood.

Come on, Ethan…

Camryn put her hands against the barrier once more and pushed with all her strength. She ground her teeth and grunted with the effort. She panted and sobbed, kicked the ground, and growled. She slammed her fist into the wall with one last primitive scream.

And her fist went through.

Her first instinct was to pull it back, but *no!* This would be her only chance. She could see the barrier now, like a pane of glass around the area where her arm had penetrated. It had shattered and cracked with the invasion of her fist, but it was repairing itself around her arm. Although the barrier tried to expel her, Camryn stretched her hand even further and opened her palm.

By some astronomical miracle, Ethan saw it.

But he didn't take it right away. He just stared at the hand as if he couldn't trust his eyes.

"Take my hand," Camryn screamed, but of course, he couldn't hear her. She sobbed through the pain and stretched a little farther.

Finally, slowly, he extended his hand and placed it in hers. As soon as he did, Camryn yanked him forward toward the wall.

He fought her at first. Who in their right mind wouldn't? But she dug in her fingers, still blistered from her own escape. No way in hell was she letting go.

She yanked again, pulled with such force that they both flew backward and landed hard on the rocky ground. She landed with an umph, and Ethan tumbled through the barrier, flopping down on top of her.

His eyes widened with surprise. He scrambled back onto his knees, staring.

"It's me." Camryn reached a hand toward him and tried to smile, but he pulled back from her.

"Ethan, it's me. Can't you—" She placed her other hand on her chest. "Can't you feel it? It's really me."

He took two more breaths, contemplating, before he crawled to her, examining every inch of her face, her eyes, her lips. He touched her hand, brushing his fingers gently over hers.

"How did you—" He gestured back toward the wall that had just held him captive. "How did you know I could get through?"

"No reflection," she said, gesturing to the pools of black water dotting the ground.

"God, you're a genius," he said, taking her face in his hands.

Camryn closed her eyes, letting an errant tear escape down her cheek.

"Don't cry." He swiped the tear with his thumb. "We're going to get out of here."

Camryn glanced around. "You know where we are, right? No one escapes from here."

Ethan looked around, his face pale and gaunt. What hell had he just gone through?

Camryn couldn't find it within herself to argue with him when he finally looked back at her with haunted eyes and said, "We at least have to try."

DAY SIX

THIRTY-EIGHT

Michael paced his cell like a restless lion, glaring at the backsides of the dozen guards surrounding his square enclosure.

Imbeciles.

He would kill them. Kill them all when he got the chance.

On instinct, he brought his hand to his side—his sword side—for the hundredth time since his capture, but his weapons had been stripped from him...just like everything else that he loved.

Michael let out a low growl—all he had the heart for anymore. For the past two days, he'd yelled at the guards, cursed them, demanded they release him immediately, but they'd studiously ignored him.

He touched the bars one more time, but his fingers sizzled against the Hell Fire. Jerking back, he cursed, glaring at the soldiers as if they'd been the ones to burn him.

Without a wall to lean on, he sank to the floor, defeated. Did he dare let go of this anger? He'd held onto it for days, waiting for someone to come—to torture him, to interrogate him—so he could unleash his fury on the unlucky victim. But no one had come.

What were their plans for him? If last time were any indication...

Michael remembered the hours of torture and torment he'd endured at Dagon's hand after Arael had betrayed him in the valley of the Alborz.

First Arael. Now Raphael.

Would it never end?

As detrimental as his time with Dagon had been, though, he would take that torture again and again—a thousand times over if it would reverse what Raphael had done to him.

He placed his head in his hands with a sigh.

"Have you finally calmed down?" a quiet voice came from behind.

Michael stood and whirled in one quick motion. "What are you doing here?" he snarled.

Raphael appeared unphased by the venom in Michael's words as he dismissed the guards surrounding the cell. "We didn't get a chance to talk before. I wanted to—"

"I don't care what you want." Michael turned his back to his former *qanima*. "There is nothing you could say that I want to hear."

"Of course, there is." Raphael circled the cage to face Michael again. "You need to understand what is happening."

"I understand perfectly well."

"You understand nothing!" Raphael's nostrils flared. "You never even *tried* to understand."

Michael pinned him with a cold, flat stare. "So, this is about her then?"

Her… The one thing he and Raphael had disputed for centuries. Obsession, Raphael had called it. Michael called it penance.

"Of course, this is about her," Raphael said. "What else is there?"

Michael turned away from him again, but Raphael was undeterred. "You've been so blinded by your guilt over her exile that nothing else has mattered to you. Not your decaying world. Definitely not me."

Michael's voice was eerily quiet. "I did what I had to do."

"And I'm doing what *I* have to do. Surely you can understand that."

Michael worked his jaw but didn't answer.

"Do you have any idea what it was like for me all those years, watching her try to destroy you? And you…acting like it didn't matter?"

"It didn't."

"It should have!" Raphael shouted. "And what she did to you in the Alborz—" Raphael shook his head, unable to speak the words. "When she carried you out of the Void…you were unrecognizable. It took me days to heal you. And even then, I wasn't sure you'd ever be the same."

Michael's voice remained flat. "You severed our bond."

"I had to get you away from her. I tried other ways—on the ship, in the church—but you were always there. Always hovering. Apollyon needed her alone."

A roiling heat swelled in Michael's belly, a swimming feeling Michael had never felt before. "So, you work for Apollyon now?"

Raphael took a step back. "Did you ever think…" He seemed to measure his words carefully. "Did you ever think that maybe the world isn't as black or white as you make it out to be? Maybe the *right thing* isn't always so clear."

"How long?"

Raphael shifted uncomfortably. "How long what?"

"How long have you been working for him?"

Raphael closed his eyes with a sigh. "I'm not—"

"It was you...during the battle. In the First War. You weren't supposed to be there." Michael turned to face Raphael. "Were you working for him then, too?"

When Raphael didn't answer right away, Michael knew the answer.

"Get out."

Michael turned so Raphael wouldn't see the pain written all over his face. Raphael knew how much Michael blamed himself, how much he mourned for Arael after her banishment. And he had said nothing...all this time.

"It was—" Raphael stammered. "It was only supposed to be Uriah... I suppose that was Apollyon's idea of punishment for Arael's treason."

"You blame me for protecting her all those years when all this was your fault to begin with?"

When Raphael looked up, he at least had the decency to look ashamed. "He threatened you. I did what I had to, as you say. And don't forget...I was mortified that Arael got caught in the crossfire of Apollyon's wrath, but it was her choice to come after you, so do not blame me...or yourself for the choices she made."

"You should have come to me!"

"I know that now. Millennia of conflict has taught me that, but back then...we were all so naïve. We knew nothing of war. I've hated myself for centuries because I didn't come to you right away, but the damage had already been done."

Michael spread his arms wide. "And yet here we are."

"This was different. I couldn't have come to you with this. Not with so much at stake."

"'So much at stake…'" Michael repeated slowly, letting the words marinate in the air between them.

"You know that's not what I meant. I don't care about Apollyon's plans. I don't care about the earth or those repugnant humans. I care about you. I understand that protecting them has been your assignment for the past millennia, and you've done your job—the best anyone could have done—but you must remember, you had a purpose before their creation. You'll have a purpose after they're gone."

"You know…" Michael began to pace again. "You say you hate her, but you are just like her." He stopped and stepped closer to the bars until he and Raphael were face to face. "All those years with her heart filled with so much hate and revenge. That is what I see when I look at you."

Raphael's eyebrows twitched only a fraction, but Michael knew his words had hit their mark.

"You won't have to stay here long," Raphael said quietly. "And no one will hurt you. I have Apollyon's vow. Once he has what he needs from her, I will come for you."

"Don't bother."

"Michael, please." Raphael sighed.

Michael turned his back on Raphael one last time. "I hope you realize the cost of all this…before it's too late."

THIRTY-NINE

Camryn stumbled through the thicket of thorns that suddenly appeared under her feet. For what seemed like hours, she and Ethan had watched the landscape blur and shift around them. One moment, they walked on small, black pebbles, and the next they trudged through thick, wet sand. The sky changed from black rolling clouds to dark-purple, dotted with stars.

Of course, they weren't real stars. Where they were, such things didn't exist.

Ethan reached to steady her but didn't bother with words. They walked in silence, with just the occasional sigh or groan to break the monotony.

Keeping her eyes trained on the steady motion of Ethan's shoulders in front of her, Camryn thought of the illusion of him she'd experienced in her prison, the words she'd spoken to him about his mother, the gut-wrenching apology that had spewed from her.

She studied the profile of Ethan's face—the real Ethan. Could she force herself to repeat those words again? It had been hard enough the first time when she'd thought he was dead. Camryn wasn't sure she could summon them again.

On the verge of collapse, Ethan pointed to something up ahead. "Look. We just have to make it to that rock. Then we can rest."

"I can't." Camryn shook her head.

"Yes, you can. You can do anything you put your mind to," Ethan urged.

"You are the worst at pep talks. Did anyone ever tell you that?"

"Just keep moving."

Annoyingly enough, Ethan was right. With his help, Camryn did make it to the rock and practically fell onto it, exhausted. "I don't know how much longer I can do this," she said, leaning forward and bracing her elbows on her knees.

Ethan joined her, wiping the sweat from his face. He leaned back on the rock and pulled his ivory token from his pocket, twisting it in his fingers. Camryn snatched it from his hand mid-twirl.

"What's wrong?" Ethan pulled himself up from the rock.

"This shouldn't be possible. Physical objects don't pass between realms. Not unless it's linked to your appearance, like clothes or something. This should still be in your pocket wherever your body is."

Ethan eyed it curiously. "That's true…" He took the object back from Camryn and examined it. "What do you think it means?"

"I have no idea." Camryn sighed. "Maybe Michael will know—if we can ever find him."

"You really think we can free him?"

Camryn shook her head. "All I know is, I've done it once before."

She'd explained it all to him on their journey—all the gory details, from her role in Michael's capture to her helping him escape—about the heavenly army that came to rescue him and about Raphael's threat.

Ethan had listened in silence. He hadn't yelled or fumed or cursed, so Camryn was left to wonder how bad it would be if Ethan ever came face to face with Raphael again.

"Before we can free him, though, we have to find him," Ethan said, looking around. "And I don't think this particular hell has an end."

Camryn squinted into the dark expanse in front of them, then turned back from where they'd just come. With a startled cry, Camryn shot up. Ethan turned and drew in a sharp breath.

Behind them—where a thorn-blanketed desert had just been—stood a wall stretching out in either direction for as far as Camryn could see, with nothing marking its face except one dark tunnel directly in front of them.

"What the—"

"We need to go." Camryn grabbed Ethan's arm, pulling him in the opposite direction.

"Wait." Ethan pulled back. "The tunnel. It may be our way out of here."

"That tunnel," Camryn exclaimed, "mysteriously appeared when we started talking about Michael. There's no way I'm stepping foot in it."

Ethan ran his tongue over the metal ring in his lip. "Yeah, you're probably right."

Camryn had just released Ethan's arm when a voice echoing from the darkness froze her feet to the ground. The muscles in her neck tensed, and her mouth turned to cotton.

"Are you two just going to stand there conversing about the complexities of the Void?" the voice drawled. "I was hoping for a chase."

Camryn didn't turn to look. She couldn't have even if she'd wanted to. By the way Ethan's body tensed, she knew he was just as terrified.

They locked eyes for one terrible, agonizing moment, so many apologies in that one look.

Then the chains snapped around their wrists.

FORTY

With hair the color of chestnut, braided beard hanging low on his chest, and blue-green scales shaping each side of his face, disappearing into the bare flesh of his neck—Dagon stepped from the tunnel, fiery staff in hand.

"Hmmm…" he harumphed. "It seems my hunch was correct." He raked his eyes over his two captives, taking in their youthful and very human appearance.

Never an angel to waste words, Dagon turned swiftly and said with no emotion in his voice, "Come with me."

Camryn's legs turned to jelly. Dagon—the Punisher—had captured them, and power-dampening chains encircled their wrists.

Two Fallen soldiers stepped forward and grabbed Camryn and Ethan by the arm, leading them into the tunnel after Dagon.

Camryn stumbled forward.

She could do nothing but stare straight ahead. Even Ethan seemed to understand. They wouldn't free Michael. They would never find a way out of here. They would follow Dagon into the depths of Hell, never to be heard from again.

Inside the tunnel, darkness swelled from the cave walls, too thick for Camryn's human eyes. But the soldiers yanked their restraints and prodded them along, guiding them to their destination.

Camryn hadn't experienced many moments like these in her life—moments of resignation. Moments that drained all the fight from her and made her willing to accept whatever fate lay in front of her.

Risking the consequences, Camryn extended her hand in the darkness. Somehow, her fingers found Ethan's straight away. As soon as her skin brushed his, his fingers opened, taking hers with a grip that reminded Camryn how strong she was. He wouldn't be gentle with her. Neither of them needed that.

Eventually, they emerged from the darkness into a large, dimly-lit chamber. Camryn recognized the space from her memories, the place where Apollyon had penetrated her mind and hijacked her thoughts after he'd figured out how to steal the powers of other angels—Apollyon's throne room.

Seraphim stood guard at each exit, just as they had since Apollyon had claimed the title of Lord of the Underworld. A circle of small flames lit the room, casting long shadows on the stone walls.

And right smack in the middle of the space sat Apollyon.

Even in this underground chamber, Apollyon wore a light gray tailored suit, the silk pocket square the same color as his onyx throne.

It never mattered what he chose to wear, though. Apollyon blended perfectly into any environment—the deadliest chameleon. His wide-set eyes greeted them—eyes that appeared kind at first glance, but Camryn knew better. Spend any time gazing into them, and you would fall into the emptiness of their depths.

"Arael, my dear." He raised his hand in greeting. "Or should I call you Camryn?" Apollyon rose from his throne, not waiting for an answer. Approaching them both, he spoke only to Camryn, eyeing her up and down. "Look at you. Still presenting yourself as a child. Even here."

Camryn held up her hands. She'd noticed that, too. She and Ethan had both retained their earthly forms, even free of the physical bodies that had held them.

"Is that a problem?"

"Not at all. I'm just surprised. I thought you would manifest here in your more powerful form."

Camryn had expected the same thing, but after surviving her prison of insurmountable fears and managing to break Ethan out of his, she had determined that, perhaps, this was her more powerful form.

Without taking his eyes from her, Apollyon flicked his wrist, a signal to two of the closest guard who closed in, securing Ethan on either side. Before Camryn knew what was happening, Dagon had sliced his staff across Ethan's chest, not deep enough to send his soul to the death pits, but deep enough to elicit a roar of pain. Ethan doubled over as the Heavenly Fire scorched his skin.

Camryn caught the weight of him, lowering him to the floor. Black streaks spread from the wound, but he wasn't disintegrating into smoke. Ethan hissed through his teeth and squeezed her hand with enough strength to let her know his injury wasn't fatal.

She slung a venomous glance back to Apollyon. "What the hell did you do that for?"

"To ensure your cooperation," Apollyon said, striding back to his throne. "I'm sure you understand that it could get much worse for him."

Dagon and the guards stepped back, leaving Ethan panting on his knees and Camryn kneeling beside him.

"I'm fine," Ethan said. "Don't let him distract you."

Michael had warned her. Apollyon would use everyone she loved against her. He'd already killed her parents—just to cause her pain. She had no doubt that Ethan would suffer the same fate many times over. And she would be forced to witness it.

"You've got my attention." Camryn stood. "And my word." She glanced down at Ethan, still trying to gather the strength to stand. "I won't give you any trouble. As long as he isn't hurt."

Apollyon slapped a hand to his knee. "That is exactly what I hoped to hear," he exclaimed. "Come. Sit." Apollyon waved his hand, and another throne appeared beside him.

Ethan raised a hand to her, indicating that he was okay.

Camryn padded over and lowered herself onto the hard, flat seat of the throne, not letting more than a few seconds pass before checking a glance back toward Ethan.

"So, you've got us here. What now?"

"So hasty," Apollyon *tsk*ed. "We have so much catching up to do. So much has happened for the both of us. Let's chat."

"Why?" Camryn's confusion was getting harder to disguise. "You're wasting time on small talk when you have a world to destroy?"

Camryn knew there were questions that Apollyon would kill to have the answers to, but one look into her mind would tell him that she didn't have the answers that he desired.

Apollyon sighed. "I am not *destroying* the world." He leaned in as if sharing a secret. "I am cleansing it. Cleansing it of those parasitic vermin that Elohim created." He straightened in his seat again. "Did you know that I was once the protector of Earth?"

Ethan's labored breathing cut through their conversation, but Camryn forced her eyes to remain focused on Apollyon. *Keep his attention on me.*

"That's right. I stood at the entrance of Eden, sword in hand, and proudly defended what I was told would be mine one day." His eyes lost focus for a brief moment. "It was beautiful. As you well remember."

Then his face grew dark and his voice hard as stone. "And then He created man—the worst blite upon all of Creation. I thought Him infallible until that moment. I thought He could do no wrong. But you see what they've done. They are overcome with greed and lust and pride."

"You made them that way."

"They were born that way," Apollyon spat. "I just pulled it out of them—to make Him see. To show Him how vile they were. But He couldn't accept it. Always blamed me—as you're doing now."

"And after you've purged them, then what? Harriet didn't mention ruling the earth with you. She thinks she will rule the heavens. Is that your next conquest?"

"Perhaps," Apollyon said with a shrug.

"You tried that once. Didn't turn out too well for you."

"Ah, but I've learned so much since then. And am much more powerful."

"But Harriet isn't. She's a vulnerable human. How have you convinced her that she will even be able to rule with you?"

Apollyon's eyes shrank the tiniest degree. He studied Camryn, calculating. "Harriet is stronger than you assume," he said finally.

"I don't know. The world is…unpredictable. Especially right now."

"She is in the safest place she could possibly be," he said, his voice growing impatient. "Enough about her. I want to talk about you."

Camryn threw a cautious glance at Ethan. He was standing now—shaky but upright—and she decided she really didn't care what they talked about, as long as they kept talking.

"What do you want to know?"

Apollyon surprised her by taking her hand in his. "Camryn, my dear—I assume you want me to call you Camryn, is that right?"

Camryn nodded, staring at her hand enveloped in Apollyon's.

"There are so many questions that I want to ask you—so much I want to know. But right now…" He squeezed her hand, encouraging her to meet his eyes. "Right now, there is only one question you can answer for me."

Camryn swallowed, waiting.

"Will you join me in my quest?"

Camryn stared at his mouth as if this were a badly dubbed foreign film, sure she'd heard wrong.

"Well?" Apollyon prodded after a moment.

"I'm waiting for the punchline," she managed to say.

Apollyon chuckled. "This is no joke, I assure you. I have wanted you by my side since you escaped from me in Syria. It was then that I realized just how smart and resourceful you are. What an asset you'd be to my court."

Camryn wrinkled her nose. This was wrong. A lie. A stumbling disorientation clouded her mind—the same awkward daze that she'd felt after waking from his mind control the first time she visited this place. She'd been standing in one place, then blinked, waking up in another. It was the bending of reality. The twisting of truth.

"I thought you wanted to kill me."

Apollyon put a hand to his chest with a soft gasp. Anyone who didn't know him would presume his astonishment genuine.

"Why would you think that?"

Fifty years of memories ran through her head—her years as Arael, hiding in New York City, being approached by Dagon and offered a seat in Apollyon's court in exchange for capturing Michael. And now, even in Harriet's appeals for them to turn themselves in…yes, she'd threatened Camryn's family, but never her or Ethan directly.

Camryn's mind raced. Could that be right? Surely there was something she wasn't remembering.

But… Camryn shook her head. It didn't matter.

"I don't care if you'd spent the last fifty years actively protecting me, it will never make up for the pain you've caused me." She looked to Ethan, thinking of his mother lying lifeless on the dirty ground outside the temple. "The pain you've caused us."

She brought her eyes to meet Apollyon's with conviction. "I will *never* work for you again."

Apollyon sighed. "I was afraid you'd say that." He pushed himself to his feet and turned to face her. "And I am truly sorry to hear it."

Camryn blinked as his hands began moving toward her. What was he going to do? Kill her right here? So quickly?

Only then did Michael's warning come back to her. "*You have something that he wants. Don't let him take it from you.*"

Of course. Camryn flinched away from Apollyon's approaching hands.

Of course, that's why we're here.

"Don't fight me," he commanded, and as if his words held infinite power, Camryn lost all ability to resist. She sat, frozen, not even able to glance away from Apollyon's pulsating eyes.

"You've left me with no other choice. I'm afraid we've run out of time for persuasion."

"I–I don't have anything you want. My powers are useless."

Apollyon gripped Camryn's chin and lowered his face so close to hers that his breath licked her cheek as he spoke. "Why do you lie to yourself? You know it's there. You've felt it already."

Camryn shook her head again. She didn't feel anything.

A glazed look had come into Apollyon's eyes, his voice nothing more than a whisper now. "If I can see it, so can you." He ran his nose along her cheekbone as if he could smell it on her skin.

"But perhaps it is better this way." He drew back, looking her in the eyes again. "You aren't even aware of the potential that lies within you. It could be years before you can properly utilize it."

Words erupted from Camryn like vomit. "Whatever you think you see—this power you think I have—how do you think you can control it so quickly? A power that isn't even yours?" Camryn didn't know what she was saying, her only desire to postpone whatever Apollyon had planned for her.

Apollyon pulled back his lips to reveal sparkling teeth. "Of course, I can." His eyes grew wide with unchecked hunger. "And it will give me unlimited power."

He grasped her face, the same cold grip that had held her hand just moments before. Camryn braced herself for the horror that would follow, but instead of her own cries, it was Ethan's roar that filled the room.

Apollyon whirled, and Camryn shot up, trying in vain to bring the electricity back to her fingers. "What did you do to him?"

Dagon frowned down at Ethan as the boy toppled to the floor.

Apollyon's outrage matched Camryn's as he shouted at Dagon. "You were not ordered to harm him!"

"I haven't touched him."

Dagon leveled his staff at Ethan as if he suspected a ruse.

Camryn took a step toward Ethan—Apollyon's chains be damned—when an incinerating fire sliced through her. Her eyes shot to Dagon, but he stood just as he'd been, staff directed at Ethan, looking as confused as everyone else.

Camryn doubled over in pain. She crashed to her knees as her insides were shredded and her bones crushed to dust. Her face contorted and the scream that ripped from her shook the walls of the chamber.

Ethan reached for her but was overtaken by his own pain. He struggled to his knees, gasping for breath.

And then he disappeared.

FORTY-ONE

Camryn coughed then groaned as she rolled to her side in what felt like slow motion. A soul-splitting scream escaped her throat as her broken bones cracked and popped into place.

Bones? Actual bones?

Then she noticed other things as well: the cool air on her skin, the breeze brushing her face—each item her mind registered bringing her out from under the oppressive weight of the Void.

I'm free.

But the pain… The pain was too much. It was like surgery without anesthesia, her insides mending inside her.

All the damage that had been rendered by the explosion—her shredded skin, her broken bones, even her punctured lung—was being repaired…ever so slowly.

Even before she attempted to pry open her eyes, Camryn ran her fingers through the dirt under her hand and hitched a breath of fresh, cool air into her lungs. *Concentrate on that. Not the pain.*

Not the pain.

"Son of a *bitch*," she gritted through her teeth.

No matter how much she tried to push it from her mind, the harder it pressed on her. She felt everything—every bone healing, every tissue reconnecting, every hole closing.

"Give it a moment," a rough voice echoed. "It's not every day that I bring someone back from the dead."

Oh, God… She knew that voice.

Camryn looked up to see Raphael kneeling beside her, one arm casually propped on a knee, the purple sky of dusk over his shoulder, and the sounds of gunfire echoing in the distance.

Ethan? The quick jerk of her head sent a shooting pain down her spine, but she had to see him.

And there he was. Sitting in the road beside her with his head in his hands.

She eyed Raphael with caution. "You…saved us?"

Raphael flicked his gaze upward. "Well, I didn't have much choice, now did I?"

"I…have no idea what that means." Camryn wiggled her toes and took a few deep breaths, assessing her pain.

"How long were we—" Ethan started.

"Not long." Raphael surveyed the area. "Eighteen hours or so."

Camryn followed Raphael's gaze around the courtyard. The dust had settled, but evidence of the battle lay heaped in ruins and scattered in the streets. All the angels who'd fought here had either died or moved their fight elsewhere.

The blinking red lights of the cameras had long since died out. The courtyard was quiet. Camryn wondered if the reporters were still nearby and what the world was being told about this supernatural battle they'd been witness to.

"Why?" was the only thing Camryn could think to say.

Raphael stared for a moment before answering. "Pockets of fighting have cropped up all over the globe," he began. "Mostly angelic, but some humans have joined them."

Camryn tried to sit up. "They're here? In the physical realm?"

"Does it matter? The video those children took of you disposing of those guards and Ethan's bullet wounds healing could be written off as fancy editing, but this…" Raphael motioned to the dust-covered cameras that had first captured the battle. "The world knows about us now. There is no going back from this. No one on our side knows what is happening, and without Michael to guide them, angels from every order are joining the fight; Guardians and Seraphim—angels who've never wielded a weapon before—and they're being slaughtered."

Camryn couldn't hide the horror on her face.

"Eventually there won't be any of us left."

Ethan scoffed. "You can't tell me you didn't see this coming."

"I didn't," Raphael said a little too quickly. "I didn't have any idea it would come to this. If I had…" He exhaled slowly. "I never would have agreed to help him."

Camryn's head flopped back onto the tire of the burned-out van. "Vengeance is a nearsighted bitch, isn't she?"

Raphael snorted. "She's exhausting is what she is." He extended his hand and hauled them both to their feet. "This doesn't mean I've forgiven you," he said to Camryn. "I never will."

"That's fair," Camryn replied.

Raphael looked into the distance and rested his hand on his sword. "But your friends need you now. And I'm sure my help wouldn't be welcome, no matter how much they need it."

Camryn and Ethan exchanged a look. "Where are they?"

Arriving a few moments later on a small hill overlooking the salty bank of the Dead Sea, Camryn blinked several times at the sight before them. Akira was there, along with Ronan and Zephaniah. But barely a sound could slip through Camryn's lips at what she saw rising from the water.

"Mother of God..."

FORTY-TWO

Apollyon had tried his hand at Creation over the centuries—hideous creatures that could never survive in the physical realm; hybrid beasts with a scorpion body and a fish-like tail, a serpent with three heads, or the abomination before them now.

"It's a leviathan," Raphael explained. "A rather small one compared to the other beasts he has waiting to be unleashed."

Akira's scream reached them as the monster loomed over her, taunting her with its thick tongue. No matter that the torso of the snake-like monster stood twelve feet tall with three rows of razor-sharp teeth chomping at the arrows she continued to lob its way. Even from where they stood, its white eyes glowed with growing menace.

Ronan and Zephaniah stood on either side of the creature, swinging swords and fiery chains, trying to lasso it like a bucking bull.

"We have to get down there," Ethan said. "We have to help them."

"I'll leave you two to it." Raphael backed away from them and flared his massive wings. "Someone will be coming to collect me soon. And I have one more thing to do before I go."

Before Camryn and Ethan could say goodbye, Raphael disappeared.

Ethan studied the scene below him, the leviathan's teeth snapping closer and closer to Akira with every nip. "We'll never get to them in time. They're too far away."

Camryn scanned the area between them and the angels on the beach. "You're right," she said, running down the hill toward the water's edge. A good seventy-five yards separated them from the monster, but Camryn touched her hand to the water, sending her electric current its way.

"Come on!" Akira screamed. "Just a little closer, you slimy bastard!" She taunted the leviathan, trying to lure the thing onto the beach so Ronan and Zephaniah could secure it in their chains. He slithered closer—so close she could smell its rancid breath with every chomp of its yellowed teeth. Just a few more arrows and then…

The leviathan reared back its head, readying to lunge for her again when it let out a roar, slinging its head from side to side. It convulsed once. Twice. Then collapsed onto the salty beach, its eyes rolling.

Yes! One of her arrows must have hit its mark.

Ronan tossed the fiery rope over the leviathan's head and into Zephaniah's waiting hand. They each held one edge of the rope as Akira vaulted herself onto the beast's skull and slung her legs around the creature's neck. She leaned forward, toward its massive ears. `

"Not so tough, now, are you?" She yanked on the rope, bringing its head back a little farther. "I ought to slice out your slimy tongue and mount it on my wall."

Coming out of its paralysis, the leviathan strained against the ropes that held him in place.

"Stop playing around and just kill it already," Zephaniah called to her as he and Ronan held tight to the restraints.

"Fine," Akira said as she brought her blade up and thrust it down into the leviathan's neck, slicing upward then letting its head fall back to the ground into the puddle of blood that had already accumulated there. "You guys never let me have any fun."

She raised her sword, readying to plunge the blade into the leviathan's skull when something in the distance caught her eye.

Her sword dropped, and the two males turned to see what had caused her such alarm. They all stared as two figures ran toward them on the beach.

Akira stood atop the leviathan's neck, her fiery curls billowing across her face. "Are you two seeing what I'm seeing?"

Even Zephaniah remained speechless. When the two figures reached them, Ethan flashed a wide grin and slapped Ronan on the back. "You guys looked like you could use some help."

Akira stared, not trusting her eyes. "You were dead." *This doesn't make any sense.*

The boy standing before her now had a smile on his face—not the Ethan she'd come to know over the last week.

Ethan lifted his hands in the air. "And now we're not."

Akira hopped off the neck of the leviathan, her boots burrowing into the sand. "How?"

"Raphael," Ethan answered, "if you can believe it."

"The prophecy didn't say anything about this," Ronan offered.

The girl standing beside Ethan remained silent, observing. Could this be some kind of a trap? Shapeshifters of some kind? But the aura around them reassured her that she wasn't losing her mind. Something like that couldn't be faked.

Akira approached them cautiously, focusing her eyes on Ethan's face.

Camryn cleared her throat but said nothing.

"Raising the dead—it's forbidden." Akira's eyes locked on Ethan's. "Even for him."

Ethan nodded solemnly. "He said as much before he took off. I imagine we won't be seeing him again any time soon."

I saw you die, she wanted to say, *and with you, a piece of me died, too.* But she would never say that, not even to Ethan. She reached to touch his arm. Could she let herself believe he was really okay?

Ronan didn't have the same problem. He ran to Camryn and crushed her into a hug, swinging her around until she laughed.

She smacked him on the back. "Put me down, you idiot."

Zephaniah frowned. "Raphael is the idiot," he said, pulling the bloody rope back into his belt. "Not that–not that I'm not grateful for what he did," he stammered as if just realizing his blunder. "You two saved our asses just then." He shoved his thumb toward the creature bleeding out on the beach.

"No worries," Ethan said. "I think we can all agree; Raphael is definitely an idiot."

They all laughed. All except Akira. She planted her fists on her hips and finally turned away from Ethan. "We have to find President Kaya and put an end to this."

Ronan shrugged. "We don't even know where to start."

"I think I have an idea," Camryn said. "But we're going to need a portal. Transporting isn't going to get us where we need to go."

Akira snorted. "Well, good luck with that."

"Actually..." Zephaniah regarded Camryn with a knowing eye. "I think I know someone who can help us."

FORTY-THREE

"*M*e?" Camryn blurted at Zephaniah's suggestion. "I can't—I wouldn't even know where to start."

"Nonsense. I'm sure you've conjured plenty of portals in your day. And you're the only Archangel who isn't in prison or on the run. If you want a portal, you're going to have to make one."

"I'm *not* an Archangel…" Camryn stammered. But she was. At least…she had been.

"Stop," Ethan said, interrupting her stammering. "Stop saying you can't." He pulled her away from the others, speaking in a whisper. "You do this every time. You think you can't do something, but you always figure it out in the end. Stop doubting yourself. Stop saying you can't, and just do it."

"This is a little diff—"

"No. it's not. Logistically, it should work. You have your Tempest powers. We have our *qanima* connection back. You should be able to do this, too. Stop overthinking. You are the strongest, smartest, cutest person I know. Don't even let yourself imagine that it doesn't work. It's going to work. That's it. Simple as that."

"Look at you." Camryn cleared her throat. "I knew you had a good pep talk in you somewhere."

Ethan pulled one corner of his mouth into a grin and lowered his gaze. "We all know you can do this. You don't have to prove anything to us."

"Okay, well." Camryn pointed at a spot a few yards down the beach. "I'm just gonna..." She walked to the spot and, facing away from her friends, planted her feet. She turned back to find everyone staring after her, and they quickly averted their eyes.

Okay...remember the words. She thought back to her memories of Michael conjuring the portal in the church in New York. *Aperta sunt in nominee Domini*—that's what he'd said.

Camryn was heartened to realize she understood the meaning of each word this time—that had to mean something, right? She stretched her hands in front of her and repeated, "*Aperta sunt in nominee Domini,*" with as much authority as she could muster.

Nothing happened.

"Does anyone have a sword I could borrow?"

Ronan rushed up and handed over his broadsword with an encouraging nod.

The sword fell into her hand like a long-lost friend. She hadn't held such a weapon since her celestial days, but it felt light and...*perfect* in her grip. Camryn turned back to the beach in front of her. *Come on. This has to work.*

She stretched out the sword, just as she remembered Michael doing, just as she had done so many times before, and repeated the words again. "*Aperta sunt in nominee Domini.*"

Something sparked from the end of the sword, and Akira squealed. Camryn's jaw dropped. Something had *happened*. Not the thing they had wanted, but something.

She set her feet, closed her eyes, picturing the place she needed to go, and repeated the words one more time.

She heard the hushed whispers behind her before she dared to open her eyes. When she did, a swirling blue portal lay open in front of her.

"I could be wrong about this," Camryn said a few moments later after she'd explained her suspicions to the others. "But just in case, we should be ready for a fight."

"If you're right, you won't be able to kill her there," Akira said. "We'll have to get her back to this realm."

Camryn stared into the portal she'd somehow managed to create. "I'm sure we'll figure something out."

The group took one collective step toward the portal when Zephaniah's Halo buzzed in his pocket. His face fell when he looked at the message displayed there.

"Raphael?" Ronan asked.

Camryn didn't think she'd ever seen a more regretful nod. "Duty calls," he said with a dramatic bow. "Good luck in there." And then Zephaniah vanished from in front of them.

Ronan's face grew somber. "Well, I guess it's up to the four of us then."

Thankfully there was no time to think of all the ways things could go south as they stepped through to the other side of the portal. Camryn took in the vast expanse of orange dirt to her left. To her right—the backside of Conclave Hall.

"Wow…" Ethan mumbled. "Welcome to Eden, I guess."

Camryn gripped Ronan's sword in her hand. He'd drawn his daggers and readied himself for battle.

Akira nodded toward the front of the structure. "Let's go."

They eased their way around the building but were spotted straight away. Three Fallen guards landed in front of them, swords drawn.

"Well, it looks like you were right," Akira said to Camryn.

One soldier, as pale as death, ran his eyes over Camryn, Akira, and Ronan, sizing up their weapons. Apparently, the weaponless Ethan didn't even warrant a glance. Ronan jerked to the side, drawing their attention while Ethan threw two balls of flame into the middle of the group of guards, knocking them all to the ground.

"Come on!" Ethan shouted to the others, jumping around the stunned guards.

His tiny inferno may have stunned them, but they wouldn't stay that way for long.

As Camryn and the others rounded the corner, running into three more guards, the others caught up to them. Akira turned, hurling a dagger right into the pale one's throat. She didn't wait to see the puff of black dust he turned into before whirling back around to find another guard almost upon her. She flinched with no time to react, but Ronan's dagger sliced across her attacker, misting him into a cloud of smoke.

Camryn stood, watching her friends fight off the guards, unsure of herself and the weapon she held. Even Ethan fought them with only the fire in his hands.

She looked down at the sword. Could she even use it? Did she need to? She had other weapons at her disposal—inside her.

She was just about to toss the weapon back to Ronan when another guard lunged at her. On instinct, Camryn swung the sword, colliding with her attacker's in a deafening clang.

Her eyes traveled up the blade, across the hilt, up the chest, and to the face of the angel on the other end of the weapon.

He growled at her and lunged again. She twisted and brought the sword around and down, never faltering when it met soft flesh.

When the angel disappeared, Camryn stared down at the sword, dripping with the angel's insides. "The sword of the Lord is bathed in blood."

The sword of the Lord.

"Last one," Akira said, rising from the ground and stabbing her dagger back into its spot on her belt as the last guard misted away in a gray cloud. "But, why were there only six of them?"

Ethan stepped past her, his hands burning a light blue. "Something doesn't feel right."

They all trudged through the Hall, memories assaulting Camryn from all sides. How many times had she been here, assembled with her Order, receiving Gabriel's message?

They approached the stage in the center of the space, the one where Michael had stood during the last Conclave and sentenced so many Fallen—the Founders—to their eternal prisons.

From atop the stage, they stopped and turned.

"Where could she be?" Ronan mumbled just as a legion of Fallen soldiers emerged from every section, descending from the rafters, leaving them no path of escape.

"Uh, guys…" Ethan said. "That's a lot more than six guards."

A soft laugh echoed through the Hall before Harriet Kaya emerged from behind the stage, her hands clasped in front of her and a look of pure joy on her face.

Camryn's heart pounded in her ears as she gazed at the once polished and professional Harriet Kaya now clad in black fighting leather from head to toe.

"You have no idea how happy I am to see you two." The woman shook her head as if she couldn't believe her luck. "I have to admit, your death in the plaza was a bit of a miscalculation on my part." She wagged a finger at them as if they were naughty children who'd pulled off a devious prank.

"See, I was under the impression that you couldn't be killed, so when you died…" Her eyes grew wide and she blew out a breath. "That landed me in a bit of hot water for a bit…until you popped up in your little cages and got me off the hook. I guess I owe you a debt of gratitude for that," she said, whipping a gun from her waistband.

"But now that we know you can die and what will happen to you when you do," she said, glancing between Camryn and Ethan. "I'm afraid I'm going to have to kill you again." She shrugged noncommittally. "Get me back in Apollyon's good graces, you know?"

Camryn knew she and Ethan couldn't be killed here, in the same way that Harriet couldn't, but that didn't appease her much. Just like their plan to remove Harriet from Eden and kill her on the beach, Camryn and Ethan could be removed and disposed of just as easily. Easier, actually, as she didn't think Ronan and Akira could do much to defend them against the encroaching horde.

But it looked like they were willing to try.

Akira and Ronan raised their daggers. Ethan brought up his hands, ready to ignite at his command.

I guess this is it, then. Camryn raised Ronan's sword, but thoughts raced through her mind at such speed, if someone asked her name in that moment, she might not be able to answer.

She'd just taken a staggering step forward when a loud swishing sound drew everyone's attention overhead.

A swarm of severely disfigured, winged creatures hovered in the open space above the Conclave Hall. They held a celestial form, but their faces were mutilated beyond recognition, their bodies covered in layers upon layers of scars. If they had once been angels, what were they now?

Wary of these interlopers' intentions, Camryn wasn't sure if she should run or rejoice. Even when Harriet's soldiers turned their attention from Camryn and her friends to rush up to meet the zombie-like angels in the air, colliding with a deafening clang, she remained on guard.

Where had these angels come from? And how had they known where to find them?

The feral creatures held no weapons but defended themselves with a ferocity that told Camryn that even if they weren't there on behalf of Harriet Kaya, she should probably still steer clear.

Her gawking only lasted a moment before the few soldiers left on the ground closed in. She raised her blade to the soldier in front of her.

"Get to President Kaya," she yelled to Akira, who sprouted two ash-colored wings and flew through the airborne battle toward the stage where the President stood with her gun as her only defense. Akira descended upon the woman and, with her guards busy with the Founders, was no match for Akira's celestial strength and speed.

"Meet me at the portal!" Akira called to the others.

But there was no way through, by foot or by air. Camryn slung her blade left and right as Fallen soldiers sprung at her from all sides. Another angel dove for her with a speed almost faster than her eyes could track. She raised her sword, but the angel stopped in his tracks and his eyes focused on something behind her. The shock on his face gave her pause—right before she was snatched into the air.

Camryn screamed and kicked and jabbed the sword upward. "Careful with that thing!" a voice called down to her.

"Ronan!" she cried, but he continued to haul her through the air like a hawk with its prey. He flew directly toward a dueling pair of angels in the crowded sky above the Conclave stage. "Look out!" Camryn shouted.

Ronan banked to the left, and Camryn's stomach rose in her throat. She clamped her mouth shut to keep from emptying its contents all over the battle below her.

Dip.

Turn.

Spin.

Oh, God...I'm going to vomit. She wanted to close her eyes, but angels flew through the air, blocking their escape. Ronan wielded his dagger in his free hand, fending them off at every turn.

"Put that sword to some use, why don't you?" Ronan called down to her.

"You just better hang on to me!" she screamed back, slicing the weapon at the soldiers flying toward them as they fell one by one.

"On your left!" Ronan called to her, but the circular blade had already spun past, slicing into her side. Camryn sucked in a breath, bracing for the pain.

But none came. Camryn said another prayer of thanks for her humanity when the flying weapon went straight through her without a mark.

I don't think I'll ever get used to that, she thought as Ronan broke through the wall of soldiers and into the air above the Hall. Speeding toward the portal, Camryn looked back to see a dozen of Apollyon's men following close behind.

"Hurry! They're coming!"

"Let's go! Let's go!" Ronan called to Akira and Ethan, who stood with Harriet Kaya on the crest of the portal.

"Took you long enough," Akira shouted as they followed Ronan and Camryn through.

Ronan crashed onto the beach on the other side of the portal, Camryn in tow. The portal snapped shut behind them, but not before two of their pursuers tumbled through and landed beside them.

"Get me out of here!" Harriet called to her soldiers as she struggled in Akira's celestial grasp.

Akira yanked the woman behind her as easily as if she were a child.

Ronan stood and straightened his armor. He spun his daggers through the air as the two soldiers lunged for Akira. The weapons found the spot of vulnerability in their armor, and the angels disintegrated into smoke.

Camryn blinked at the spot where the two soldiers had been. At the closed portal. At the dead leviathan still lying on the beach.

We made it.

She gripped her head in her hands as her knees gave out. Ethan caught her by the arm, pulling her back to her feet. "I can't believe we just did that."

Her relief was interrupted, though, by Harriet's delirious laughter.

Akira snarled. "What is so funny?"

"What are you going to do now?" The woman laughed. "Hold me for ransom? Demand Apollyon clean up his mess and leave the nice people alone?" she finished with a fake pout.

"No," Akira said, eyeing Camryn's gun and shoving Harriet toward her. "Now we're going to kill you."

FORTY-FOUR

Camryn pulled the gun from her waistband. *Oh yeah*. That *was* the plan, wasn't it? And Camryn had been fine with that arrangement when the woman had been trying to kill her friends. But now…with Harriet Kaya standing here on the beach, outnumbered and docile, Camryn couldn't imagine herself pulling the trigger.

"He's promised you so much," Camryn said, still staring at the gun. "Why do you believe him?"

"Because he's her father," Ronan stated, coming to stand in front of the woman. "Isn't that right, Harriet?"

Ethan's lips parted, and Akira almost dropped Harriet's arm. "*What?*"

"I should have figured it out when I fought you back at the embassy," Ronan continued. "I mean, no human sheds light out of a wound."

"And what if he is?" Harriet's eyes narrowed. "That changes nothing."

Ronan glanced at the gun in Camryn's hand. "I think it changes everything."

Camryn's eyes darted from Harriet to Ronan and back again.

"Is that true?" Camryn asked.

"Well, she's not going to answer you now." Akira rolled her eyes.

"You saw it for yourself," Ronan said. "It's the only thing that makes sense. It's the reason he hid her in Eden. The only reason she's still alive.

"How old are you?" Ronan asked Harriet. "Fifty-seven?"

Akira's eyes widened as if things were starting to make sense. "You must have been his backup plan when our mission in Syria failed."

"How dare you," Harriet seethed. "I was born to rule with him. This was his plan all along. I am no one's back up plan."

"So, it's true." Ethan took a step forward.

Camryn took this all in, wondering what it would mean for their plan. Could Harriet even be killed? Ronan or Akira certainly couldn't do it. She was still half human, after all.

Can I?

"Camryn, stop wasting time and just do it," Akira yelled.

Camryn leaned her head back and peered up at the clouds. If she'd learned anything in the past few days, it was to trust her instincts. What were they telling her now?

"Camryn..."

"You're asking me to kill someone right now. Just give me a minute, will you?" Camryn dug out the memories from the plaza that she'd tucked away for this very occasion. Images of her parents fighting and dying and Elizabeth crying on her knees before her. She'd wanted to kill Harriet so badly in that moment. She would have if Raphael's cuffs hadn't been on her wrists.

Her grip tightened on the gun as she immersed herself in the anguish and grief she hadn't yet allowed herself to feel.

The tears she'd cried in the Void had been for her parents and what they'd had to endure. The tears that welled in her eyes now were selfish tears—tears for her own loss and pain.

Her throat burned. Her chest ached as if it would crack in two. But she still couldn't make herself level the gun.

"She can't do it." Harriet laughed again.

Ethan yanked the gun from Camryn's hand. "Well, I can."

Camryn started to protest, but Harriet took advantage of the distraction and lunged for her, grabbing Camryn by the shoulder and spinning her around with a leather-clad arm around her neck.

"Hand over the gun."

"Not a chance in hell." Ethan almost laughed.

"Willing to risk your little girlfriend's life, are you? What gall you have." Harriet smiled. "Your mother would have been proud. Too bad she isn't around to see you now."

The gun faltered in Ethan's grip. "What about my mother?" he asked with a hitch in his voice.

Harriet pulled away enough to peer at Camryn before bursting into laughter again. "Oh, dear. You haven't told him?"

Camryn's face had already gone numb at the mention of Ethan's mother. "Don't," she whispered. But it was already done.

"Oh, this is too good." Harriet continued to laugh. "Now, I have to hear this. Please." She inclined her head. "Please tell him that his mother is dead. That you could have saved her, but you chose yourself instead."

Camryn shook her head in the crook of Harriet's elbow. *That isn't how it happened...*

"You...what?" Ethan's shoulders dropped and shadows filled his eyes. Camryn wanted to run to him, to sling her arms around him, to take away his pain like she had in Yon's apartment.

But Harriett had her in a pretty efficient choke hold, so the best she could offer was a grief-stricken expression.

"It–it's not like that," Camryn stammered. "It didn't happen like that at all."

"So, it's true? My mother is dead?"

Camryn swallowed hard, her eyes holding the answer to his question.

Tears filled Ethan's eyes, but the gun remained trained on Harriet. "You let her die?"

"I couldn't..." Camryn couldn't force the words over the lump in her throat.

"Well." Harriet sighed. "This has been oddly satisfying, but now that we've gotten that out of the way..." She nodded toward the weapon in Ethan's hand.

Ethan shook his head and adjusted his grip. "This doesn't change anything between me and you."

"Then she dies," Harriet said as she tightened her elbow under Camryn's chin.

With one last apologetic look to Ethan, Camryn dropped, letting her body weight pull Harriet forward. Bringing her hands up at the same time, she grabbed the woman's head and rolled her up and over, slamming her onto the beach in front of her. Camryn slung her body around to straddle the woman, but Harriet bucked her hips to the left, sending Camryn tumbling onto the sand.

Camryn sprang to her feet in a flash, facing the woman again. Harriet met her with a flying fist, connecting squarely with Camryn's jaw. Her head rang, but she'd been dealt worse. She threw her own punch, but Harriet caught her wrist and spun her around again. This time, Harriet pulled a knife from her belt and held it to Camryn's throat.

All three of her friends moved then, but Harriet stared them down through the mess of hair that had fallen from her neat bun. "Don't move." She blew a strand of hair out of her eyes. "I'm not going to tell you again."

"Don't do it," Camryn called to Ethan, prompting Harriet to press the blade into the soft skin on the side of Camryn's neck.

Camryn closed her eyes, offering a silent prayer. She'd been through scenarios like this with her dad so many times. *"What will you do if he has a gun? What if he has a knife?"* But those were all hypothetical situations played out with a person who wasn't actually trying to kill her. Would his instructions work in this all-too-real situation? Only one way to find out.

Camryn brought her hand up and gripped the blade. This would do some damage, but nothing that wouldn't heal. She pushed the weapon away while spinning out of Harriet's grasp. The knife sliced into Camryn's hand, but she'd been prepared for that. She stumbled away, but Harriet grabbed Camryn by the hair. Ethan leveled the gun at the woman, hesitating.

"Don't shoot!" Camryn screamed.

They were too close. And moving too fast. And Ethan had never held a gun before a day in his life.

Camryn dropped to the ground, bringing Harriet down on top of her, acutely aware that the woman still held the blade securely in her hand. Harriet raised the knife just as a shot rang out, ricocheting off the surrounding hills. Harriet dropped onto Camryn's chest, spewing blood onto her already mud-covered clothes.

Dead. She's dead. She's on top of me, and she's dead.

Camryn kicked and pushed the woman's lifeless husk off of her, then scrambled to a sitting position, her breath hitching in her throat.

When Ethan turned his back from the scene, Ronan stepped forward. "Hey, hey, it's okay. Slow down." Camryn tried to obey him, tried to catch the breath that evaded her.

"Is she—" Camryn gasped in another gulp of air.

"Yeah," Ronan said as Akira came to stand behind him, her fists planted on her hips.

"What the hell happened?" Akira asked right before her eyes landed on the gun in Camryn's hand. "Where did that come from?"

Camryn dropped the tiny revolver she'd had secured to her back since they'd left Yon's apartment. "My dad always told me..." she said, looking up at them, "to be prepared for anything."

Camryn leaned to the side, coughing and heaving with every breath. She fought the invisible hand that seemed to be clamped over her airway as she wiped Harriet's blood from her face.

She'd killed someone. An actual human. *Half-human*. She'd held someone's life in her hands and ended it. So quickly. She knew there had been no other choice, but it didn't make it any easier to accept.

Ronan rubbed his hand over Camryn's back, but his reassurance wasn't what she needed. She cast a timid eye toward Ethan, but the look on his face was one Camryn never thought she'd see directed at her. He wiped his thumb over his lips as he turned and walked away.

FORTY-FIVE

Akira had just raised her hand to knock when the apartment door flew open and two bewildered faces stared back at them. Camryn couldn't imagine how they must look, standing in the dim glow of the hall light, covered in sweat and sand and blood.

They'd contemplated going back to the office complex, but with Harriet Kaya dead, they weren't sure what Apollyon's next move would be. Yon and his family were likely in more danger without them around.

"We thought you were dead," Levana breathed, pulling Camryn into a hug.

"That's kind of a long story."

"Are you in danger?" Yon asked, peering out into the hall.

Levana swatted her husband's arm and waved them inside.

"You're hurt," she grasped Camryn's hand, pulling her toward the bathroom as the group entered the apartment and collapsed onto the first available surface they came to; Akira on the sofa, Ronan in the plush purple chair, and Ethan in the dining chair by the kitchen window.

"You are going to need stitches on that," Levana said as she finished bandaging Camryn's hand a few moments later. "That is the best I can do with what I have."

Camryn nodded her thanks and joined Akira on the couch, cradling her throbbing hand.

"You must be starving," Levana said, pulling items from the refrigerator and banging pots onto the stove. Just the mention of food made Camryn's stomach rumble. She could have fallen asleep listening to the sounds of Levana in the kitchen and probably would have if Ethan's anger wasn't hanging so heavy in the air. Camryn pulled herself from the couch and trudged over to him.

"How's your hand?" Ethan asked without looking at her.

"My hand's fine," she said. "Can we talk?"

Ethan shook his head, staring out the window.

"Okay." Camryn picked at a spot of chipped paint on the table. "I need to talk. You can just listen." She looked around the apartment at the other faces in the cramped space. "But...maybe someplace more private."

Ethan rubbed his hair out of his eyes and pushed back from the table so quickly that Camryn flinched away from him. "Fine. Let's go."

On the roof a few minutes later, Camryn stood beside Ethan, looking out at the city. A day of rain had washed the remaining blood from the streets and the city appeared untouched from Apollyon's hands. For now.

Camryn propped her elbows on the edge of the roof wall. "I'm sorry," she said without looking at him. "I'm sorry for so many things, but mostly because I didn't tell you about your mother."

She looked down at her hands twisting in front of her. "I thought— I thought I was protecting you."

"You were protecting yourself."

"Maybe," Camryn rubbed her thumb in her uninjured palm.

"But that isn't the whole truth. I couldn't have saved them. What Harriet was asking… It was beyond my control. I wasn't lying about that. I tried. I tried…" Camryn tilted her head back to stop the tears from spilling down her face.

Camryn wished he would just touch her—just one brush of his hand against her back or his fingers against hers that would tell her all was well between them. But he wouldn't even look at her.

"I think she would want you to know," Camryn placed a hand on Ethan's arm, "that she wasn't scared. Not at the end."

Ethan pulled his arm away from her, his jaw clenched tight.

Camryn let her fingers slide off his arm and eased away from him. Maybe he just needed some space, some time to process his mother's death…for the second time. But his silence was a chisel in her already splintered soul.

She wished he would yell at her, scream at her, at God, at anyone. But he just turned his back to her, a stark, impenetrable wall.

"Tell us everything," Yon demanded when they were all showered and sitting around the dining table with steaming plates of food in front of them.

And so, they told them. The whole story. From the beginning—the Fall, the Flood, New York City, the Void…all of it. Each filling in the parts that they knew.

Why not? The celestial battles had been plastered all over the news for the past twenty-four hours. There was nothing the world hadn't seen.

Camryn kept her eyes on Ethan the entire time, even though he wouldn't meet them.

Myria woke from her nap halfway through their tale and ran immediately to a startled Ethan. "You're okay!" she squealed, hugging him around his neck. He returned the girl's hug with a pleading look around the table.

"Come, Myria," Levana said with a laugh.

By the time the tale was through, they'd settled themselves around the apartment, and the room sat in relative silence, save for the occasional sniffle from Levana.

"I don't understand." Levana glanced around. "You say portal, like a doorway, but I saw them—we saw them," she said, gesturing to herself and her husband. "Just disappear and reappear." She raised her hands in the air, indicating her confusion.

"What you saw is called transporting," Ronan explained. "Like this." He vanished from before them only to reappear across the room a half second later, eliciting a gasp from Yon and Levana. Myria clapped and squealed with delight.

"That is how we move around within a realm." He gave a small bow to the little girl. "If you liked that, watch this," he said, vanishing again. "I'm still in this world, but without my physical body." His voice could be heard, but Ronan was nowhere in sight.

The little girl whipped her head around, looking for him. "I'm still here, but you can't see me."

He materialized again, back in the same spot he'd been. "Portaling is mostly only used to move between realms. And only the most powerful angels can do it," Ronan said with a wink in Camryn's direction.

No one spoke for a moment, letting that all sink in.

"And your parents?" Levana asked finally. "Are they really dead?"

Ethan stood suddenly and stomped to the bathroom, slamming the door. Camryn flinched at the sound.

"Yes," she whispered.

"Do you believe us?" Akira asked.

Yon pointed at the note Camryn had left, still stuck to the front of the refrigerator. The words were large enough for everyone to see.

Keep your family indoors for a few days.
Don't eat or drink anything that isn't already
in your apartment.
You said God sent us to you–for our protection,
but maybe it was the other way around.
Thanks for everything.
Sorry about your rug.
-Cam

"How could we not?"

"But how does this end?" Levana asked. "What is he planning now?"

Camryn cleared her throat and rubbed her shoe across the tiled floor. Apollyon had been eerily quiet since Harriet's death. They'd expected some retaliation. But nothing so much as an errant missile attack or volcanic eruption had been reported. Camryn wished he'd do something if only to kill the suspense that was building.

"I'm sure whatever it is, it will be worse than anything we've seen."

"Will you be able to stop him?" Levana asked in a hushed tone.

"That's a good question." Akira shrugged.

"I wish you all didn't carry this burden," Levana said, taking Camryn and Ronan by the arm. "But if what I've seen is any indication, you will rise to the challenge."

Levana rose from the table a few minutes later. "Please make yourselves comfortable." She glanced at Akira, who had her muddy boots propped on the coffee table. "But not too comfortable," she teased.

Camryn smacked Akira's feet off the table. "We're sorry for barging in like this again," she said. "We don't have to stay. We just wanted to make sure you guys were safe."

"Nonsense." Yon gestured to the pile of blankets and pillows still on the couch from their last stay. "We hoped you'd return."

Yon and Levana excused themselves to bed, but as they turned to leave, Camryn caught the woman by the arm.

"Thank you, Levana." Camryn hugged her again. "You have no idea how grateful we are for all you've done. I hope we can repay you someday."

Levana took Camryn's hands and gave a gentle squeeze. "Kill the bastard," Levana said, glancing to the muted television that still broadcast replays of the battles that had shaken the globe. "That will be payment enough."

Camryn hadn't realized she'd fallen asleep until she was roused by Ronan's shaky voice.

"Guys..." he whispered from the darkened window ledge.

Camryn jumped to her feet, wiping the sleep from her eyes. "What is it?"

Ronan stared down at a green light blinking in the corner of the Halo in his hand. "Someone's tracking us."

"Well, who could—"

A loud knock interrupted her question, and all eyes flew to the door.

Roused by the noise, Yon and Levana raced from their bedroom. "What's happening?"

Camryn held her hand up to stop the couple. "Get Myria. Take her to your room and lock the door."

Thankfully, they didn't argue. Levana grabbed the little girl and followed Camryn's instructions.

When Ronan peered out the peephole a few seconds later, he released a nervous laugh before swinging open the door for three larger than average men to step through.

No, not men.

Angels.

Camryn rushed forward. "Michael!" She practically jumped into his arms. Akira, Ronan, and Ethan rushed to Jay and Sam, who entered behind Michael.

"How?" Camryn asked, hugging the other two with just as much fervor.

"Raphael." Michael's face drooped at the name. "He led us out before…"

Camryn's joy sank a notch at the sadness in Michael's eyes. "And now he's…?"

"Gone," was Michael's only response.

Camryn's heart ached for her brother, for the loss of his *qanima*. She knew that heartache, would never forget the agony of it. But she couldn't help being a little relieved. It was Raphael, after all, who had given their location to Harriet Kaya. It was his fault their parents were dead. He would never suffer enough for that.

If only Michael didn't have to be included in that suffering.

Yon emerged from the bedroom at the apparent lack of danger. "What is going on?" he demanded.

"Yon, this is Michael, and Samael, and Japhael." Camryn was in the middle of her introductions when Levana and Myria made their way out of the bedroom behind Yon. The little girl tucked her head into her mother's neck at the sight of the three imposing strangers.

Michael appeared startled as if just realizing they were dressed in their angel armor. "We didn't mean to…" he trailed off, backing toward the door.

"Oh, believe me." Ethan began, "you're not the craziest thing they've seen today."

"I do apologize if this is rude," Samael said. "But we should probably be going. We do have a global war to attend to."

FORTY-SIX

Ethan knew he should be happy. Happy Michael had returned. Happy they were all still alive. *Well, we're not* all *still alive.* But the only thought in his brain—the one that plagued him like a persistent fly buzzing around his head—was how his mother had died alone…again.

He worked his jaw and stared at his shoes, letting his hair fall over his eyes.

Michael took his Halo from Ronan and pressed a few buttons. "I've sent our location to Zephaniah. He needs to know we've been released, and I need an update on his progress."

"President Kaya is Nephilim," Akira blurted. "Or she was until Camryn killed her. There's some progress for you."

The three Archangels stared at her.

Samael thumbed his sword. "Nephilim?"

"That explains a lot," Michael said.

"I'm more concerned about the *dead* part." Japhael held out his Halo, displaying a news alert of President Kaya making an impromptu speech on the grounds of the Turkish presidential complex just hours before. "How did she give a press conference if she's supposed to be dead."

"Apollyon?" Akira wondered aloud.

"It has to be."

Ethan's heart sank to his gut. "So killing Harriet changed nothing. Great," he said turning away from the group. He didn't even care anymore.

As they talked, Ethan absently pulled his mother's token from his pocket and rubbed it between his fingers, realizing it was the only thing he had left of her.

Michael stopped mid-sentence and stared at the item. When everyone grew quiet around him, Ethan finally looked up to find all eyes glued to him.

"May I?" Michael opened his palm, and Ethan placed the token in it. Everyone cast questioning glances while Michael examined it with a meticulous eye.

"Where did you get this?"

"It's just a good luck charm," Ethan said flatly. "My mom gave it to me."

Michael pinned him with a hard glare. "This is much more than a simple good luck charm." He turned the token over in his hand. "This is an angelic weapon, entrusted by Gabriel to a human king long ago, to keep it from Apollyon's hands. When Gabriel returned to retrieve it, he discovered that the weapon was missing."

Michael looked as if he couldn't breathe. "We need to get this to Gabriel right away." He extended the item to Samael. "He's the only one who can wield it."

Sam reached to take the item, but Ethan snatched it from Michael's hand. "You're wrong," he snapped. "It's just a stupid plastic token."

But was it? It had traveled with him between realms, which, as Camryn had pointed out, shouldn't have been possible for a normal physical object. And something else had happened down there—in the presence of Apollyon—something that made Ethan think that Michael might be right.

Michael reached to take it back, but Zephaniah chose that moment to make his appearance in the street beside them, concern etched on his face. He glanced around the group, nodding in greeting. When his eyes landed on Michael, he bowed. "Glad you're back, sir. Couldn't have come at a better time."

Michael narrowed his eyes. "What's happened?"

"Meteor, sir. Bigger than last time," he said, breathless. "Headed straight for us. Broke into the earth's orbit about five minutes ago."

Everyone looked to the sky as if they might see it careening toward them through the clouds.

Ethan hoped the news had saved his charm from further inspection, but he couldn't get that lucky.

Michael looked back to Ethan and the token in his hand. "I'll send for Gabriel. Find Apollyon and send us your location. Do not engage him alone. I'll send him to wherever you are, and we can end this once and for all."

With that, the four angels sprouted luminous wings and shot into the air.

Akira rolled her eyes. "I hate when they do that."

Ethan stared down at the token he'd owned all his life like it was something foreign to him now.

"So, how are we supposed to find Apollyon if he's parading around as the Turkish president?" Ronan asked.

"I might be able to help."

Everyone spun to see Yon standing on the sidewalk behind them. "I know people." He shrugged.

Less than five minutes later, Yon's contact had relayed the needed information, the group had sent Michael the coordinates to relay to Gabriel and transported to the presidential complex in Turkey. From what Ronan could detect, Apollyon lingered in Harriet's office, despite the late hour.

"Let's go." Akira started for the building, but was stopped by a firm grip on her wrist.

"Shouldn't we wait for Gabriel?" Ronan asked. "Michael said not to engage him alone."

A roaring sound overhead turned their eyes to the sky. A light flashed as if someone had snapped a picture from the clouds, then the sound of a freight train came roaring through the heavens.

"No time," Akira said. "If Michael can't stop that thing, we have five minutes, tops, before the only weapon with a chance of stopping Apollyon is destroyed."

"Fuck it." Ethan threw up his hands. "We're all gonna die anyway."

Akira punched him lightly on the shoulder. "That's the spirit."

"And what are we going to do when we get in there?" Ronan asked. "Ask him to have tea?"

"We just have to have faith," Camryn said, glancing around at her friends. "We'll figure something out."

Surprisingly, the building was deserted. No staff, no security.

"Apollyon must have sent them all to die at home," Akira said after scanning the building for threats.

They raced through the quiet halls of the dark building, Akira and Ronan in the lead, with Camryn and Ethan following at a slight distance.

Ethan continued to cast swift glances at Camryn, who avoided his eyes. She hadn't spoken to him directly since their time on the roof of Yon's apartment, but Ethan couldn't blame her. He'd basically given her the silent treatment since he'd found out about his mother's death on that beach. And for what reason? Was Camryn the one who deserved his animosity?

Ethan wanted nothing more than to stop and spend their last few minutes on this earth telling her all the things he'd been holding inside, but he'd have to settle for a lame attempt at an apology as they hurried through the halls.

As Akira and Ronan slowed around one particular corner, Ethan put a hand on Camryn's arm, startling her. "I'm sorry," he said. "For what I said earlier."

Camryn blinked up at him with lips slightly parted. When she didn't immediately respond, Ethan's chest began to burn. What if she wouldn't forgive him?

Arriving at President Kaya's office moments later, Apollyon spun in Harriet's chair to face them. "How did you get in here?" he asked, though he didn't sound surprised to see them.

"Ah yes," he glanced at Akira. "You do have a few parlor tricks up your sleeve, don't you?" Apollyon stood. "I'm glad you're here, actually." He turned toward the window, toward the fiery ball of rock falling from the sky.

Ethan's eyes widened at the sight. It was like something from a movie; a rock the size of New Mexico hurtling through the air, dragging a tail of fire behind it, a collage of color against a black sky.

It's too close. Even if Michael and his army were successful in blowing it to bits, it was too close to the ground.

Apollyon stood, straightening his suit jacket. "I know it's rude to leave guests unattended, but I must be going. Don't want to be around for this," he said, gesturing toward the rock. "Might be dangerous, you know?"

"Leaving so soon?" Akira chided. "But we just got here."

"Akira, my dear." Apollyon shook his head as if he were truly sad. "You are a true gem. A soldier I'm going to miss in my ranks. You had such potential. Such talent. I was devastated to learn of your disloyalty all those years ago."

Akira scoffed. "If you knew, why keep up the farse? Why even let me live?"

"I had my reasons. How's the saying go? Something about keeping your enemies close…" He turned back to stare out the window.

"Rumor has it," Apollyon mused, "a US satellite changed the trajectory of that asteroid that's about to decimate the entirety of the middle east. It seems they blame us for the plague that's ravaging the earth and wanted to teach us a lesson without diplomatic sanctions." He *tsk*ed for a moment with the shake of his head. "It may be reason enough for retaliation."

Something sparked inside Ethan, and his fingers twitched. Camryn would struggle with the fact that she'd killed Harriet for the rest of her life, and for what? So Apollyon could masquerade as a powerful world leader and take over where Harriet had left off? It was as if she'd never even died.

Ethan reached into his pocket and fingered his good luck charm again. If he'd ever needed the damn thing to work, it was now.

But the time for luck had run out. Gabriel hadn't come. Camryn wrapped her fingers around Ethan's arm and clung to him as if he were the only thing holding her up. *This is it. This is where we die.*

Before Ethan could finish the thought, the fiery rock exploded in the air, breaking into thousands of smaller, but still just as dangerous pieces. Camryn gasped beside him as the pieces continued their path toward the earth, bracing to be blown away by the concussive force that would surely follow their impact.

But after a moment, the smaller fragments of the meteor slowed their descent and seemed to hover, weightless, in the air before shooting back toward the inky black sky.

Disbelief escaped in a laugh as Ethan imagined Michael's army crashing into the rock, obliterating it into thousands of pieces, then carrying each piece back into orbit, away from the earth.

Akira threw a hand in the air with a shout before Apollyon spun and pinned her with his invisible grip.

"What is happening?" he demanded, squeezing her with all his might.

"It's Michael," Akira managed to say through her obvious pain.

"Let her go," Camryn shouted as Ronan unsheathed his sword.

Apollyon whipped his other hand to Ronan, sending the Dominion smashing through the farthest wall.

"Michael is in my dungeon," Apollyon roared.

"Not anymore, he's not." Camryn raised her palms toward Apollyon but before the power sparked from her fingers, she was frozen by his suffocating power.

Ethan's eyes darted between Apollyon and the two females. He pulled the fire into his hands, but something shook in his pocket, his token burning with a strange heat, just as it had back in Apollyon's throne room. He'd been too consumed with pain from Dagon's staff to give it much thought at the time, but it had happened. Just as it was happening now.

"Ah!" Ethan exclaimed as the token scorched his skin.

He pulled the medallion out, ready to toss it to the floor, but what he saw in his hand stopped him short. The charm seemed to be growing, shifting into…something different than what he'd known it to be. Still a round ivory disk, but glowing orange barbs now rotated around the item like a saw blade.

What the hell…

"Ethan!" Ronan called from under the debris of the demolished wall.

Ethan looked up in time to see a red ball of Apollyon's power flying straight for Camryn and Akira.

"Camryn!" Ethan screamed, and the token began to spin. He pulled back his arm and released it, just as he'd practiced in the basement with Michael. As it left his hand, he dove for Camryn, knocking her to the floor just as the wall behind her exploded in smoking flames.

Ethan watched in horror as Camryn's body tremored with Apollyon's residual paralysis, but she waved him away. "Go!" she shouted.

Ethan sprang to his feet and sprinted across the room, stopping to scoop up one of Ronan's lost daggers. He slid across the top of the desk, coming face to face with a stricken Apollyon.

Apollyon stared in disbelief at the glowing orange weapon in his chest. He reached to remove it, but his power was draining quickly. Ethan knocked Apollyon's hand away and shoved the weapon in farther. "That's for Camryn," he said through his teeth.

Then he thrust Ronan's Heavenly Fire-infused dagger between Apollyon's ribs, directly into his heart. Apollyon sank to the floor as Ethan watched the power exit his body.

Ethan brought his face down just inches from the monster responsible for his mother's death. "And this is for my mother," he said with a twist of the blade.

Apollyon sucked in a breath before dissolving into a smoking pile of ash.

Ethan scanned the floor around him, weapon still in hand. Was Apollyon truly gone?

With the last, dying whisp of black smoke, Ethan heard Ronan's armor scraping across the carpet. "Akira…" Ronan groaned.

Ethan stood from behind the desk to see Akira, a hole the size of Apollyon's fist blasted right through her middle.

Camryn knelt beside her, examining the wound with hopelessness in her eyes.

Ethan was around the desk and at her side before Ronan had made it halfway across the room. He knelt beside her and pulled her head into his lap, but her eyes were fixed on something on the opposite wall. He touched her cheek. "Akira, look at me."

"It's okay," she said, turning her eyes to him. "It doesn't hurt."

Ethan placed his palm over the wound, praying for a miracle to flow through his hand.

Akira closed her eyes and bobbed her head as a soft smoke drifted from the wound.

"No," Ethan said, trying to stop the hole from widening.

Akira latched onto his hand and pulled it to her chest. "I've been preparing for this moment since I followed you through that portal out of Eden." Her mouth remained open as if she wanted to say more, but she didn't have to.

Ethan thought back to the first time he'd seen her, looking so innocent and timid right before she'd offered to help him find his *qanima*. She'd offered to help despite the danger to herself. And she had never stopped.

He stared into her eyes until they were nothing but black smoke.

FORTY-SEVEN

Camryn and Ethan stood silently outside the now-familiar building, their ragged, weary appearance much the same as the first time they'd knocked on the apartment door. Camryn should have felt relieved, being back here, knowing that this family could now be safe, but Camryn felt nothing.

Michael and the other Archangels waited nearby. But even with Ethan standing inches away, she'd never felt so alone. What would she do now? Where would she go?

She knew that Michael would work out the details, and Ethan would be by her side. But in that moment, those questions seemed impossible to answer.

"Do you have to go?" Myria's big, brown eyes gazed up at them, puffy from sleep. The little girl clung to her mother, having just awakened moments before to say goodbye to her new friends.

Camryn reached to touch the girl's pudgy cheek. "Yeah, we do. But we'll come back to visit, I promise." Camryn's words and reassuring smile seemed to appease the child, who stuck her thumb back in her mouth and leaned her head on her father's shoulder.

Yon stepped forward and offered his hand for Camryn and Ethan to shake. "I'm sure it will take a while to process everything that's happened, but I feel as though some thanks are in order. You pulled it off. I don't know how, but you did."

The legions of Fallen that had terrorized the earth for nearly two days had weakened with Harriet Kaya's death and totally dispersed with Apollyon's. Without a leader, their purpose had vanished like the angels being slaughtered in the streets.

"I'm not really sure either," Camryn replied. "But we actually came here to thank *you*."

Ethan stuffed his hands deep into his pockets. "We never would have found Apollyon in time."

Levana leaned her head onto her husband's shoulder. "God will always lead us where we need to be."

Camryn pulled her lips into a tight smile. She wanted to believe those words, wanted to believe that everything had all worked out according to some grand plan, but how could that be? How could that be when so many had died and so much had been lost?

Perhaps He'd allowed Camryn and Ethan to survive, to defeat Apollyon, but at what cost?

Levana lowered her eyes and gave Camryn a look that only a mother could pull off. "I think with time, you will come to realize that your family… They are still with you." She took Camryn and Ethan by the hand and squeezed, unearthing a twinge of warmth from within Camryn with the intensity of her gaze.

"All of them."

DAY SEVEN

FORTY-EIGHT

The plane ride from Jerusalem to Virginia was a bumpy one. *New fear unlocked*, Camryn thought, shaking Ethan awake. They'd both slept most of the trip, making up for several days of lost sleep and mental exhaustion. But Camryn had awakened with the horrific events of the past week roiling in her stomach, dashing any hope of further rest.

"We're home," she said to Ethan as the plane broke through the clouds and the green and brown hues of dry land came into view.

She pointed to the pristine buildings and intact roads, all seemingly untouched by Apollyon's hand. Ethan put his chin on her shoulder, and together, they peered out the window as the plane made its descent into Kentucky.

She'd only been gone a week, but Camryn hadn't been sure what to expect of the home she'd left behind. Two major earthquakes had rocked the west coast and the heart of the country, and from the air, they'd witnessed the still-blazing wildfires, felled bridges, ravaged cities—carnage from the battles that had raged all over the world.

A lump swelled in her throat, knowing that even though so much damage had been done and so many lives lost… some things remained the same.

If only her parents were here to see it.

"Are you sure they're still here?" Camryn asked Jay as they bumped along the asphalt road that surely hadn't been repaved in decades.

Dressed in a very human outfit of jeans and a plain t-shirt, Jay smiled from the driver's seat of the old pickup truck that had been waiting for them at the airport. "Safe and sound, just like I left them."

"They probably didn't even realize you were gone," Ethan said from the backseat, eliciting a swift swish of Camryn's ponytail as she whipped her head around to glare at him.

"I was kidding." He laughed, holding up his hands. "Sheesh."

Camryn was practically bouncing in her seat as the truck pulled to a stop at the end of a long drive. Unable to contain her excitement, she opened the door and hopped out before Jay had even turned off the ignition.

She spotted the stable right away, standing rust-red in the distance. Camryn didn't wait for an invitation before she took off running toward the aged building.

A familiar whinny hit Camryn's ears before she even saw them, and she ran toward the sound until she reached the end of a long row of well-kept stalls. And there they were, side by side—Rebel and Romeo; her horses, her pets, her friends—all she had left from her life before.

As she neared their stall, they came forward and offered their snouts in greeting. After the past few days, Camryn didn't think she had any tears left inside, but she couldn't stop the salty trail etching down her face as she felt the softness of their manes and the fullness of their bellies. They seemed better off than how she'd left them.

"I think they've missed you more than you've missed them," Ethan said from the doorway.

Romeo extended his long, slick tongue and ran it up the side of Camryn's face. "Come on, boys," she said with a laugh. "I'm taking you home."

The afternoon sun sent daggers of light slicing through the canopy of trees, creating a shimmering orange blanket on top of the water. For a brief moment, Ethan wondered what would happen if he just slipped off this pier and let himself sink to the bottom of this old, forgotten lake. *Just one little scooch.*

But he wouldn't do it. No matter how much he was dreading the coming hours, he would endure it. Two weeks ago, it would have been a different story. But now...

"I thought you'd already gone home," Ethan said before his companion spoke.

"You're getting good at that," Ronan said, easing himself down beside Ethan on the pier. Ethan glanced at his friend but didn't speak. The words that would ease their losses didn't exist.

"I wanted to say goodbye first."

Ethan nodded. "Back to old Dominion business?"

"Something like that."

They both stared out at the water as the squawk of geese sounded overhead.

"So this is your new home, huh?"

"I guess." Ethan shrugged. "Michael said we'd be safe here for a few months, at least till we turn eighteen."

"If only he'd let everyone continue to think you two were dead, then you could just be whoever you wanted to be," Ronan said with a laugh.

Ethan had thought of that. He'd tried to convince Michael to just make up new identities for them. It wouldn't be hard. But Michael had refused. Too many people had seen their faces. And apparently, *some people* needed to know they were alive.

"Yeah. If only…"

"I'm…really sorry about your mother."

"It's okay." Ethan waved off the comment. And it really was. He'd found peace with it. He'd said goodbye to his mother once, after all, and then been blessed with another few days with her after that. If anything, he was grateful that they'd ended on a good note. That he had some happy memories to look back on.

"And Akira—" Ronan started but Ethan cut him off with a slash of his hand across his throat. He didn't think he could talk about her just yet.

"I don't have to tell you that it wasn't your fault, do I?" Ronan finally asked.

Ethan hung his head. "I thought I was going to have to tell you that."

Ronan smiled. "So it was no one's fault."

Ethan nodded. "Right."

Ronan slapped him on the back and stood. "Right," he repeated in a tone that let Ethan know he didn't believe that any more than Ethan did.

Ethan turned to peer up at his friend. "Don't let it be a hundred more years before I see you again."

"I'm thinking fourth of July." Ronan pointed both index fingers at Ethan. "Fireworks."

Ethan nodded. “It’s a date.” He chuckled but when he looked back, Ronan was gone.

Ethan was alone once again.

He’d left Camryn back at the barn an hour ago, excusing himself to the solitude of this lake. Her shoulders had slumped, but she’d been busy getting Rebel and Romeo settled in, so she hadn’t complained.

He knew what Camryn suspected—that he was still upset with her about his mother—but that wasn’t the source of the weight in his chest.

The wood creaked with Camryn’s footfalls as she made her way toward him on the splintered pier.

“Look what I found,” she said, dropping a dozen yellow dandelions into his hand.

“You picked me flowers?”

“I made you dinner,” Camryn corrected.

Ethan grimaced at the flowers in his hand. “I have to eat these?”

Camryn snatched them out of his palm and cradled them like a found treasure. “You don’t *have* to. We can eat the disgusting cans of soup Michael left us, loaded with fake meat and preservatives if you’d rather.” She nudged him with her shoulder.

“But just so you know, there’s enough foragable vegetation around here to keep us alive all year.”

“Well, thank goodness we only have to stay here a few months.”

“Have you given any thought to what we’re going to do once we turn eighteen? We won’t have to worry about being orphans after that.”

Ethan looked around. “I don’t know. I think I like the idea of staying here with you. For a while, at least.”

Camryn followed his gaze around the algae-topped lake and the overgrown weeds surrounding the ivy-covered hunting cabin. "I could stay here forever."

"Akira would have liked it here."

"Really?" Camryn wrinkled her nose.

"There was a lot about her that would surprise you."

Camryn swung her feet and looked out at the water. "I wish I'd taken the time to get to know her better."

Ethan brushed his fingers over Camryn's hand that rested between them on the pier. "You were jealous."

"I was not." She gave him a playful nudge.

"She was never a threat to you, you know?" He looked into the honey oceans of Camryn's eyes. "When you're around, I can't even look at anyone else."

That had always been true—in any lifetime. But sitting with Camryn here on this pier, the image of Akira dying in his arm barged into Ethan's mind again. Standing there in President Kaya's office, he'd held both of their lives in his hands. An impossible choice. But it hadn't been a choice, really, which was the most unfair thing about it. Akira had never had a chance.

Camryn smiled a tight smile, a blush rushing to her pale cheeks. "If you ever want to talk about her…about the time you spent together, I'd love to hear about it."

He entwined her fingers with his and pulled her hand into his lap. Ethan knew she meant it, but he wasn't ready for that just yet. "Maybe someday."

After a few more minutes, Ethan stood and brushed off his jeans. "Let's go," he said, offering a hand to Camryn and pulling her to her feet. "We have a big night tonight."

Inside the cabin, Ethan pulled a soda from the fridge. Michael had left them a few hours earlier, saying he had things to prepare before the evening.

"But don't worry," he'd said. "You have everything here that you'll need."

"No guards?" Camryn had teased, remembering the Guardians that had stealthily stalked her for most of her life.

"No need," Michael answered with a smile.

Camryn smiled back. Apollyon was dead—in the Fallen angel sense, anyway. He was locked away in the deepest, most secure death pit in the Void. Ethan worried at first that he would find a way out, that someone would release him, as Camryn had with Michael. But Michael's army had made swift work of rounding up the rest of his loyal Fallen army and confining them there as well.

The Founders had returned to their eternal punishment, and all entrances to the Void had been sealed. Michael had promised them a lesser sentence and the temporary respite from their cages in exchange for their aid in getting Ethan and his group out of Eden. Ethan imagined they would have accepted if he'd offered them only one breath of fresh, cool air.

Apart from Jay and Michael, most of the Righteous had returned to the spirit realm after the remainder of the loosed chemicals had been cleansed from the water supply, but Ethan noticed a difference in the air, just knowing they were near.

As For him and Camryn, nothing much had changed since Apollyon's defeat. They were still two seventeen-year-old humans who had lost their parents in the crossfire of their battle with the underworld. Perhaps they would return to their former state when these bodies died. But if their trip to the Void was any indicator, they would remain as they were in that moment in time.

Ethan popped open the soda can and slumped down onto the couch. "Want to watch something?" he pointed to the television.

Camryn sat down facing him, propping one arm on the back of the couch. "You sure there's nothing you want to…" she hesitated, biting her lip, "talk about?"

Ethan turned to face her. "Not really." He tossed his hair back out of his eyes.

Camryn pressed her lips together and nodded, looking down at her hands in her lap.

"Camryn."

Her face reddened with suppressed tears as she picked at a loose strand on the cushion.

"Cam." Ethan took her hands in his and leaned down to look into her glistening eyes. "I don't blame you. If that's what you want to know. I said some awful things to you…" he wrapped his fingers around her wrists with just enough force to make her look at him. "Maybe it's what I didn't say that was worse."

Camryn exhaled a breath as if she'd been holding it for some time.

"I was a dick to you, and no matter how long I live, it won't be long enough to make it up to you."

"Stop." Camryn's voice was as soft as a fallen leaf on autumn grass. "You aren't the one who should be apologizing. I should have told you. I wanted to, I just…" She stared at something over Ethan's shoulder.

"You were right—I was scared. And saying it out loud—that they were all dead—made it too real, you know?"

Ethan leaned forward and pressed his forehead to hers. "I swear to you on my mother's grave…you will never have to be scared of anything ever again, especially not of me."

Camryn pinched his shirt between her fingers and pulled him toward her.

The storm that had raged for days in Ethan's chest finally calmed as he took her face in his hands and kissed her—a kiss that put the others to shame. Camryn leaned back, never breaking her lips from his, and pulled him down on top of her. He smiled against her mouth.

I love you. Those words echoed in Ethan's mind once again—words that he'd been struggling to speak for days now.

"What's not to love?" Camryn answered before pulling him toward her.

Ethan's eyes widened. "You heard that? How—" but Camryn brought her lips up to meet his once again.

He stopped trying to apologize and just kissed her.

And this time…no one was around to stop them.

FORTY-NINE

Ethan woke with a start, the dread that Camryn's lips had momentarily abolished returning like a lead weight in his gut. He inched his arm from around a sleeping Camryn and reached to check the time on the new phone Michael had procured for him: 5:17PM. Less than an hour before Michael would be back around to get him—to deliver him to his doom.

That's how it felt, anyway. Even through the events of the past few weeks and the unpredictable life he'd led, Ethan had never been so nervous.

He turned toward Camryn, who stretched and smiled beside him. For a brief moment, he thought he'd woken her, but the smile faded, and a soft snore echoed in her throat. Ethan bit his lip to keep from laughing. She was just too damn cute.

"Time to go?" she asked without opening her eyes.

"Yeah." Ethan sat up and put his feet on the floor but couldn't force himself to stand.

"I can wait for you here if you want."

Ethan turned to look at her over his shoulder. "I don't think I can do this alone."

Camryn placed her hands on his back and shoved. "Okay then. Let's go."

Thirty minutes later, Camryn, Ethan, and Michael stood beside a metal gate at the end of a dusty, gravel road.

"It's the first house on the left," Michael said. "They're expecting you."

Ethan swallowed hard and peered down the road. When Camryn's hand reached for his, he latched onto it as if he were scared to let go.

"This isn't going to be easy," he said as they walked toward the house, mainly just to have something to say.

"It'll be easier than you think."

Ethan laughed. "I love this new optimism you have."

"Shut up." Camryn poked him in the ribs.

Thankfully, they didn't have to walk far. Ethan had already decided to turn back and abandon this business altogether when the house came into view.

Before they even reached the drive, the faded yellow door opened, and a man stepped out. Ethan stopped in his tracks, his heart skipping in his chest.

The man stood with hands in his pockets and a hard glare in his eyes. His massive frame blocked the doorway from which he'd just emerged.

Camryn took a step forward and tugged Ethan's hand.

When they reached the house, the man didn't speak, only continued to stare. Ethan's heart galloped faster. A small cat made its way out from under the porch, providing a welcome distraction for Ethan's nerves.

Camryn sighed and took a step forward. "Are you Elias?"

The man nodded.

"Hi. I'm Camryn," she said, placing a hand on her chest, "and this is Ethan." She pushed Ethan forward. "Your grandson."

Ethan held his breath as Elias clomped down the rickety steps and came to stand in front of him. He forced himself to meet the man's eye and visibly relaxed as he found glimpses of his mother in the man's face, his chin, his eyes.

Michael had said the man would be expecting them, but he hadn't said how this stranger had reacted to hearing about the existence of a long-lost grandson.

Ethan didn't have to wait long for the answer to that question, though, because as the man studied Ethan's face, tears filled his life-hardened eyes. Maybe he saw the same thing in Ethan's face that Ethan saw in his.

Elias took Ethan by the shoulders and pulled him in, almost swallowing Ethan in his thick arms.

Ethan heard Camryn's sniffles and looked to see her wiping her eyes.

"Come," Elias said, wrapping his other arm around Camryn's shoulders and leading them into the house. "Marjorie is preparing dinner."

A few phone calls and a few hours later, the yard was filled with food and people Ethan would come to know as family; aunts, uncles, cousins of all ages. They told stories of his mother and those family members who'd been lost to the chemical contaminants.

But more than anything, they wanted to talk about his time in Jerusalem. He told the story as best he could, with Camryn filling in the blanks where possible. But Ethan was relieved to find that they didn't treat him any differently.

He and Camryn had chosen to keep their angel pasts a secret for now, and they hadn't mentioned the supernatural token either, as they still weren't sure why Ethan had been able to wield it.

"This is so weird," he whispered to Camryn during a rare, quiet moment. Since his grandmother's death, Ethan had come to accept that he didn't have a family, had told himself that he preferred it that way—the fewer people you cared about, the fewer people who could hurt you.

But Camryn had changed all of that. And now his heart swelled knowing that all these people were a part of him now, that he had a small place in this world.

It felt good. But it would take some getting used to.

"I hope you don't mind," Elias said, glancing at a notification on his phone. "But there is one more person who wants to meet you."

Ethan put down his third plate of the evening and followed Elias back into the house, where a man with a long, dark ponytail stood staring out the front window. He wore jeans and a dark t-shirt, and Ethan had to appreciate his style.

When Ethan and Elias entered the room, the man turned from the window and seemed to stop breathing when his eyes landed on Ethan.

Ethan looked from the man to Elias, wondering who this new person could be.

Elias took a step into the room. "Ethan, this is Liam. He had a pretty long drive, so I wasn't sure he would make it today, but uh..." He hesitated as if he weren't sure how Ethan would react. "Ethan, this is your father."

Elias kept talking, but Ethan didn't hear any of it.

Father.

I have a father.

Ethan hadn't even entertained the thought, not since he was a kid.

The man stepped toward him, wringing his hands in front of him. "You look just like your mother."

Ethan shrugged. "I've heard that a few times today."

The man smiled. "I saw you on the news. When the girl—Camryn… When she said your name, I knew. Somehow, I knew you were Elizabeth's son. I didn't know you were *my* son, but I could see her in you even through the television.

"You…" Ethan hesitated on the man's words, "didn't know about me?"

Liam stared at the floor for a moment. "No. She never told me. I was…" He looked out the window again. "I would not have been a good father to you. She made the right decision by not telling me. And by the time I grew some sense in my brain, well, I had no way of contacting her, and like I said, I didn't even know you existed. She was probably terrified to reach out to me, and I honestly wouldn't blame her. I wasn't always the nicest to her."

Ethan shook out his fists, another piece of the puzzle of his life falling into place.

"So," Liam cleared his throat. "You and your friend, how did you even find yourselves in the middle of all that? And more importantly," he asked with a curious smile, "how did you survive that explosion?"

The last thing the cameras in the plaza had captured was the van explosion and Camryn and Ethan's evident death. No one knew the part they played in Harriet Kaya's demise. Or anything about Apollyon's involvement in it at all. Ethan hoped it stayed that way.

Obviously, people wanted to know all the details, but Ethan had managed to evade their questions every time before. But this time, he felt compelled to answer. Maybe because no mockery could be found in his father's face, only pure curiosity and concern.

Instead of dodging the question like he had every time before, Ethan pulled the plastic token from his pocket. "We had a little luck, I guess."

At the sight of the item in Ethan's hand, Liam went rigid. "Where did you get that?"

Why is that always everyone's reaction? "My mother gave it to me."

The man relaxed, shaking his head. "Elizabeth..." he said with a smile.

"Was it yours?"

"Not exactly," the man replied. "It belonged to my father. Well, actually...it didn't *belong* to anyone. Legend has it, it was entrusted to our ancestor long ago by the Great Spirit. And each chief after him had been tasked with its protection. I remember the ruckus around the reservation when it disappeared. But I was a dumb kid and couldn't be bothered with silly legends. And besides, I had my own disappearance to worry about at the time."

"My mother?"

The man nodded. "Your mother."

Liam pointed to the token. "We came across it one night, not long before she left. We were messing around where we shouldn't have been, of course." He chuckled as if the memories were fond ones. "We found a cache of other tribal artifacts in my father's office, and your mother took an interest. I told her this one was important, but I didn't tell her why. She must have taken it when she decided to leave. Maybe to remember me by, I don't know."

Ethan thought of the story his mother had told him about the token, about his ancestors watching over him.

"Maybe it was her way of sharing you with me," Ethan said, twisting the token in his hands. After a moment, he offered it back to the man. "Do you want it back?"

Liam shook his head. "It's not mine to give or take. The Great Spirit decides who is worthy to wield it."

"I thought that was only supposed to be the angel who brought it."

"That must have been part of its protection." The man shrugged with knowing eyes. "Who would steal a weapon they wouldn't be able to use?"

"Someone who doesn't know it's a weapon." Ethan laughed, running his thumb over the face of the token and sliding it back into his pocket.

He stood and followed the man back outside to Camryn and his waiting family.

Someone had turned on a radio, and several of the kids danced in a circle in the dirt. Camryn turned to him when he stepped out the door, her face shining with a smile. He once again wondered how she could be so incredibly strong. She hadn't mentioned her own loss all day. How could he let himself fully experience the joy of finding his family when Camryn had lost hers?

But the green mist surrounding her told him the truth. In that moment at least, she was truly happy.

He sauntered over and slid a hand around her waist. She returned the gesture and gazed up at him with her nose crinkled in laughter.

The sound was medicine to his healing heart.

Camryn collapsed onto the couch, exhausted—but in a good way this time. She studied Ethan's face as he lay staring at the ceiling, wanting to take in every detail of him to store in her mental file of all things that are beautiful.

He wasn't smiling or laughing—his expression was somber, actually—but she could feel his contentment inside her own heart, an old canoe drifting on an ocean wave.

The other guests had left hours ago, returning to their own homes as the children had gradually curled up against their mothers to drop off to sleep, and because of the late hour, Elias and Marjorie had insisted they postpone their departure until morning.

"You okay?" Ethan turned to her, catching her staring.

Camryn nodded. "Just can't sleep."

"Me either," he said, turning the rest of his body to face her. "I'm sorry if any of this has made you uncomfortable today. I know your family—"

Camryn shushed him with a finger to his lips. "My family is with me. All the time." She paused. "I had seventeen perfect years with my parents. Those memories will get me through until I see them again."

Ethan pulled his lips into a half-grin. "You're amazing, you know that?" He continued rubbing his thumb over the top of her hand, even as his smile faded into a look of concern.

"What's bothering you?"

"I just keep thinking…what if this isn't over? I mean, we have no idea what our future looks like. I just keep expecting something else to fall from the sky."

Camryn pulled her lips into a knowing smile. "Well, let me tell you a little secret." She moved closer and whispered. "Our future looks pretty damn great."

Ethan's eyes widened. "Did you see something?"

Camryn shrugged. "Not much. But enough." She leaned forward and pressed her forehead against his. "So you can stop worrying, okay?"

Ethan let out a pent-up breath, visibly relaxing beside her. She turned over to stare into the darkness, letting her hand fall into his.

Now that she understood the visions that had plagued her were not simply premonitions—that they were a power that Apollyon had wanted for himself—she'd been able to conjure them more often. Not as often as she liked and never anything more than a flash, but perhaps they were the source of her new-found peace.

One thing still bothered her, though. A question that still remained unanswered. Neither of them had yet remembered the specifics of the mission that had sent them to earth to be born as the humans they now were. And maybe they never would. Maybe it was safer that way, a secret safe from falling into the wrong hands.

The wrong hands...

They may have killed Apollyon and eradicated his influence from the earth, but that didn't mean this would now become a perfect world. Apollyon had been right about one thing. He didn't make people do bad things. And just because he was gone, evil would not cease to exist. It was the nature of man, and as long as man walked the earth, evil would, too.

And maybe a few Nephilim as well. Camryn couldn't shake the fear that Harriet Kaya hadn't been the only one. And since she'd appeared completely human, not the giants of Noah's days, there would be no way to tell until they showed their hand.

So, she was okay with not knowing if it meant the world could be safe from other celestials getting the same ideas as Apollyon.

And she would remain prepared for battle, as her father had always taught her.

The thought brought a grimace to her face, but if the time came—if called upon again...she would be ready.

She owed the universe that much.

During their millennium of existence, she and Ethan had committed some heinous acts—against each other, against Michael, Apollyon, and countless others. The guilt of it all had plagued her for centuries, and surely Ethan, too.

But somehow, through all the chaos and destruction and death they had found each other again and again, and this time, maybe they'd find something else as well. Perhaps they'd finally find their redemption.

THE END

ACKNOWLEDGEMENTS

And here we are at my favorite part of writing a book—THE END! I'm kidding! It's the part where I get to thank everyone who helped me along the way.

Without getting too emotional, let me just start by thanking my daughter, Ava, who gave up lots of snuggle time in the last few months as I tried *to just get this dang book finished!* We have lots of TV to catch up on.

A huge shout out to my beta readers, Robert Hecksher and Ellie Headley. To my dear friend, Michelle Mars from TikTok, who grew up in Israel and was instrumental in helping bring Tel Aviv to life in this story. And to my wonderful editor, Gina Salamon. Thank you. Thank you. Thank you all…

ABOUT THE AUTHOR

AE Winstead grew up in west Tennessee where she lives with her husband, two children, three cats, and one dog. You can find her online at aewinstead.com

www.ingramcontent.com/pod-product-compliance
Lightning Source LLC
Chambersburg PA
CBHW030538310726
48979CB00010B/1953/J